new skies

**The Best in Today's Fiction . . .
for Today's Readers**

Finder
by Emma Bull

Briar Rose
by Jane Yolen

Wildside
by Steven Gould

Sister Light, Sister Dark
by Jane Yolen

City of Darkness
by Ben Bova

The One-Armed Queen
by Jane Yolen

Dogland
by Will Shetterly

White Jenna
by Jane Yolen

War for the Oaks
by Emma Bull

new skies

AN ANTHOLOGY OF TODAY'S SCIENCE FICTION

EDITED BY
PATRICK NIELSEN HAYDEN

TOR

A TOM DOHERTY ASSOCIATES BOOK
NEW YORK

This is a work of fiction. All the characters and events portrayed in this book are fictitious or are used fictitiously.

NEW SKIES: AN ANTHOLOGY OF TODAY'S SCIENCE FICTION

A Tor Book
Published by Tom Doherty Associates, LLC
175 Fifth Avenue
New York, NY 10010

www.tor.com

Tor® is a registered trademark of Tom Doherty Associates, LLC.

ISBN 0-765-34004-6
EAN 978-0765-34004-7

First Tor Teen edition: July 2004

Printed in the United States of America

0 9 8 7 6 5 4 3 2 1

Copyright Acknowledgments

For Soren DeSelby

Contents

Contents

Introduction

What If the world were different?

What if aliens arrived? Or if a world war disrupted all our lives? What if we colonized Mars, and learned to play baseball there? What if children could divorce their parents? Or if the South had won the American Civil War?

Science fiction stories ask these questions, and then try to answer them. And what a good science fiction story shows is that once you start asking questions, it's hard to stop. What if aliens *did* arrive? Would they mean well toward us? Would we treat them fairly? How would we feel if it turned out that they were wiser and smarter than we? How could we be sure they were what they seemed? How could they be sure of us? And that's just the beginning.

All of these questions are as much about *us* as they are about the made-up aliens. We may actually encounter real aliens someday. But right now what we have is ourselves, the world of human beings, and imagining aliens and humans confronting one another turns out to be an interesting way of thinking about ourselves, about how we think, how we react, how we tick.

Science fiction is like that. It's very definitely about the future, the far horizons of adventure and discovery. But it's also about ourselves, at home, trying to figure out a world in which things often don't seem to be the way they ought to be. Sometimes, the ways school and work and home are set up seem as strange and alien as any distant planet. Science fiction often helps us think about that, too.

It's a big world, and the things that seem normal and permanent in one neighborhood often turn out to be utterly strange in another. Science fiction constantly reminds us of this, which is one reason readers of all ages have been turning to it for stimulation, for recreation, for imagination, for as long as science fiction has been published.

In these pages you'll find a selection of some of the best science fiction stories of the last two decades. All of them ask questions, imagine answers, and ask more questions in turn. Get on board, enjoy the ride—and feel free to ask your own questions.

—PATRICK NIELSEN HAYDEN

Sometimes, it's the most routine details that seem the strangest to outsiders.

Terry Bisson is known for pungent, often very funny short stories like "Bears Discover Fire" and sharp, original novels like Talking Man and The Pickup Artist.

They're Made Out of Meat

TERRY BISSON

"They're made out of meat."

"Meat?"

"Meat. They're made out of meat."

"Meat?"

"There's no doubt about it. We picked up several from different parts of the planet, took them aboard our recon vessels, and probed them all the way through. They're completely meat."

"That's impossible. What about the radio signals? The messages to the stars?"

"They use the radio waves to talk, but the signals don't come from them. The signals come from machines."

"So who made the machines? That's who we want to contact."

"*They* made the machines. That's what I'm trying to tell you. Meat made the machines."

"That's ridiculous. How can meat make a machine? You're asking me to believe in sentient meat."

"I'm not asking you, I'm telling you. These creatures are the only sentient race in that sector and they're made out of meat."

"Maybe they're like the orfolei. You know, a carbon-based intelligence that goes through a meat stage."

"Nope. They're born meat and they die meat. We studied them for several of their life spans, which didn't take long. Do you have any idea what's the life span of meat?"

"Spare me. Okay, maybe they're only part meat. You know, like the weddilei. A meat head with an electron plasma brain inside."

"Nope. We thought of that, since they do have meat heads, like the weddilei. But I told you, we probed them. They're meat all the way through."

"No brain?"

"Oh, there's a brain all right. It's just that the brain is *made out of meat!* That's what I've been trying to tell you."

"So . . . what does the thinking?"

"You're not understanding, are you? You're refusing to deal with what I'm telling you. The brain does the thinking. The meat."

"Thinking meat! You're asking me to believe in thinking meat!"

"Yes, thinking meat! Conscious meat! Loving meat. Dreaming meat. The meat is the whole deal! Are you beginning to get the picture or do I have to start all over?"

"Omigod. You're serious, then. They're made out of meat."

"Thank you. Finally. Yes. They are indeed made out of meat.

And they've been trying to get in touch with us for almost a hundred of their years."

"Omigod. So what does this meat have in mind?"

"First it wants to talk to us. Then I imagine it wants to explore the Universe, contact other sentiences, swap ideas and information. The usual."

"We're supposed to talk to meat."

"That's the idea. That's the message they're sending out by radio. 'Hello. Anyone out there. Anybody home.' That sort of thing."

"They actually do talk, then. They use words, ideas, concepts?"

"Oh, yes. Except they do it with meat."

"I thought you just told me they used radio."

"They do, but what do you think is *on* the radio? Meat sounds. You know how when you slap or flap meat, it makes a noise? They talk by flapping their meat at each other. They can even sing by squirting air through their meat."

"Omigod. Singing meat. This is altogether too much. So what do you advise?"

"Officially or unofficially?"

"Both."

"Officially, we are required to contact, welcome, and log in any and all sentient races or multibeings in this quadrant of the Universe, without prejudice, fear, or favor. Unofficially, I advise that we erase the records and forget the whole thing."

"I was hoping you would say that."

"It seems harsh, but there is a limit. Do we really want to make contact with meat?"

"I agree one hundred percent. What's there to say? 'Hello, meat. How's it going?' But will this work? How many planets are we dealing with here?"

"Just one. They can travel to other planets in special meat containers, but they can't live on them. And being meat, they can only travel through C space. Which limits them to the speed of light and makes the possibility of their ever making contact pretty slim. Infinitesimal, in fact."

"So we just pretend there's no one home in the Universe."

"That's it."

"Cruel. But you said it yourself, who wants to meet meat? And the ones who have been aboard our vessels, the ones you probed? You're sure they won't remember?"

"They'll be considered crackpots if they do. We went into their heads and smoothed out their meat so that we're just a dream to them."

"A dream to meat! How strangely appropriate, that we should be meat's dream."

"And we marked the entire sector *unoccupied*."

"Good. Agreed, officially and unofficially. Case closed. Any others? Anyone interesting on that side of the galaxy?"

"Yes, a rather shy but sweet hydrogen-core cluster intelligence in a class-nine star in G445 zone. Was in contact two galactic rotations ago, wants to be friendly again."

"They always come around."

"And why not? Imagine how unbearably, how unutterably cold the Universe would be if one were all alone . . ."

*Courage isn't being unafraid. Courage is doing what needs doing
when we're scared half to death.*

*A working space scientist when he's not writing highly plausible
"hard SF," Geoffrey A. Landis published his first novel,* Mars
Crossing, *in 2000. "A Walk in the Sun" won science fiction's
Hugo Award for Best Short Story in 1992.*

A Walk in the Sun

● ●

GEOFFREY A. LANDIS

The pilots have a saying: a good landing is any landing you
can walk away from.

Perhaps Sanjiv might have done better, if he'd been alive.
Trish had done the best she could. All things considered, it was
a far better landing than she had any right to expect.

Titanium struts, pencil-slender, had never been designed to
take the force of a landing. Paper-thin pressure walls had buckled
and shattered, spreading wreckage out into the vacuum and
across a square kilometer of lunar surface. An instant before
impact she remembered to blow the tanks. There was no explosion, but no landing could have been gentle enough to keep
Moonshadow together. In eerie silence, the fragile ship had
crumpled and ripped apart like a discarded aluminum can.

The piloting module had torn open and broken loose from the

main part of the ship. The fragment settled against a crater wall. When it stopped moving, Trish unbuckled the straps that held her in the pilot's seat and fell slowly to the ceiling. She oriented herself to the unaccustomed gravity, found an undamaged EVA pack and plugged it into her suit, then crawled out into the sunlight through the jagged hole where the living module had been attached.

She stood on the grey lunar surface and stared. Her shadow reached out ahead of her, a pool of inky black in the shape of a fantastically stretched man. The landscape was rugged and utterly barren, painted in stark shades of grey and black. "Magnificent desolation," she whispered. Behind her, the sun hovered just over the mountains, glinting off shards of titanium and steel scattered across the cratered plain.

Patricia Jay Mulligan looked out across the desolate moonscape and tried not to weep.

First things first. She took the radio out from the shattered crew compartment and tried it. Nothing. That was no surprise; Earth was over the horizon, and there were no other ships in cislunar space.

After a little searching she found Sanjiv and Theresa. In the low gravity they were absurdly easy to carry. There was no use in burying them. She sat them in a niche between two boulders, facing the sun, facing west, toward where the Earth was hidden behind a range of black mountains. She tried to think of the right words to say, and failed. Perhaps as well; she wouldn't know the proper service for Sanjiv anyway. "Goodbye, Sanjiv. Goodbye, Theresa. I wish—I wish things would have been different. I'm sorry." Her voice was barely more than a whisper. "Go with God."

She tried not to think of how soon she was likely to be joining them.

She forced herself to think. What would her sister have done? Survive. Karen would survive. First: inventory your assets. She was alive, miraculously unhurt. Her vacuum suit was in service-able condition. Life-support was powered by the suit's solar arrays; she had air and water for as long as the sun continued to shine. Scavenging the wreckage yielded plenty of unbroken food packs; she wasn't about to starve.

Second: call for help. In this case, the nearest help was a quarter of a million miles over the horizon. She would need a high-gain antenna and a mountain peak with a view of Earth.

In its computer, *Moonshadow* had carried the best maps of the moon ever made. Gone. There had been other maps on the ship; they were scattered with the wreckage. She'd managed to find a detailed map of Mare Nubium—useless—and a small global map meant to be used as an index. It would have to do. As near as she could tell, the impact site was just over the eastern edge of Mare Smythii—"Smith's Sea." The mountains in the distance should mark the edge of the sea, and, with luck, have a view of Earth.

She checked her suit. At a command, the solar arrays spread out to their full extent like oversized dragonfly wings and glinted in prismatic colors as they rotated to face the sun. She verified that the suit's systems were charging properly, and set off.

Close up, the mountain was less steep than it had looked from the crash site. In the low gravity, climbing was hardly more difficult than walking, although the two-meter dish made her balance awkward. Reaching the ridgetop, Trish was rewarded with the sight of a tiny sliver of blue on the horizon. The mountains on the far side of the valley were still in darkness. She hoisted the radio higher up on her shoulder and started across the next valley.

From the next mountain peak the Earth edged over the horizon, a blue and white marble half-hidden by black mountains. She unfolded the tripod for the antenna and carefully sighted along the feed. "Hello? This is Astronaut Mulligan from *Moonshadow*. Emergency. Repeat, this is an emergency. Does anybody hear me?"

She took her thumb off the *transmit* button and waited for a response, but heard nothing but the soft whisper of static from the sun.

"This is Astronaut Mulligan from *Moonshadow*. Does anybody hear me?" She paused again. "*Moonshadow*, calling anybody. *Moonshadow*, calling anybody. This is an emergency."

"*—shadow, this is Geneva control. We read you faint but clear. Hang on, up there.*" She released her breath in a sudden gasp. She hadn't even realized she'd been holding it.

After five minutes the rotation of the Earth had taken the ground antenna out of range. In that time—after they had gotten over their surprise that there was a survivor of the *Moonshadow*—she learned the parameters of the problem. Her landing had been close to the sunset terminator; the very edge of the illuminated side of the moon. The moon's rotation is slow, but inexorable. Sunset would arrive in three days. There was no shelter on the moon, no place to wait out the fourteen-day long lunar night. Her solar cells needed sunlight to keep her air fresh. Her search of the wreckage had yielded no unruptured storage tanks, no batteries, no means to lay up a store of oxygen.

And there was no way they could launch a rescue mission before nightfall.

Too many "no"s.

She sat silent, gazing across the jagged plain toward the slender blue crescent, thinking.

After a few minutes the antenna at Goldstone rotated into range, and the radio crackled to life. *"Moonshadow, do you read me? Hello, Moonshadow, do you read me?"*

"Moonshadow here."

She released the transmit button and waited in long silence for her words to be carried to Earth.

"Roger, Moonshadow. We confirm the earliest window for a rescue mission is thirty days from now. Can you hold on that long?"

She made her decision and pressed the transmit button. "Astronaut Mulligan for *Moonshadow*. I'll be here waiting for you. One way or another."

She waited, but there was no answer. The receiving antenna at Goldstone couldn't have rotated out of range so quickly. She checked the radio. When she took the cover off, she could see that the printed circuit board on the power supply had been slightly cracked from the crash, but she couldn't see any broken leads or components clearly out of place. She banged on it with her fist—Karen's first rule of electronics, if it doesn't work, hit it—and reaimed the antenna, but it didn't help. Clearly something in it had broken.

What would Karen have done? Not just sit here and die, that was certain. Get a move on, kiddo. When sunset catches you, you'll die.

They had heard her reply. She had to believe they heard her reply and would be coming for her. All she had to do was survive.

The dish antenna would be too awkward to carry with her. She could afford nothing but the bare necessities. At sunset her air would be gone. She put down the radio and began to walk.

Mission Commander Stanley stared at the x-rays of his engine. It was four in the morning. There would be no more sleep for him that night; he was scheduled to fly to Washington at six to testify to Congress.

"Your decision, Commander," the engine technician said. "We can't find any flaws in the x-rays we took of the flight engines, but it could be hidden. The nominal flight profile doesn't take the engines to a hundred twenty, so the blades should hold even if there is a flaw."

"How long a delay if we yank the engines for inspection?"

"Assuming they're okay, we lose a day. If not, two, maybe three."

Commander Stanley drummed his fingers in irritation. He hated to be forced into hasty decisions. "Normal procedure would be?"

"Normally we'd want to reinspect."

"Do it."

He sighed. Another delay. Somewhere up there, somebody was counting on him to get there on time. If she was still alive. If the cut-off radio signal didn't signify catastrophic failure of other systems.

If she could find a way to survive without air.

On Earth it would have been a marathon pace. On the moon it was an easy lope. After ten miles the trek fell into an easy rhythm: half a walk, half like jogging, and half bounding like a slow-motion kangaroo. Her worst enemy was boredom.

Her comrades at the academy—in part envious of the top scores that had made her the first of their class picked for a mission—had ribbed her mercilessly about flying a mission that would come within a few kilometers of the moon without landing. Now she had a chance to see more of the moon up close than anybody in history. She wondered what her classmates were thinking now. She would have a tale to tell—if only she could survive to tell it.

The warble of the low voltage warning broke her out of her reverie. She checked her running display as she started down the maintenance checklist. Elapsed EVA time, eight point three hours. System functions, nominal, except that the solar array current was way below norm. In a few moments she found the trouble: a thin layer of dust on her solar array. Not a serious problem; it could be brushed off. If she couldn't find a pace that would avoid kicking dust on the arrays, then she would have to break every few hours to housekeep. She rechecked the array and continued on.

With the sun unmoving ahead of her and nothing but the hypnotically blue crescent of the slowly rotating Earth creeping imperceptibly off the horizon, her attention wandered. *Moonshadow* had been tagged as an easy mission, a low-orbit mapping flight to scout sites for the future moonbase. *Moonshadow* had never been intended to land, not on the moon, not anywhere.

She'd landed it anyway; she had to.

Walking west across the barren plain, Trish had nightmares of blood and falling, Sanjiv dying beside her; Theresa already dead in the lab module; the moon looming huge, spinning at a crazy angle in the viewports. Stop the spin, aim for the terminator—at low sun angles, the illumination makes it easier to see the roughness of the surface. Conserve fuel, but remember to blow the tanks an instant before you hit to avoid explosion.

That was over. Concentrate on the present. One foot in front of the other. Again. Again.

The undervoltage alarm chimed again. Dust, already?

She looked down at her navigation aid and realized with a shock that she had walked a hundred and fifty kilometers.

Time for a break anyway. She sat down on a boulder, fetched a snackpack out of her carryall, and set a timer for fifteen minutes. The airtight quick-seal on the food pack was designed to mate to the matching port in the lower part of her faceplate. It would be important to keep the seal free of grit. She verified the vacuum seal twice before opening the pack into the suit, then pushed the food bar in so she could turn her head and gnaw off pieces. The bar was hard and slightly sweet.

She looked west across the gently rolling plain. The horizon looked flat, unreal; a painted backdrop barely out of reach. On the moon, it should be easy to keep up a pace of fifteen or even twenty miles an hour—counting time out for sleep, maybe ten. She could walk a long, long way.

Karen would have liked it; she'd always liked hiking in desolate areas. "Quite pretty, in its own way, isn't it, Sis?" Trish said. "Who'd have thought there were so many shadings of grey? Plenty of uncrowded beach—too bad it's such a long walk to the water."

Time to move on. She continued on across terrain that was generally flat, although everywhere pocked with craters of every size. The moon is surprisingly flat; only one percent of the surface has a slope of more than fifteen degrees. The small hills she bounded over easily; the few larger ones she detoured around. In the low gravity this posed no real problem to walking. She walked on. She didn't feel tired, but when she checked her readout and realized that she had been walking for twenty hours, she forced herself to stop.

Sleeping was a problem. The solar arrays were designed to be detached from the suit for easy servicing, but had no provision to power the life-support while detached. Eventually she found a way to stretch the short cable out far enough to allow her to prop up the array next to her so she could lie down without disconnecting the power. She would have to be careful not to roll over. That done, she found she couldn't sleep. After a time she lapsed into a fitful doze, dreaming not of the *Moonshadow* as she'd expected, but of her sister, Karen, who—in the dream— wasn't dead at all, but had only been playing a joke on her, pretending to die.

She awoke disoriented, muscles aching, then suddenly remembered where she was. The Earth was a full handspan above the horizon. She got up, yawned, and jogged west across the gunpowder-grey sandscape.

Her feet were tender where the boots rubbed. She varied her pace, changing from jogging to skipping to a kangaroo bounce. It helped some; not enough. She could feel her feet starting to blister, but knew that there was no way to take off her boots to tend, or even examine, her feet.

Karen had made her hike on blistered feet, and had had no patience with complaints or slacking off. She should have broken her boots in before the hike. In the one-sixth gee, at least the pain was bearable.

After a while her feet simply got numb.

Small craters she bounded over; larger ones she detoured around; larger ones yet she simply climbed across. West of Mare Smythii she entered a badlands and the terrain got bumpy. She had to slow down. The downhill slopes were in full sun, but the crater bottoms and valleys were still in shadow.

Her blisters broke, the pain a shrill and discordant singing in her boots. She bit her lip to keep herself from crying and continued on. Another few hundred kilometers and she was in Mare Spumans—"Sea of Froth"—and it was clear trekking again. Across Spumans, then into the north lobe of Fecundity and through to Tranquility. Somewhere around the sixth day of her trek she must have passed Tranquility Base; she carefully scanned for it on the horizon as she traveled but didn't see anything. By her best guess she missed it by several hundred kilometers; she was already deviating toward the north, aiming for a pass just north of the crater Julius Caesar into Mare Vaporum to avoid the mountains. The ancient landing stage would have been too small to spot unless she'd almost walked right over it.

"Figures," she said. "Come all this way, and the only tourist attraction in a hundred miles is closed. That's the way things always seem to turn out, eh, Sis?"

There was nobody to laugh at her witticism, so after a moment she laughed at it herself.

Wake up from confused dreams to black sky and motionless sunlight, yawn, and start walking before you're completely awake. Sip on the insipid warm water, trying not to think about what it's recycled from. Break, cleaning your solar arrays, your life, with exquisite care. Walk. Break. Sleep again, the sun nailed to the sky in the same position it was in when you awoke. Next day do it all over. And again. And again.

The nutrition packs are low-residue, but every few days you must still squat for nature. Your life support can't recycle solid waste, so you wait for the suit to dessicate the waste and then void the crumbly brown powder to vacuum. Your trail is marked by your powdery deposits, scarcely distinguishable from the dark lunar dust.

Walk west, ever west, racing the sun.

Earth was high in the sky; she could no longer see it without craning her neck way back. When the Earth was directly overhead she stopped and celebrated, miming the opening of an invisible bottle of champagne to toast her imaginary traveling companions. The sun was well above the horizon now. In six days of travel she had walked a quarter of the way around the moon.

She passed well south of Copernicus, to stay as far out of the impact rubble as possible without crossing mountains. The terrain was eerie, boulders as big as houses, as big as shuttle tanks. In places the footing was treacherous where the grainy regolith gave way to jumbles of rock, rays thrown out by the cataclysmic impact billions of years ago. She picked her way as best she could. She left her radio on and gave a running commentary as she moved. "Watch your step here, footing's treacherous. Coming up on a hill; think we should climb it or detour around?"

Nobody voiced an opinion. She contemplated the rocky hill. Likely an ancient volcanic bubble, although she hadn't realized that this region had once been active. The territory around it would be bad. From the top she'd be able to study the terrain for a ways ahead. "Okay, listen up, everybody. The climb could be tricky here, so stay close and watch where I place my feet. Don't take chances—better slow and safe than fast and dead. Any questions?" Silence; good. "Okay, then. We'll take a fifteen-minute break when we reach the top. Follow me."

Past the rubble of Copernicus, Oceanus Procellarum was smooth as a golf course. Trish jogged across the sand with a smooth, even glide. Karen and Dutchman seemed to always be lagging behind or running up ahead out of sight. Silly dog still followed Karen around like a puppy, even though Trish was the one who fed him and refilled his water dish every day since Karen went away to college. The way Karen wouldn't stay close behind her annoyed Trish—Karen had *promised* to let her be the leader this time—but she kept her feelings to herself. Karen had called her a bratty little pest, and she was determined to show she could act like an adult. Anyway, she was the one with the map. If Karen got lost, it would serve her right.

She angled slightly north again to take advantage of the map's promise of smooth terrain. She looked around to see if Karen was there, and was surprised to see that the Earth was a gibbous ball low down on the horizon. Of course, Karen wasn't there. Karen had died years ago. Trish was alone in a spacesuit that itched and stank and chafed her skin nearly raw across the thighs. She should have broken it in better, but who would have expected she would want to go jogging in it?

It was unfair how she had to wear a spacesuit and Karen didn't. Karen got to do a lot of things that she didn't, but how come she didn't have to wear a spacesuit? *Everybody* had to wear a spacesuit. It was the rule. She turned to Karen to ask. Karen laughed bitterly. "I don't have to wear a spacesuit, my bratty little sister, because I'm *dead*. Squished like a bug and buried, remember?"

Oh, yes, that was right. Okay, then, if Karen was dead, then she didn't have to wear a spacesuit. It made perfect sense for a few more kilometers, and they jogged along together in companionable silence until Trish had a sudden thought. "Hey, wait—if you're dead, then how can you be here?"

"Because I'm not here, silly. I'm a fig-newton of your over-active imagination."

With a shock, Trish looked over her shoulder. Karen wasn't there. Karen had never been there.

"I'm sorry. Please come back. Please?"

She stumbled and fell headlong, sliding in a spray of dust down the bowl of a crater. As she slid she frantically twisted to stay face-down, to keep from rolling over on the fragile solar wings on her back. When she finally slid to a stop, the silence echoing in her ears, there was a long scratch like a badly healed scar down the glass of her helmet. The double reinforced faceplate had held, fortunately, or she wouldn't be looking at it.

She checked her suit. There were no breaks in the integrity, but the titanium strut that held out the left wing of the solar array had buckled back and nearly broken. Miraculously there had been no other damage. She pulled off the array and studied the damaged strut. She bent it back into position as best she could, and splinted the joint with a mechanical pencil tied on with two short lengths of wire. The pencil had been only extra weight anyway; it was lucky she hadn't thought to discard it. She tested the joint gingerly. It wouldn't take much stress, but if she didn't bounce around too much it should hold. Time for a break anyway.

When she awoke she took stock of her situation. While she hadn't been paying attention, the terrain had slowly turned mountainous. The next stretch would be slower going than the last bit.

"About time you woke up, sleepyhead," said Karen. She yawned, stretched, and turned her head to look back at the line of footprints. At the end of the long trail, the Earth showed as a tiny blue dome on the horizon, not very far away at all, the single speck of color in a landscape of uniform grey. "Twelve days to walk halfway around the moon," she said. "Not bad, kid. Not great, but not bad. You training for a marathon or something?"

Trish got up and started jogging, her feet falling into rhythm automatically as she sipped from the suit recycler, trying to wash the stale taste out of her mouth. She called out to Karen behind her without turning around. "Get a move on, we got places to go. You coming, or what?"

In the nearly shadowless sunlight the ground was washed-out, two dimensional. Trish had a hard time finding footing, stumbling over rocks that were nearly invisible against the flat landscape. One foot in front of the other. Again. Again.

The excitement of the trek had long ago faded, leaving behind a relentless determination to prevail, which in turn had faded into a kind of mental numbness. Trish spent the time chatting with Karen, telling the private details of her life, secretly hoping that Karen would be pleased, would say something telling her she was proud of her. Suddenly she noticed that Karen wasn't listening; had apparently wandered off on her sometime when she hadn't been paying attention.

She stopped on the edge of a long, winding rille. It looked like a riverbed just waiting for a rainstorm to fill it, but Trish knew it had never known water. Covering the bottom was only dust, dry as powdered bone. She slowly picked her way to the bottom, careful not to slip again and risk damage to her fragile life support system. She looked up at the top. Karen was standing on the rim waving at her. "*Come on!* Quit *dawdling*, you slow-poke—you want to stay here *forever?*"

"What's the hurry? We're ahead of schedule. The sun is high up in the sky, and we're halfway around the moon. We'll make it, no sweat."

Karen came down the slope, sliding like a skier in the powdery dust. She pressed her face up against Trish's helmet and stared into her eyes with a manic intensity that almost frightened her. "The hurry, my lazy little sister, is that you're halfway around the moon, you've finished with the easy part and it's all mountains and badlands from here on, you've got six thousand kilometers to walk in a broken spacesuit, and if you slow down and let the sun get ahead of you, and then run into one more teensy little problem, just one, you'll be dead, dead, dead, just like me. You wouldn't like it, trust me. Now get your pretty little lazy butt into gear and *move!*"

And, indeed, it was slow going. She couldn't bound down slopes as she used to, or the broken strut would fail and she'd have to stop for painstaking repair. There were no more level plains; it all seemed to be either boulder fields, crater walls, or mountains. On the eighteenth day she came to a huge natural arch. It towered over her head, and she gazed up at it in awe, wondering how such a structure could have been formed on the moon.

"Not by wind, that's for sure," said Karen. "Lava, I'd figure. Melted through a ridge and flowed on, leaving the hole; then over the eons micrometeoroid bombardment ground off the rough edges. Pretty, though, isn't it?"

"Magnificent."

Not far past the arch she entered a forest of needle-thin crystals. At first they were small, breaking like glass under her feet, but then they soared above her, six-sided spires and minarets in fantastic colors. She picked her way in silence between them, bedazzled by the forest of light sparkling between the sapphire spires. The crystal jungle finally thinned out and was replaced by giant crystal boulders, glistening iridescent in the sun. Emeralds? Diamonds?

"I don't know, kid. But they're in our way. I'll be glad when they're behind us."

And after a while the glistening boulders thinned out as well, until there were only a scattered few glints of color on the slopes of the hills beside her, and then at last the rocks were just rocks, craggy and pitted.

Crater Daedalus, the middle of the lunar farside. There was no celebration this time. The sun had long ago stopped its lazy rise, and was imperceptibly dropping toward the horizon ahead of them.

"It's a race against the sun, kid, and the sun ain't making any stops to rest. You're losing ground."

"I'm tired. Can't you see I'm tired? I think I'm sick. I hurt all over. Get off my case. Let me rest. Just a few more minutes? Please?"

"You can rest when you're dead." Karen laughed in a strangled, high-pitched voice. Trish suddenly realized that she was on the edge of hysteria. Abruptly she stopped laughing. "Get a move on, kid. Move!"

The lunar surface passed under her, an irregular grey treadmill.

Hard work and good intentions couldn't disguise the fact that the sun was gaining. Every day when she woke up the sun was a little lower down ahead of her, shining a little more directly in her eyes.

Ahead of her, in the glare of the sun she could see an oasis, a tiny island of grass and trees in the lifeless desert. She could already hear the croaking of frogs: braap, braap, BRAAP!

No. That was no oasis; that was the sound of a malfunction alarm. She stopped, disoriented. Overheating. The suit air conditioning had broken down. It took her half a day to find the clogged coolant valve and another three hours soaked in sweat to find a way to unclog it without letting the precious liquid vent to space. The sun sank another handspan toward the horizon.

The sun was directly in her face now. Shadows of the rocks stretched toward her like hungry tentacles, even the smallest looking hungry and mean. Karen was walking beside her again, but now she was silent, sullen.

"Why won't you talk to me? Did I do something? Did I say something wrong? Tell me."

"I'm not here, little sister. I'm dead. I think it's about time you faced up to that."

"Don't say that. You can't be dead."

"You have an idealized picture of me in your mind. Let me go. *Let me go!*"

"I can't. Don't go. Hey—do you remember the time we saved up all our allowances for a year so we could buy a horse? And we found a stray kitten that was real sick, and we took the shoebox full of our allowance and the kitten to the vet, and he fixed the kitten but wouldn't take any money?"

"Yeah, I remember. But somehow we still never managed to save enough for a horse." Karen sighed. "Do you think it was easy growing up with a bratty little sister dogging my footsteps, trying to imitate everything I did?"

"I wasn't either bratty."

"You were too."

"No, I wasn't. I adored you." Did she? "I *worshipped* you."

"I know you did. Let me tell you, kid, that didn't make it any easier. Do you think it was easy being worshipped? Having to be a paragon all the time? Christ, all through high school, when I wanted to get high, I had to sneak away and do it in private, or else I knew my damn kid sister would be doing it too."

"You didn't. You never."

"Grow up, kid. Damn right I did. You were always right behind me. Everything I did, I knew you'd be right there doing it next. I had to struggle like hell to keep ahead of you, and you, damn you, followed effortlessly. You were smarter than me—you know that, don't you?—and how do you think that made me feel?"

"Well, what about me? Do you think it was easy for *me?* Growing up with a dead sister—everything I did, it was 'Too bad you can't be more like Karen' and 'Karen wouldn't have done it that way' and 'If only Karen had. . . .' How do you think that made me feel, huh? You had it easy—I was the one who had to live up to the standards of a goddamn *angel*."

"Tough breaks, kid. Better than being dead."

"Damn it, Karen, I loved you. I love you. Why did you have to go away?"

"I know that, kid. I couldn't help it. I'm sorry. I love you too, but I have to go. Can you let me go? Can you just be yourself now, and stop trying to be me?"

"I'll . . . I'll try."

"Goodbye, little sister."

"Goodbye, Karen."

She was alone in the settling shadows on an empty, rugged plain. Ahead of her, the sun was barely kissing the ridgetops. The dust she kicked up was behaving strangely; rather than falling to the ground, it would hover half a meter off the ground. She puzzled over the effect, then saw that all around her, dust was silently rising off the ground. For a moment she thought it was another hallucination, but then realized it was some kind of electrostatic charging effect. She moved forward again through the rising fog of moondust. The sun reddened, and the sky turned a deep purple.

The darkness came at her like a demon. Behind her only the tips of mountains were illuminated, the bases disappearing into shadow. The ground ahead of her was covered with pools of ink that she had to pick her way around. Her radio locator was turned on, but receiving only static. It could only pick up the locator beacon from the *Moonshadow* if she got in line of sight of the crash site. She must be nearly there, but none of the landscape looked even slightly familiar. Ahead—was that the ridge she'd climbed to radio Earth? She couldn't tell. She climbed it, but didn't see the blue marble. The next one?

The darkness had spread up to her knees. She kept tripping over rocks invisible in the dark. Her footsteps struck sparks from the rocks, and behind her footprints glowed faintly. Triboluminescent glow, she thought—nobody has *ever* seen that before. She couldn't die now, not so close. But the darkness wouldn't wait. All around her the darkness lay like an unsuspected ocean, rocks sticking up out of the tidepools into the dying sunlight. The undervoltage alarm began to warble as the rising tide of darkness reached her solar array. The crash site had to be around here somewhere, it had to. Maybe the locator beacon was broken? She climbed up a ridge and into the light, looking around desperately for clues. Shouldn't there have been a rescue mission by now?

Only the mountaintops were in the light. She aimed for the nearest and tallest mountain she could see and made her way across the darkness to it, stumbling and crawling in the ocean of ink, at last pulling herself into the light like a swimmer gasping for air. She huddled on her rocky island, desperate as the tide of darkness slowly rose about her. Where were they? *Where were they?*

Back on Earth, work on the rescue mission had moved at a frantic pace. Everything was checked and triple-checked—in space, cutting corners was an invitation for sudden death—but still the rescue mission had been dogged by small problems and minor delays, delays that would have been routine for an ordinary mission, but loomed huge against the tight mission deadline.

The scheduling was almost impossibly tight—the mission had been set to launch in four months, not four weeks. Technicians scheduled for vacations volunteered to work overtime, while suppliers who normally took weeks to deliver parts delivered overnight. Final integration for the replacement for *Moonshadow*, originally to be called *Explorer* but now hastily re-christened *Rescuer*, was speeded up, and the transfer vehicle launched to the Space Station months ahead of the original schedule, less than two weeks after the *Moonshadow* crash. Two shuttle-loads of propellant swiftly followed, and the transfer vehicle was mated to its aeroshell and tested. While the rescue crew practiced possible scenarios on the simulator, the lander, with engines inspected and replaced, was hastily modified to accept a third person on ascent, tested, and then launched to rendezvous with *Rescuer*. Four weeks after the crash the stack was fueled and ready, the crew briefed, and the trajectory calculated. The crew shuttle launched through heavy fog to join their *Rescuer* in orbit.

Thirty days after the unexpected signal from the moon had

revealed a survivor of the *Moonshadow* expedition, *Rescuer* left orbit for the moon.

From the top of the mountain ridge west of the crash site, Commander Stanley passed his searchlight over the wreckage one more time and shook his head in awe. "An amazing job of piloting," he said. "Looks like she used the TEI motor for braking, and then set it down on the RCS verniers."

"Incredible," Tanya Nakora murmured. "Too bad it couldn't save her."

The record of Patricia Mulligan's travels was written in the soil around the wreck. After the rescue team had searched the wreckage, they found the single line of footsteps that led due west, crossed the ridge, and disappeared over the horizon. Stanley put down the binoculars. There was no sign of returning footprints. "Looks like she wanted to see the moon before her air ran out," he said. Inside his helmet he shook his head slowly. "Wonder how far she got?"

"Could she be alive somehow?" asked Nakora. "She was a pretty ingenious kid."

"Not ingenious enough to breathe vacuum. Don't fool yourself—this rescue mission was a political toy from the start. We never had a chance of finding anybody up here still alive."

"Still, we had to try, didn't we?"

Stanley shook his head and tapped his helmet. "Hold on a sec, my damn radio's acting up. I'm picking up some kind of feedback—almost sounds like a voice."

"I hear it too, Commander. But it doesn't make any sense."

The voice was faint in the radio. "Don't turn off the lights. Please, please, don't turn off your light. . . ."

Stanley turned to Nakora. "Do you . . . ?"

"I hear it, Commander . . . but I don't believe it."

Stanley picked up the searchlight and began sweeping the horizon. "Hello? *Rescuer* calling Astronaut Patricia Mulligan. Where the hell are you?"

The spacesuit had once been pristine white. It was now dirty grey with moondust, only the ragged and bent solar array on the back carefully polished free of debris. The figure in it was nearly as ragged.

After a meal and a wash, she was coherent and ready to explain.

"It was the mountaintop. I climbed the mountaintop to stay in the sunlight, and I just barely got high enough to hear your radios."

Nakora nodded. "That much we figured out. But the rest—the last month—you really walked all the way around the moon? Eleven thousand kilometers?"

Trish nodded. "It was all I could think of. I figured, about the distance from New York to LA and back—people have walked that and lived. It came to a walking speed of just under ten miles an hour. Farside was the hard part—turned out to be much rougher than nearside. But strange and weirdly beautiful, in places. You wouldn't believe the things I saw."

She shook her head, and laughed quietly. "*I* don't believe some of the things I saw. The immensity of it—we've barely scratched the surface. I'll be coming back, Commander. I promise you."

"I'm sure you will," said Commander Stanley. "I'm sure you will."

As the ship lifted off the moon, Trish looked out for a last view of the surface. For a moment she thought she saw a lonely figure standing on the surface, waving her goodbye. She didn't wave back.

She looked again, and there was nothing out there but magnificent desolation.

A fast-moving adventure set in (and outside of) an immense
future high-rise, this is a story with more going on in it than some
full-length novels.

Steven Gould is the author of many works of SF, including
Jumper, one of the most acclaimed "young adult" SF novels of
the last two decades.

Peaches for Mad Molly

. . . .

STEVEN GOULD

Sometime during the night the wind pulled a one-pointer off
the west face of the building up around the 630th floor. I heard
him screaming as he went by, very loud, like this was his last
chance to voice an opinion, but it was all so sudden that he didn't
know what it was. Then he hit a microwave relay off 542 . . .
hard, and the chance was gone. Chunks of him landed in Buffalo
Bayou forty-five seconds later.

The alligators probably liked that.

I don't know if his purchase failed or his rope broke or if the
sucker just couldn't tie a decent knot. He pissed me off though,
because I couldn't get back to sleep until I'd checked all four of
my belay points, the ropes, and the knots. Now if he'd fallen
without expressing himself, maybe?

No, I would have heard the noise as he splattered through the
rods of the antennae.

Stupid one-pointer.

The next morning I woke up a lot earlier than usual because someone was plucking one of my ropes, *adagio*, thrum, thrum, like the second movement of Ludwig's seventh. It was Mad Molly.

"You awake, Bruce?" she asked.

I groaned. "I am now." My name is not Bruce. Molly, for some reason, calls everyone Bruce. "*Shto etta*, Molly?"

She was crouched on a roughing point, one of the meter cubes sticking out of the tower face to induce the micro-turbulence boundary layer. She was dressed in a brightly flowered scarlet kimono, livid green bermuda shorts, a sweatshirt, and tabi socks. Her belay line, bright orange against the gray building, stretched from around the corner to Molly's person where it vanished beneath her kimono, like a snake hiding its head.

"I got a batch to go to the Bruce, Bruce."

I turned and looked down. There was a damp wind in my face. Some low clouds had come in overnight, hiding the ground, but the tower's shadow stretched a long ways across the fluffy stuff below. "Jeeze, Molly. You know the Bruce won't be on shift for another hour." Damn, she had me doing it! "Oh, hell. I'll be over after I get dressed."

She blinked twice. Her eyes were black chips of stone in a face so seamed and browned by the sun that it was hard to tell her age. "Okay, Bruce," she said, then stood abruptly and flung herself off the cube. She dropped maybe five meters before her rope tightened her fall into an arc that swung her down and around the corner.

I let out my breath. She's not called Mad Molly for nothing.

I dressed, drank the water out of my catch basin, urinated on the clouds (seems only fair) and rolled up my bag.

Between the direct sunlight and the stuff bouncing off the clouds below, the south face was blinding. I put my shades on at the corner.

Molly's nest, like a mud dauber's, hung from an industrial exhaust vent off the 611th floor. It was woven, sewed, tucked, patched, welded, snapped, zipped, and tied into creation. It looked like a wasp's nest on a piece of chrome. It did not blend in.

Her pigeon coop, about two floors lower down, blended in even less. It was made of paper, sheet plastic, wire, and it was speckled with pigeon droppings. It was where it was because only a fool lives directly under *under* defecating birds, and Molly, while mad, was not stupid.

Molly was crouched in the doorway of her nest balanced on her feet like one of her pigeons. She was staring out at nothing and muttering angrily to herself.

"What's wrong, Molly? Didn't you sleep okay?"

She glared at me. "That damn Bruce got another three of my birds yesterday."

I hooked my bag onto a beaner and hung it under her house. "What Bruce, Molly? That red tailed hawk?"

"Yeah, that Bruce. Then the other Bruce pops off last night and wakes me up so I can't get back to sleep because I'm listening for that damn hawk." She backed into her nest to let me in.

"Hawks don't hunt at night, Molly."

She flapped her arms. "So? Like maybe the vicious, son-of-a-bitchin' Bruce gets into the coop? He could kill half my birds in one night!" She started coiling one of her ropes, pulling the line with short, angry jerks. "I don't know if it's worth it anymore, Bruce. It's hot in the summer. It's freezing in the winter. The Babs are always hassling me instead of the Howlers, the Howlers keep hassling me for free birds or they'll cut me loose one night. I can't cook on cloudy days unless I want to pay an arm and a leg for fuel. I can't get fresh fruit or vegetables. That crazy social worker who's afraid of heights comes by and asks if he can help me. I say 'Yeah, get me some fresh fruit.' He brings me applications for readmittance! God, I'd kill for a fresh peach! I'd be better off back in the home!"

I shrugged. "Maybe you would, Molly. After all, you're getting on in years."

"Fat lot you know, Bruce! You crazy or something? Trade this view for six walls? Breathe that stale stuff they got in there? Give up my birds? Give up my freedom? Shit, Bruce, who the hell's side are you on anyway?"

I laughed. "Yours, Molly."

She started wrapping the pigeons and swearing under her breath.

I looked at Molly's clippings, bits of faded newsprint stuck to the wall of the tower itself. By the light coming through some of the plastic sheeting in the roof, I saw a picture of Molly on Mt. McKinley dated twenty years before. An article about her second attempt on Everest. Stories about her climbing buildings in New York, Chicago, and L.A. I looked closer at one that talked about her climbing the south face of El Capitan on her fourteenth birthday. It had the date.

I looked twice and tried to remember what day of the month it was. I had to count backwards in my head to be sure.

Tomorrow was Mad Molly's birthday.

The Bruce in question was Murry Zapata, outdoor rec guard of the south balcony on the 480th floor. This meant I had to take the birds down 131 stories, or a little over half a kilometer. And then climb back.

Even on the face of Le Bab tower, with a roughing cube or vent or external rail every meter or so, this is a serious climb. Molly's pigeons alone were not worth the trip, so I dropped five floors and went to see Lenny.

It's a real pain to climb around Lenny's because nearly every horizontal surface has a plant box or pot on it. So I rappeled down even with him and shouted over to where he was fiddling with a clump of fennel.

"Hey, Lenny. I'm making a run. You got anything for Murry?"

He straightened up. "Yeah, wait a sec." He was wearing shorts and his climbing harness and nothing else. He was brown all over. If I did that sort of thing I'd be a melanoma farm.

Lenny climbed down to his tent and disappeared inside. I worked my way over there, avoiding the plants. I smelled dirt, a rare smell up here. It was an odor rich and textured. It kicked in memories of freshly plowed fields or newly dug graves. When I got to Lenny's tent, he came out with a bag.

"What'cha got," I asked.

He shrugged. "Garlic, cumin, and anise. The weights are marked on the outside. Murry should have no trouble moving it. The Chicanos can't get enough of the garlic. Tell Murry that I'll have some of those tiny *muy caliente* chilis for him next week."

"Got it."

"By the way, Fran said yesterday to tell you she has some daisies ready to go down."

"Check. You ever grow any fruit, Lenny?"

"On these little ledges? I thought about getting a dwarf orange once but decided against it. I grow dew berries but none of them are ripe right now. No way I could grow trees. Last year I grew some cantaloupe but that's too much trouble. You need a bigger bed than I like."

"Oh, well. It was a thought." I added his bag to the pigeons in my pack. "I'll probably be late getting back."

He nodded. "Yeah, I know. Better you than me, though. Last time *I* went, the Howlers stole all my tomatoes. Watch out down below. The Howlers are claiming the entire circumference from 520 to 530."

"Oh, yeah? Just so they don't interfere with my right of eminent domain."

He shrugged. "Just be careful. I don't care if they want a cut. Like maybe a clump of garlic."

I blinked. "Nobody cuts my cargo. Nobody."

"Not even Dactyl?"

"Dactyl's never bothered me. He's just a kid."

Lenny shrugged. "He's sent his share down. You get yourself pushed off and we'll have to find someone else to do the runs. Just be careful."

"Careful is what I do best."

Fran lived around the corner, on the east face. She grew flowers, took in sewing, and did laundry. When she had the daylight for her solar panel, she watched TV.

"Why don't you live inside, Fran. You could watch TV twenty-four hours a day."

She grinned at me, a not unpleasant event. "Nah. Then I'd pork up to about a hundred kilos eating that syntha crap and not getting any exercise and I'd have to have a permit to grow even one flower in my cubicle and a dispensation for the wattage for a grow light and so on and so forth. When they put me in a coffin, I want to be dead."

"Hey, they have exercise rooms and indoor tracks and the rec balconies."

"Big deal. Shut up for a second while I see if Bob is still mad at Sue because he found out about Marilyn's connection with her mother's surgeon. When the commercial comes I'll cut and bundle some daisies."

She turned her head back to the flat screen. I looked at her blue bonnets and pansies while I waited.

"There, I was right. Marilyn is sleeping with Sue's mother. That will make everything okay." She tucked the TV in a pocket and prepared the daisies for me. "I'm going to have peonies next week." I laced the wrapped flowers on the outside of the pack to avoid crushing the petals. While I was doing that Fran moved closer. "Stop over on the way back?"

"Maybe," I said. "Of course I'll drop your script off."

She withdrew a little.

"I want to, Fran, honest. But I want to get some fresh fruit for Mad Molly's birthday tomorrow and I don't know where I'll have to go to get it."

She turned away and shrugged. I stood there for a moment, then left, irritated. When I looked back she was watching the TV again.

The Howlers had claimed ten floors and the entire circumference of the Le Bab Tower between those floors. That's an area of forty meters by 250 meters per side or 40,000 square meters total. The tower is over a kilometer on a side at the base but it tapers in stages until it's only twenty meters square at three thousand meters.

Their greediness was to my advantage because there's only thirty-five or so Howlers and that's a lot of area to cover. As I rappelled down to 529 I slowly worked my way around the building. There was a bunch of them in hammocks on the south face, sunbathing. I saw one or two on the east face but most of them were on the west face. Only one person was on the north side.

I moved down to 521 on the north face well away from the one guy and doubled my longest line. It was a hundred-meter blue line twelve millimeters thick. I coiled it carefully on a roughing cube after wrapping the halfway point of the rope around another roughing cube one complete circuit, each end trailing down. I pushed it close into the building so it wouldn't slip. Then I clipped my brake bars around the doubled line.

The guy at the other corner noticed me now and started working his way from roughing cube to roughing cube, curious. I kicked the rope off the cube and it fell cleanly with no snarls, no snags. He shouted. I jumped, a gloved hand on the rope where it came out of the brake bars. I did the forty meters in five jumps, a total of ten seconds. Halfway down I heard him shout for help and heard others come around the corner. At 518 I braked and swung into the building. The closest Howler was still fifteen meters or so away from my rope, but he was speeding up. I leaned against the building and flicked the right hand rope hard, sending a sinusoidal wave traveling up the line. It reached the top and the now loose rope flicked off the cube above and fell. I sat down and braced. A hundred-meter rope weighs in at eight kilos and the shock of it pulling up short could have pulled me from the cube.

They shouted things after me, but none of them followed. I heard one of them call out, "Quit'cha bitchin. He's got to pass us on his way home. We'll educate him then."

All the rec guards deal. It's a good job to have if you're inside. Even things that originate inside the tower end up traveling the outside pipeline. Ain't no corridor checks out here. No TV cameras or sniffers either. The Howlers do a lot of that sort of work.

Murry is different from the other guards, though. He doesn't deal slice or spike or any of the other nasty pharmoddities, and he treats us outsiders like humans. He says he was outside once. I believe him.

"So, Murry, what's with your wife? She had that baby yet?"

"Nah. And boy is she tired of being pregnant. She's, like, out to *here*." He held his hands out. "You tell Fran I want something special when she finally dominoes. Like roses."

"Christ, Murry. You know Fran can't do roses. Not in friggin pots. Maybe day lilies. I'll ask her." I sat in my seat harness, hanging outside the cage that's around the rec balcony. Murry stood inside smelling the daisies. There were some kids kicking a soccer ball on the far side of the balcony and several adults standing at the railing looking out through the bars. Several people stared at me. I ignored them.

Murry counted out the script for the load and passed it through the bars. I zipped it in a pocket. Then he pulled out the provisions I'd ordered the last run and I dropped them, item by item, into the pack.

"You ever get any fresh fruit in there, Murry?"

"What do I look like, guy, a millionaire? The guys that get that sort of stuff live up there above 750. Hell, I once had this escort job up to 752 and while the honcho I escorted was talking to the resident, they had me wait out on this patio. This guy had apples and peaches and *cherries* for crissakes! *Cherries!*" He shook his head. "It was weird, too. None of this cage crap." He rapped on the bars with his fist. "He had a chest-high railing and that was it."

"Well of course. What with the barrier at 650 he doesn't have to worry about us. I'll bet there's lots of open balconies up that way." I paused. "Well, I gotta go. I've got a long way to climb."

"Better you than me. Don't forget to tell Fran about the special flowers."

"Right."

They were waiting for me, all the Howlers sitting on the south face, silent, intent. I stopped four stories below 520 and rested. While I rested I coiled my belay line and packed it in my pack. I sat there, fifteen kilos of supplies and climbing paraphernalia on my back, and looked out on the world.

The wind had shifted more to the southwest and was less damp than the morning air. It had also strengthened but the boundary layer created by the roughing cubes kept the really high winds out from the face of the tower.

Sometime during the day the low clouds below had broken into patches, letting the ground below show through. I perched on the roughing cube, unbelayed and contemplated the fall. 516 is just over two kilometers from the ground. That's quite a drop—though in low winds the odds were I'd smack into one of the rec balconies where the tower widened below. In a decent southerly wind you can depend on hitting the swamps instead.

What I had to do now was rough.

I had to free ascend.

No ropes, no nets, no second chances. If I lost it the only thing I had to worry about was whether or not to scream on the way down.

The Howlers were not going to leave me time for the niceties.

For the most part the Howlers were so-so climbers, but they had a few people capable of technical ascents. I had to separate the good from the bad and then out-climb the good.

I stood on the roughing cube and started off at a run, leaping two meters at a time from roughing cube to roughing cube moving sideways across the south face. Above me I heard shouts but I didn't look up. I didn't dare. The mind was blank, letting the body do the work without hindrance. The eyes saw, the body did, the mind coasted.

I slowed as I neared the corner, and stopped, nearly falling when I overbalanced, but saving myself by dropping my center of gravity.

There weren't nearly as many of them above me now. Maybe six of them had kept up with me. The others were trying to do it by the numbers, roping from point to point. I climbed two stories quickly, chimneying between a disused fractional distillation stack and a cooling tower. Then I moved around the corner and ran again.

When I stopped to move up two more stories there were only two of them above me. The other four were trying for more altitude rather than trying to keep pace horizontally.

I ran almost to the northwest corner, then moved straight up.

The first one decided to drop kick me dear Jesus through the goal posts of life. He pulled his line out, fixed it to something convenient and rappelled out with big jumps, planning, no doubt, to come swinging into me with his feet when he reached my level. I ignored him until the last minute when I let myself collapse onto a roughing cube. His feet slammed into the wall above me then rebounded out.

As he swung back out from the face I leaped after him.

His face went white. Whatever he was expecting me to do, he wasn't expecting *that*! I latched onto him like a monkey, my legs going around his waist. One of my hands grabbed his rope, the other punched with all my might into his face. I felt his jaw go and his body went slack. He released the rope below the brake bars and started sliding down the rope. I scissored him with my legs and held onto the rope with both hands. My shoulders creaked as I took the strain but he stopped sliding. Then we swung back into the wall and I sagged onto a cube astride him.

His buddy was dropping down more slowly. He was belayed but he'd seen what I'd done and wasn't going to try the airborne approach. He was still a floor or two above me so I tied his friend off so he wouldn't sleepwalk and took off sideways, running again.

I heard him shout but I didn't hear him moving. When I paused again he was bent over my friend with the broken jaw. I reached an external exhaust duct and headed for the sky as fast as I could climb.

At this point I was halfway through Howler territory. Off to my right the group that had opted for height was now moving sideways to cut me off. I kept climbing, breathing hard now but not desperate. I could climb at my current speed for another half hour without a break and I thought there was only one other outsider that could keep up that sort of pace. I wondered if he was up above.

I looked.

He was.

He wasn't on the wall.

He didn't seem to be roped on.

And he was dropping.

I tried to throw myself to the side, in the only direction I could go, but I was only partially successful. His foot caught me a glancing blow to my head and I fell three meters to the next roughing cube. I landed hard on the cube, staggered, bumped into the wall, and fell outward, off the cube. The drop was sudden, gut wrenching, and terrifying. I caught the edge of the cube with both hands, wrenching my shoulders and banging my elbow. My head ached, the sky spun in circles and I knew that there was over a kilometer of empty space beneath my feet.

Dactyl had stopped somehow, several stories below me, and, as I hung there, I could see the metallic gleam of some sort of wire, stretched taut down the face of the tower.

I chinned myself up onto the cube and traversed away from the wire, moving and climbing fast. I ignored the pain in my shoulders and the throbbing of my head and even the stomach-churning fear and sudden clammy sweat.

There was a whirring sound and the hint of movement behind me. I turned around and caught the flash of gray moving up the face. I looked up.

He was waiting, up on the edge of Howler territory, just watching. Closer were the three clowns who were trying to get above me before I passed them. I eyed the gap, thought about it, and then went into overdrive. They didn't make it, I passed them before they reached the exhaust duct. For a few stories they tried to pursue and one of them even threw a grapple that fell short.

That left only Dactyl.

He was directly overhead when I reached 530. I paused and glanced down. The others had stopped and were looking up. Even the clothesliners had made it around the corner and were watching. I looked back up. Dactyl moved aside about five meters and sat down on a ledge. I climbed up even with him and sat too.

Dactyl showed up one day in the middle of Howler territory. Three Howlers took the long dive before it was decided that maybe the Howler should ignore Dactyl before there were no Howlers left. He's a loner who does a mixed bag: some free ascent, some rope work, and some fancy mech stuff.

There was something about him that made him hard to see, almost. Not really, but he did blend into the building. His nylons, his climbing shoes, his harness were gray like the roughing cube he sat on. His harness was strung with gray boxes and pouches of varying sizes, front and back, giving his torso a bulky appearance, sort of like a turtle with long arms. He was younger than I'd thought he'd be, perhaps twenty, but then I'd only seen him at a distance before now. His eyes looked straight at me, steady and hard. He wasn't sweating a bit.

"Why?" I said.

He shrugged. "Be natural, become a part of your environment. Who said that?"

"Lot's of people said that. Even I said that."

Dactyl nodded. "So, like I'm doing that thing. I'm becoming a part of the environment. One thing you should know by now, dude . . ."

"What's that?" I asked warily.

"The environment is hostile."

I looked out, away from him. In the far distance I saw white sails in Galveston Bay. I turned back. "What did I ever do to you?"

He smiled. "You take it too personal. It's more random than that. Think of me as an extra-somatic evolutionary factor. You've got to evolve. You've got to adapt. *Mano a Mano* shit like that."

I let that stew for a while. The Howlers were gathering below, inside their territory. They were discussing something with much hand waving and punctuated gestures.

"So," I finally said. "You ever walk through downtown Houston?"

He blinked, opened his mouth to say something, then closed it. Finally, almost unwillingly, he said, "On the ground? No. They eat people down there."

I shrugged. "Sometimes they do. Sometimes they don't. Last time I was in Tranquillity Park they were eating alligator tail with Siamese peanut sauce. Except when the alligators were eating them."

"Oh."

"You even been down below at all?"

"I was born inside."

"Well, don't let it bother you," I said as I stood up.

He frowned slightly. "What's that supposed to mean?"

I grinned. "It's not where you were born that matters," I said. "It's where you die."

I started climbing.

The first half-hour was evenly paced. He waited about a minute before he started after me and for the next seventy floors it was as if there was an invisible fifteen-meter rope stretched between us. About 600 he lowered the gap to ten meters. I picked up the pace a little, but the gap stayed the same for the next ten floors.

I was breathing hard now and feeling the burn in my thighs and arms. My clothes were soaked in sweat but my hands were dry and I was in rhythm, climbing smooth and steady.

Dactyl was also climbing fast, but jerky, his movements inefficient. The gap was still ten meters but I could tell he was straining.

I doubled my speed.

The universe contracted. There was only the wall, the next purchase, the next breath. There were no peaches, no birthdays, no flowers, and no Dactyl. There was no thought.

But there *was* pain.

My thighs went from burning to screaming. I started taking up some of the slack with my arms and they joined the chorus. I climbed through the red haze for fifteen more stories and then collapsed on a roughing cube.

The world reeled as I gasped for the first breaths. I felt incipient cramps lurking in my thighs and I wanted those muscle cells to have all the oxygen I could give them. Then, as the universe steadied, I looked down for Dactyl.

He wasn't on the north face.

Had he given up?

I didn't know and it bothered me.

Five stories above was the barrier—a black, ten-meter overhang perpendicular to the face. It was perfectly smooth, made of metal, its welds ground flush. I didn't know what was above it. There were rumors about automatic lasers, armed guards, and computer monitored imaging devices. I'd worry about them when I got past that overhang.

I was two stories short of it when Dactyl appeared at the northeast corner of the building.

Above me.

It wasn't possible. I almost quit then but something made me go on. I tried to blank my mind and began running toward the west face, doing the squirrel hopping from block to block, even though my muscles weren't up to it. I almost lost it twice, once when my mind dwelt too much on how Dactyl had passed me and once when my quadriceps gave way.

I stopped at the corner, gasping, and looked back. Dactyl was working his way leisurely after me, slowly, almost labored. I ducked around and climbed again, until I was crouched on a roughing cube, the dark overhang touching my head. I peeked around the corner. Dactyl had paused, apparently resting.

I took off my pack and pulled out a thirty-meter length of two-ton-test line, a half-meter piece of ten-kilo-test monofilament, and a grapple. I tied the monofilament between the heavier line and the grapple.

I peeked around the corner again. Dactyl was moving again, but slowly, carefully. He was still two-hundred meters across the face. I dropped down two meters and stepped back around the corner. Dactyl stopped when he saw me, but I ignored him, playing out the grapple and line until it hung about fifteen meters below me. Then I started swinging it.

It was hard work, tricky, too. I didn't think I had the time to rig a quick belay before Dactyl got there. At least the grapple was light, three kilos at most, but as it swung wider and wider it threatened to pull me off at each end of its swing, especially as the corner formed by the barrier concentrated the wind somewhat.

Finally the grapple raised far enough on the swing away from the corner. As it dropped to the bottom of its swing I began pulling it in. As the moment arm decreased the grapple sped up, gaining enough speed to flip up above the edge of the overhang. I had no idea how thick the overhang was or even if there was something up there for the grapple to catch on. I held my breath.

There was a distant clinking noise as it struck something and the rope slackened. For an instant I thought it was dropping back down and I was scared because I was already off balance and I didn't know how far Dactyl was behind me. Then the rope stopped moving and the grapple didn't drop into sight.

I risked a quick look behind. Dactyl was still a hundred meters away. I took the rope and moved back around the corner, pulling the rope cautiously tight. As luck would have it, with the line pulled over, Dactyl wouldn't be able to see any part of the rope until he rounded the corner.

It took me two minutes to tie the lower end of the rope around a roughing cube and then to two more cubes for backup. Then I recklessly dropped from cube to cube until I was three stories down and hidden behind a Bernoulli exhaust vent.

He stuck his head around the corner almost immediately. Saw the dangling line and tugged it hard. The ten-kilo test line hidden above the barrier held. Dactyl clipped a beaner over the line and leaped out, almost like a flying squirrel, his hands reaching for the rope. He was halfway out before his full weight hit the rope.

The ten-kilo test snapped immediately. I heard his indrawn breath, but he didn't swear. Instead, as he arched down, he tried to twist around, to get his legs between him and the face as he swung into it.

He was only partially successful, slamming hard into the corner of a roughing cube, one leg taking some of the shock. I heard the breath leave his lungs in an explosive grunt and then he was sliding down the rope toward the unattached end, grabbing weakly to stop himself, but only managing to slow the drop.

I moved like a striking snake.

I was already lower down the tower from where he'd hit the wall and took three giant strides from cube to cube to get directly beneath him. Then he was off the end of the rope and dropping free and my hand reached out, snared his climbing harness, and I flattened myself atop the cube *I* was on.

For the second time that day I nearly dislocated my shoulder. His weight nearly pulled me off the tower. The back of my shirt suddenly split. I heard his head crack onto the cube and he felt like a sack of dirt, lifeless, but heavy as the world.

It took some time to get him safely onto the cube and lashed in place.

It took even longer to get my second grapple up where the first one was. It seemed my first attempt was a fluke and I had to repeat the tiring process six more times before I could clip my ascenders to the rope and inchworm up it.

The building had narrowed above the barrier, to something like 150 meters per side. I was on the edge of a terrace running around the building. Unlike the recreation balconies below, it was open to the sky, uncaged, with only a chest-high railing to contain its occupants. Scattered artfully across the patio were lounge chairs and greenery-topped planters.

I saw a small crowd of formally dressed men and women mingling on the west terrace, sheltered from the northeast wind. Servants moved among them with trays. Cocktail hour among the rich, the influential, and the cloudy.

I pulled myself quickly over the edge and crouched behind a planter, pulling my rope in and folding my grapples.

The terrace areas unsheltered by the wind seemed to be deserted. I looked for cameras and IR reflectors and capcitance wires but I didn't see any. I couldn't see any reason for any.

Above me, the face of the tower rose another five hundred meters or so, but unlike the faces below, there were individual balconies spotted here and there among the roughing cubes. On more than one I could see growing plants, even trees.

I had more than a hundred floors to go, perhaps 400 meters.

My arms and legs were trembling. There was a sharp pain in the shoulder Dactyl had kicked, making it hard for me to lift that arm higher than my neck.

I nearly gave it up. I thought about putting down my pack, unbuckling my climbing harness, and stretching out on one of these lounge chairs. Perhaps later I'd take a drink off of one of those trays.

Then a guard would come and escort me all the way to the ground.

Besides, I could do a hundred stories standing on my head, right? Right.

The sun was completely down by the time I reached 700 but lights from the building itself gave me what I couldn't make out by feel. The balconies were fancy, sheltered from the wind by removable fairings and jutting fins. I kept my eye out for a balcony with fruit trees, just in case. I wouldn't climb all the way up to 752 if I didn't have to.

But I had to.

There were only four balconies on 752, one to each side. They were the largest private balconies I'd ever seen on the tower. Only one of them had anything resembling a garden. I spent five minutes looking over the edge at planter after planter of vegetables, flowers, shrubs, and trees. I couldn't see any lights through the glass doors leading into the building and I couldn't see any peaches.

I sighed and pulled myself over the edge for a closer look, standing upright with difficulty. My limbs were leaden, my breath still labored. I could hear my pulse thudding in my ears, and I still couldn't see any peaches.

There were some green oranges on a tree near me, but that was the closest thing to fruit I could see. I shivered. I was almost two kilometers above sea level and the sun had gone down an hour ago. My sweat-soaked clothes were starting to chill.

Something was nagging me and, at first, the fatigue toxins wouldn't let me think clearly. Then an important fact swam into my attention.

I hadn't checked for alarms.

They were there, in the wall above the railing, a series of small reflectors for the IR beams that I'd crawled through to enter the balcony.

Time to leave. Long past time. I stepped toward the railing and heard a door open behind me. I started to swing my leg up over the edge when I felt something stick me in the side. And then the universe exploded.

All the muscles on my right side convulsed spasmodically and I came down onto the concrete floor with a crash, slamming my shoulder and hip into the ground. My head was saved from the same fate by the backpack I wore.

Taser, I thought.

When I could focus, I saw the man standing about three meters away, wearing a white khaftan. He was older than I was by decades. Most of his hair was gone and his face had deep lines etched by something other than smiling. I couldn't help comparing him to Mad Molly, but it just wasn't the same. Mad Molly could be as old but she didn't look anywhere as *nasty* as this guy did.

He held the taser loosely in his right hand. In his left hand he held a drink with ice that he swirled gently around, clink, clink.

"What are you doing here, you disgusting little fly?"

His voice, as he asked the question, was vehement and acid. His expression didn't change though.

"Nothing." I tried to say it strongly, firmly, reasonably. It came out like a frog's croak.

He shot me with the taser again. I caught the glint on the wire as it sped out, tried to dodge, but too late.

I arched over the backpack, my muscles doing things I wouldn't have believed possible. My head banged sharply against the floor. Then it stopped again.

I was disoriented, the room spun. My legs decided to go into a massive cramp. I gasped out loud.

This seemed to please him.

"Who sent you? I'll know in the end. I can do this all night long." I said quickly, "Nobody sent me. I hoped to get some peaches."

He shot me again.

I really didn't think much of this turn of events. My muscles had built enough lactic acid without electro-convulsive induced contractions. When everything settled down again I had another bump on my head and more cramps.

He took a sip from his drink.

"You'll have to do better than that," he said. "Nobody would risk climbing the outside for peaches. Besides, there won't be peaches on that tree for another five months." He pointed the taser. "Who sent you?"

I couldn't even talk at this point. He seemed to realize this, fortunately, and waited a few moments, lowering the taser. Then he asked again, "Who sent you?"

"Get stuffed," I told him weakly.

"Stupid little man." He lifted the taser again and something smashed him in the arm, causing him to drop the weapon. He stooped to pick it up again but there was a streak of gray and the thud of full body contact as someone hit him and bowled him over onto his back.

I saw the newcomer scoop up the taser and spin sharply. The taser passed over my head and out over the railing.

It was Dactyl.

The man in the khaftan saw Dactyl's face then and said, "You!" He started to scramble to his feet. Dactyl took one sliding step forward and kicked him in the face. The man collapsed in a small heap, his khaftan making him look like a white sack with limbs sticking out.

Dactyl stood there for a moment looking down. Then he turned and walked slowly back to me.

"That was a nasty trick with the rope."

I laughed, albeit weakly. "If you weren't so lazy you would have made your own way up." I eyed him warily, but my body wasn't up to movement yet. Was he going to kick me in the face, too? Still, I had to know something. "How did you pass me down there, below the barrier? You were exhausted, I could see it."

He shrugged. "You're right. I'm lazy." He flipped a device off his back. It looked like a gun with two triggers. I made ready to jump. He pointed it up and pulled the trigger. I heard a *chunk* and something buried itself in the ceiling. He pulled the second trigger and there was a whining sound. Dactyl and gun floated off the floor. I looked closer and saw the wire.

"Cheater," I said.

He laughed and lowered himself back to the floor. "What the hell are you doing here?" he asked.

I told him.

"You're shitting me."

"No."

He laughed then and walked briskly through the door into the tower.

I struggled to stand. Made it. I was leaning against the railing when Dactyl came back through the door with a plastic two-liter container. He handed it to me. It was ice cold.

"What's this?"

"Last season's peaches. From the freezer. He always hoards them until just before the fresh ones are ready."

I stared at him. "How the hell did you know that?"

He shrugged, took the peaches out of my hand and put them in my pack. "Look, I'd get out of here before he wakes up. Not only does he have a lot nastier things than that taser, but security will do whatever he wants."

He swung up over the edge and lowered himself to arm's length. Just before he dropped completely from sight he added something which floated up with the wind.

"He's my father."

• • • • • •

I started down the tower not too long after Dactyl. Physically I was a wreck. The taser had exhausted my muscles in a way that exercise never had. I probably wasn't in the best shape to do any kind of rope work, but Dactyl's words rang true. I didn't want anybody after me in the condition I was in, much less security.

Security is bad. They use copters and rail cars that run up and down the outside of the building. They fire rubber bullets and water cannon. Don't think this makes them humane. A person blasted off a ledge by either is going to die. Security is just careful not to damage the tower.

So, I did my descent in stages, feeling like an old man tottering carefully down a flight of stairs. Still, descent was far easier than ascent, and my rope work had me down on the barrier patio in less than ten minutes.

It was nearing midnight, actually lighter now that the quarter moon had risen, and the patio, instead of being deserted, had far more people on it than it had at sunset. A few people saw me coiling my rope after my last rappel. I ignored them, going about my business with as much *panache* as I could muster. On my way to the edge of the balcony I stopped at the buffet and built myself a sandwich.

More people began looking my way and talking. An elderly woman standing at one end of the buffet took a long look at me, then said, "Try the wontons. I think there's really pork in them."

I smiled at her. "I don't know. Pork is tricky. You never know who provided it."

Her hand stopped, a wonton halfway to her mouth, and stared at me. Then, almost defiantly, she popped it into her mouth and chewed it with relish. "Just so it's well cooked."

A white-clad steward left the end of the table and walked over to a phone hanging by a door.

I took my sandwich over to the edge and set it down while I took the rope from the pack. My legs trembled slightly. The woman with the wontons followed me over after a minute.

"Here," she said, holding out a tall glass that clinked. "Ice tea."

I blinked, surprised. "Why, thank you. This is uncommonly kind."

She shrugged. "You look like you need it. Are you going to collapse right here? It would be exciting, but I'd avoid it if I were you. I think that nasty man called security."

"Do I look as bad as all that?"

"Honey, you look like death warmed over."

I finished playing out the rope and clipped on my brake-bars. "I'm afraid you're right." I took a bite out of the sandwich and chewed quickly. I washed it down with the tea. It wasn't one of Mad Molly's roast pigeons but it wasn't garbage, either.

"You'll get indigestion," the woman warned.

I smiled and took another large bite. The crowd of people staring at me was getting bigger. There was a stirring in the crowd from over by the door. I took another bite and another swig, then swung over the edge. "We must do this again, some-time," I said. "Next time, we'll dance."

I dropped into the dark, jumping out so I could swing into the building. I didn't reach it on the first swing, so I let out more rope and pumped my legs. I came within a yard of the tower and swung out again. I felt better than before but was still weak. I looked up and saw heads looking over the edge at me. Something gleamed in the moonlight.

A knife?

I reached the wall and dropped onto a roughing cube, unbalanced, unsure of my purchase. For a moment I teetered, then was able to heave myself in toward the wall, safe. I turned, to release one end of the rope, so I could snake it down from above.

I didn't have to. It fell from above, two new ends whipping through the night air.

Bastards. I almost shouted it, but it seemed better to let them think I'd fallen. Besides, I couldn't be bothered with any action so energetic. I was bone weary, tired beyond reaction.

For the next hundred stories I made like a spider with arthritis, slow careful descents with lengthy rests. After falling asleep and nearly falling off a cube, I belayed myself during all rest stops. At one point I'm sure I slept for over an hour because my muscles had set up, stiff and sore. It took me another half hour of careful motion before I was moving smoothly again.

Finally I reached Mad Molly's, moving carefully, quietly. I unloaded her supplies and the peaches and put them carefully inside her door. I could hear her snoring. Then, leaving my stash under her house as usual, I climbed down, intending to see Fran and make her breakfast.

I didn't make it to Fran's.

In the half dark before the dawn they came at me.

This is the place for a good line like "they came on me like the wolf upon the fold" or "as the piranha swarm." Forget it. I was too tired. All I know is they came at me, the Howlers did. At me, who'd been beaten, electroshocked, indigested, sliced at, and bone wearified, if there exists such a verb. I watched them come in dull amazement, which is not a suit of clothes, but an amalgam of fatigue and astonished reaction to the last straw on my camellian back.

Before I'd been hurt and felt the need to ignore it. I'd been challenged and felt the need to respond. I'd felt curiosity and felt the need to satisfy it. I'd felt fear and the need to overcome it. But I hadn't yet felt what I felt now.

I felt rage, and the need to express it.

I'm sure the first two cleared the recreation balcony, they had to. They came at me fast unbelayed and I used every bit of their momentum to heave them out. The next one, doubtless feeling clever, landed on my back and clung like a monkey. I'd passed caring, I simply threw myself to the side, aiming my back at the roughing cube two meters below. He tried, but he didn't get off in time. I'm grateful though, because the shock would have broken my back if he hadn't been there.

I don't think he cleared the rec balcony.

I ran then, but slowly, so angry that I wanted them to catch up, to let me use my fists and feet on their stubborn, malicious, stupid heads. For the next ten minutes it was a running battle only I ran out of steam before they ran out of Howlers.

I ended up backed into a cranny where a cooling vent formed a ledge some five meters deep and four meters wide, when Dactyl dropped into the midst of them, a gray blur that sent three of them for a dive and two more scrambling back around the edges.

I was over feeling mad by then and back to just feeling tired.

Dactyl looked a little tired himself. "I can't let you out of my sight for a minute, can I?" he said. "What's the matter? You get tired of their shit?"

"Right . . ." I laughed weakly. "Now I'm back to owing *you*."

"That's right, suck-foot. And I'm not going to let you forget it."

I tottered forward then and looked at the faces around us. I didn't feel so good.

"Uh, Dactyl."

"Yeah."

"I think you better take a look over the edge."

He walked casually forward and took a look down, then to both sides, then up. He backed up again.

"Looks like you're going to get that chance to repay me real soon," he said.

The Howlers were out there—all of the Howlers still alive— every last one of them. In the predawn gray they were climbing steadily toward us from all sides, as thick as cannibals at a funeral. I didn't think much of our chances.

"Uh, Dactyl?"

"Yeah."

"Do you think that piton gun of yours can get us out of here?"

He shook his head. "I don't have anything to shoot into. The angles are all wrong."

"Oh."

He tilted his head then and said, "I do have a parachute."

"What?"

He showed me a gray bundle connected to the back of his climbing harness between batteries.

"You ever use it?"

"Do I look crazy?" he asked.

I took a nine-meter length of my strongest line and snapped one end to my harness and the other to his.

The Howlers were starting to come over the lip.

"The answer is yes," I said.

We started running.

I took two of them off with me, and Dactyl seemed to have kicked one man right in the face. The line stretched between us pulled another one into the void. I was falling, bodies tumbling around me in the air, the recreation deck growing in size. I kept waiting for Dactyl to open the chute but we seemed to fall forever. Now I could see the broken Howlers who'd preceded us, draped on the cage work over the balcony. The wind was a shrieking banshee in my ears. The sun rose. I thought, *here I am falling to my death and the bloody sun comes up*!

In the bright light of the dawn a silken flower blossomed from Dactyl's back. I watched him float up away from me and then the chute opened with a dull boom. He jerked up away from me and there came a sudden, numbing shock. Suddenly, I was dangling at the end of a three-meter pendulum, tick, tick and watching four more bodies crash into the cage.

The wind took us then, far out, away from the tower, spinning slowly as we dropped. I found myself wondering if we'd land on water or land.

Getting out of the swamp, past alligators and cannibals, and through the Le Bab Security perimeter is a story in itself. It was hard, it took some time, but we did it.

While we were gone there was a shakeup in the way of things. Between my trespassing and Howlers dropping out of the sky, the Security people were riled up enough to come out and "shake off" some of the fleas. Fortunately most of the victims were Howlers.

To finish this story up neatly I would like to add that Molly liked the peaches—but she didn't.

It figures.

This is one of those stories that sneaks up on you.

*Spider Robinson is the author of the wildly popular "Callahan"
series of comic SF novels, along with stand-alone works such as
Stardance (with Jeanne Robinson) and The Free Lunch.*

Serpents' Teeth

. . . .

SPIDER ROBINSON

LOOKOVER LOUNGE
House Rules, Age 16 And Up:

IF THERE'S A BEEF, IT'S YOUR FAULT. IF YOU BREAK IT, YOU PAY FOR
IT, PLUS SALES TAX AND INSTALLATION. NO RESTRICTED DRUGS. IF YOU
ATTEMPT TO REMOVE ANY PERSON OR PERSONS FROM THESE PREMISES
INVOLUNTARILY, BY FORCE OR COERCION AS DEFINED BY THE HOUSE,
YOU WILL BE SURRENDERED TO THE POLICE IN DAMAGED CONDITION.
THE DECISIONS OF YOUR BARTENDER ARE FINAL, AND THE MANAGE-
MENT DOESN'T WANT TO KNOW YOU. THE FIRST ONE'S ON THE HOUSE
HAVE A GOOD TIME.

Teddy and Freddy both finished reading with slightly raised
eyebrows. Any bar in their own home town might well have had
nearly identical—unofficial—house rules. But their small town
was not sophisticated enough for such rules to be so boldly committed to printout.

"You can surrender those sheets at the bar for your complimentary drink," the door-terminal advised them. *"Good luck to you both."*

Freddy said "Thank you." Teddy said nothing.

The soft music cut off; a door slid open. New music spilled out, a processor group working the lower register, leaving the higher frequencies free for a general hubbub of conversation. Smells spilled out as well: beer, mostly, with overlays of pot, tobacco, sweat, old vomit, badly burned coffee and cheap canned air. It was darker in there; Teddy and Freddy could not see much. They exchanged a glance, shared a quick nervous grin.

"Break a leg, kid," Teddy said, and entered the Lounge, Freddy at her heels.

Teddy's first impression was that it was just what she had been expecting. The crowd was sizable for this time of night, perhaps four or five dozen souls, roughly evenly divided between hunters and hunted. While the general mood seemed hearty and cheerful, quiet desperation could be seen in any direction, invariably on the faces of the hunters.

Teddy and Freddy had certainly been highlighted when the door first slid back, but by the time their eyes had adjusted to the dimmer light no one was looking at them. They located the bar and went there. They strove to move synchronously, complimentarily, as though they were old dance partners or old cop partners, as though they were married enough to be telepathic. In point of fact they were all these things, but you could never have convinced anyone watching them now.

The bartender was a wiry, wizened old man whose hair had once been red, and whose eyes had once been innocent—perhaps a century before. He displayed teeth half that age and took their chits. "Welcome to the Big Fruit, folks."

Freddy's eyebrows rose. "How did you know we're not from New York?"

"I'm awake at the moment. What'll it be?"

Teddy and Freddy described their liquid requirements. The old man took his time, punched in their order with one finger, brought the drinks to them with his pinkies extended. As they accepted the drinks, he leaned forward confidentially. "None o' my business, but . . . you might could do all right here tonight. There's good ones in just now, one or two anyways. Don't push is the thing. Don't try quite so hard. Get me?"

They stared at him. "Thanks, uh—"

"Pop, everybody calls me. Let them do the talking."

"We will," Freddy said. "Thank you, Pop."

"Whups! 'Scuse me." He spun and darted off at surprising speed toward the far end of the bar, where a patron was in danger of falling off his stool: Pop caught him in time. Teddy would have sworn that Pop had never taken his eyes from them until he had moved. She had smuggled a small weapon past the door-scanner, chiefly to build her morale, but she resolved now not to try it on Pop even in extremis. "Come on, Freddy."

Teddy found them a table near one of the air-circulators, with a good view of the rest of the room. "Freddy, for God's sake quit staring! You heard what the old fart said: lighten up."

"Teddy!"

"I like him too; I was trying to get your attention. Try to look like there isn't shit on your shoes, will you?"

"How about that one?"

"Where?"

"There."

"In the blue and *red*?" Teddy composed her features with a visible effort. "Look, my love: apparently we have 'HICK' written across our foreheads in big black letters. All right. Let's not make it 'DUMB HICK,' all right? Look at her *arms*, for God's sake."

"Oh." Freddy's candidate was brazenly wearing a sleeveless shirt—and a cop should not miss track marks.

"I'm telling you, slow down. Look, let's make an agreement: we're not going to hit on *any*body for the first hour, all right? We're just out for an evening of quiet conversation."

"I see. We spent three hundred and sixty-seven New dollars to come to New York and have a few drinks."

Teddy smiled as though Freddy had said something touching and funny, and murmured, *"God damn it, Freddy, you promised."*

"All right, but I think these people can spot a phony a mile away. The one in pink and yellow, on your left."

"I'm not saying we should be phony, I'm—" Teddy made an elaborate hair-adjusting gesture, sneaked a look, then frankly stared. "Wow. That's more like it. Dancing with the brunette, right?"

"Yes."

Freddy's new choice was golden-haired and heart-breakingly

beautiful, dressed daringly by their standards but not shockingly. Ribs showed, and pathetically slender arms, and long smooth legs. Intelligence showed in the eyes, above lips slightly curled in boredom.

"Too good to be true," Teddy said sadly. "All these regulars here, and we walk in our first night and score that?"

"I *like* wishful thinking. You shoot for the moon, once in a while you get it."

"And end up wishing you'd settled for a space station. I'd settle for that redhead in the corner with the ventilated shoes."

Freddy followed her glance, winced, and made a small sound of pity. "Don't mock the funny-looking."

"Me? I grew *up* funny looking. I worked four summers selling greaseburgers for this chin and nose. I'll settle for anyone halfway pleasant." She lowered her voice; the musicians were taking a break.

"I love your chin and nose. I don't like him anyway. He looks like the secretive type."

"And you aren't? This drink is terrible."

"So's this—"

The voice was startlingly close. "Hey! You're in my seat, Atlas."

It was the stunning golden-haired youngman. Alone.

Freddy began to move and speak at the same time, but Teddy kicked him hard in the shin and he subsided.

"No we're not," she said firmly.

There was nothing especially grudging about the respect that came into the youngman's eyes, but there was nothing especially submissive about it either. "I always sit by a circulator. I don't like breathing garbage." He made no move to go.

Teddy refused her eyes permission to drop from his. "We would be pleased if you'd join us."

"I accept."

Before Teddy could stop him. Freddy was up after a chair. He placed it beside the youngman, who moved it slightly to give himself a better view of the room than of them, and sat without thanks.

"You're welcome," Freddy said quietly, slouching down in his own chair, and Teddy suppressed a grin. When she led firmly, her husband always followed well. For the first time Teddy became aware that she was enjoying herself.

The youngman glanced sharply at Freddy. "Thanks," he said belatedly.

"Buy you a drink?" Teddy asked.

"Sure. Beer."

Teddy signaled a waiter. "Tell Pop we'd like a couple of horses over here," she said, watching the youngman. The pacification of Mexico had made Dos Equis quite expensive, but his expression did not change. She glanced down at her own glass. "In fact, make it three pair."

"Tab?" asked the waiter.

"Richards Richards, Ted Fred."

When the waiter had left, the blond said, "You people always know how to do that. Get a waiter to come. What is that, how do you do that?"

"Well," Freddy began, "I—"

"Which one of you is which?"

"I'm Freddy."

"Oh God, and you're Teddy, huh?" He sighed. "I hope I die before I get cute. I'm Davy Pangborn."

Teddy wondered if it were his legal name, but did not ask. It would not have been polite; Davy had not asked them. "Hello, Davy."

"How long have you been in the city?"

Teddy grinned broadly, annoyed. "Is there hay in my hair or something? Honest to God, I feel like there's a fly unzipped on my forehead."

"There is," Davy said briefly, and turned his attention to the room.

Teddy and Freddy exchanged a glance. Teddy shrugged.

"How old are you, Davy?" Freddy asked.

Davy turned very slowly, looked Freddy over with insolent thoroughness. "How many times a week do you folks do the hump?" he asked.

Teddy kept her voice even with some effort. "See here, we're willing to swap data, but if you get to ask questions that personal, so do we."

"You just did."

Teddy considered that. "Okay," she said finally. "I guess I understand. We're new at this."

"Is that so?" Davy said disgustedly and turned back to face the room.

"We make love about three times a week," Freddy said.

"I'm nine," Davy said without turning.

The beer arrived, along with a plate of soy crunchies garnished with real peanuts. "Compliments of the house," the waiter said, and rolled away.

Teddy glanced up, craned her head until she could see through the crowd to the bar. Pop's eyes were waiting for hers; he shook his head slightly, winked, and turned away. Total elapsed time was less than a second; she was not sure she had not imagined it. She glanced at Freddy, could not tell from his expression whether he had seen it too.

She examined Davy more carefully. He was obviously bright and quick; his vocabulary and grammar were excellent; his education could not have been too badly neglected. He was clean, his clothes were exotic but neat and well-kept. He didn't look like a welfare type; she would have given long odds that he had some kind of job or occupation, perhaps even a legal one. He was insolent, but she decided that in his position he could hardly be otherwise. He was breathtakingly beautiful, and must know it. She was sure he was not and had never been a prostitute, he didn't have that chickie look.

Her cop-sense told her that Davy had potential.

Did Pop know something she didn't? How honest was Davy? How many scars were drawn how deep across his soul, how much garbage had society poured into his subconscious? Would he grow up to be Maker, Taker, or Faker? Everyone in this room was walking wounded; how severe were Davy's wounds?

"How long have you been single, Davy?"

He still watched the roomful of hunters and hunted, face impassive. "How long since *your* kid divorced *you*?"

"Why do you assume we're divorced?"

Davy drank deeply from his beer, turned to face her. "Okay, let's run it down. You're not sterile, or if you are it was postnatal complications. You've had it before, I can see it in your eyes. Maybe you worked in a power plant, or maybe Freddy here got the measles, but once upon a time someone called you Mommy. It's unmistakable. And you're here, so the kid walked out on you."

"Or died," she suggested. "Or got sent up, or institutionalized."

"No." He shook his head. "You're hurting, but you're not hurting that bad."

She smiled. "All right. We've been divorced a year last week. And you?"

"Three years."

Teddy blinked. If Davy was telling the truth—and a lie seemed pointless—he had opted out the moment he could, and was in no hurry to remarry. Well, with his advantages he could afford to be independent.

On the other hand—Teddy looked around the room herself, studying only the hunters, the adults, and saw no one who made her feel inferior. *He never met a couple like us before*, she told herself, and she made herself promise not to offer him notarized resumé and net-worth sheets unless and until he offered them his.

"What was your kid like, Atlas?" Davy sipped beer and watched her over the rim of the glass.

"Why do you call us that?" Freddy asked.

Teddy frowned. "It's pretty obvious, darling. Atlas was a giant."

Davy grinned through his glass. "Only half the answer. The least important half. Tell me about your kid—your ex-kid—and I'll tell you the other half."

Teddy nodded. "Done. Well, his name is Eddie, and he's—"

" *'Eddie'?*" the youngman exclaimed. "Oh my God you people are too much!" He began to laugh. "If it'd been a girl it would've been Hedy, right?"

Teddy reddened but held her temper. She waited until he was done laughing, and then two seconds more, and continued, "And he's got dark brown hair and hazel eyes. He's short for his age, and he'll probably turn out stocky. He has . . . beautiful hands. He's got my temper, and Freddy's hands. And he's bright and quick, like you. He'll go far. About the divorce . . ." Teddy paused. She and Freddy had rehearsed this next part for so long that they could make it sound unrehearsed. But Davy had a Bullshit-Detector of high sensitivity. Mentally Teddy discarded her lines and just let the words come. "We . . . I guess we were slow in getting our consciousness raised. Faster than some, slower than most. We, we just didn't realize how misguided our own conditioning had been . . . until it was too late. Until we had our noses rubbed in it." Teddy sipped her beer without tasting it.

Although he had not been fed proper cues, Freddy picked it

up. "I guess we had our attention on other things. I don't mean that we fell into parenting. We thought it through—we thought we thought it through—before we decided to conceive. But some of our axioms were wrong. We . . ." He paused, blushed, and blurted it out: "We had plans for Eddie."

"Don't say another word," Davy ordered.

Freddy blinked. Teddy frowned; she was studying Davy's expression.

He finished his beer on one long slow draught, stretching the silence. He set the glass down, put both hands on the table and smiled. The smile shocked Teddy: she had never, not in the worst of the divorce, not in the worst of her work in the streets, seen such naked malice on so young a face. She ordered her own face to be inscrutable. And she took Freddy's hand under the table.

"Let me finish, it'll save time," Davy said. "And I'll still tell you why you're an Atlas." He looked them both up and down with care. "Let's see. You're hicks. Some kind of civil service or social work or both, both of you. Very committed, very concerned. I can tell you what grounds Eddie cited at the hearing, want to hear me?"

"You're doing okay so far," Teddy said tightly.

"On the decree absolute it says 'Conceptual Conditioning, Restraint of Personality, and Authoritarianism.' Guaranteed, sure as God made little green boogers. But it won't have the main reason on it: Delusions of Ownership."

They had not quite visibly flinched on the first three charges, but the fourth got to them both. Davy grinned wickedly.

"Now, the key word for both of you, the word that unlocks you both, is the word *future*. I can even sort of see why. Both of you are the kind that wants to *change* things, to make a better world. You figure like this: the past is gone, unchangeable. The present is here *right now* and it's too late. So the only part you can change is the future. You're both heavy into politics, am I right? Right?"

He knew that he was getting to them both; his grin got bigger. Teddy and Freddy were rigid in their chairs.

"So one day," the youngman went on, "it dawned on you that the best way to change the future is to colonize it. With little xeroxes of yourselves. Of course one of the first concerns of a colonizing country is to properly *condition* the colonists. To ensure their loyalty. Because a colonist is supposed to give you the things *you* want to have in exchange for the things *you* want *him* to have, and for this golden opportunity he is supposed to be properly grateful. It wouldn't do for him to get any treasonous ideas about his own destiny, his own goals." He popped a handful of soy crunchies into his mouth. "In your case, the world needed saving, and Eddie was elected. Like it or not." He chewed the mouthful, washed it down. "Let me see. Don't tell me, now. I see the basic program this way: first a solid grounding in math, history and languages—I'd guess Japanese Immersion followed by French. Then by high school begin working toward law, maybe with a minor in Biz Ecch. Then some military service, police probably, and then law school if he survived. With any luck at all old Eddie would have been governor of wherever the hell you live—one of the Dakotas, isn't it?—by the time he was thirty-five. Then Senator Richards by forty or so."

"Jesus," Teddy croaked.

"I even know what Eddie wants to be instead. A musician. And not even a respectable musician, piano or electric guitar or something cubical like that, right? He wants to play that flash stuff, that isn't even proper music, he wants to be in a processor group, right? I saw the way you looked at the band when you came in. There can't be many things on earth that are as little use to the future as flash. It doesn't even get recorded. It's not supposed to be: it's for the *present*. I wonder if Eddie's any good."

"What are you trying to do to us?"

"Now: about why you're Atlases. Atlas isn't just a giant. He's the very worst kind of giant. The one to avoid at all costs. Because he's got the weight of the whole world on his shoulders. And he wants you to take it over for him as soon as you're big enough." Suddenly, finally, the grin was gone. "Well stuff you, Atlas! You're not even cured *yet*, are you? You're still looking for a Nice Young Kid Who Wants To Make Something Of Himself, you want a god damned volunteer! You're suddenly-childless, and you're so fucking lonely you tell each other you'll settle for anything just to have a kid around the house again. But in your secret hearts you can't help hoping you'll find one with some *ambition*, can you?"

He sat back. He was done. "Well," he said in a different voice, knowing the answer, "how'd I do?" and he began eating peanuts.

• • • • • •

Teddy and Freddy were speechless for a long time. The blood had drained from both their faces; garish bar lighting made them look like wax mannequins, save that Teddy was swaying slightly from side to side. Her hand crushed Freddy's hand; neither noticed.

It was Teddy who found her voice first, and to her horror it trembled, and would not stop trembling. "You did very damned well. Two insignificant errors. It was going to be Swahili Immersion after the Japanese. Not French."

"And . . . ?"

"Our mutual occupation. You bracketed it, but no direct hit."

"So? All right, surprise me."

"We're cops."

It was Davy's turn to be speechless. He recovered faster. *"Pigs."*

Teddy could *not* get the quaver out of her voice. "Davy, how do you feel when some Atlas calls you 'punk,' or 'kid,' or 'baby'?"

Davy's eyes flashed.

The quaver was lengthening its period. Soon she would be speaking in sing-song ululation, and shortly after that (she knew) she would lose the power to form words and simply weep. She pressed on.

"Well, that's how we feel when some punk kid baby calls us 'pigs.'"

He raised his eyebrows, looked impressed for the first time. "Good shot. Fair is fair. Except that you *chose* to be pigs."

"Not at first. We were drafted at the same time, worked together in a black-and-white. After the Troubles when our hitch was up we got married and went career."

"Huh. Either of you ever work Juvenile?"

Teddy nodded. "I had a year. Freddy three."

Davy looked thoughtful. "So. Sometimes Juvie cops are all right. Sometimes they get to see things most Atlases don't. And hick cops aren't as bad as New York cops, I guess." He nodded. "Okay, I grant you the provisional status of human beings. Let's deal. I've got no eyes for anything lengthy right at the moment, but I could flash on, say, a weekend in the country or two. If we're compatible, I like your place and all, maybe we could talk something a little more substantial—*maybe*. So what's your offer?"

Teddy groped for words. "Offer?"

"What *terms* are you offering? We might as well start with your resumés and stuff, that'll give us parameters."

She stared.

"Oh, my God," he said, "don't tell me you came *here* looking for something *permanent*? On a first date? Oh, you people are the Schwartzchild Limit!" He began to laugh. "I'll bet your own contract with each other is permanent. Not even ten-year-renewable." When that sank home he laughed even harder. "Unbelievable!" He stopped laughing suddenly. "Oh Momma, you have a *lot* to learn. Now how about those resumés?"

"Shut up," Freddy said quietly.

Davy stared at him. *"What did you say?"*

"Shut up. You may not call her that."

Teddy stared as well.

Freddy's voice did not rise in volume, but suddenly there was steel in it. "You just granted us the provisional status of human beings. We do not reciprocate. You are cruel, and we would not inflict you on our town, much less our home. You can go now."

The enormity of the affront left Davy momentarily at a loss for words, but he soon found some. "How'd you like to wake up in the alley with a broken face, old man? You read the house-rules, your badges are shit in here. All I have to do is poke you right in the eye, and let the bouncers do the rest."

Freddy had the habit of sitting slouched low, curled in on himself. He sat up straight now, and for the first time Davy realized that the man topped one hundred and eighty-five centimeters and massed well over ninety kilos. Freddy's shoulders seemed to have swollen, and his eyes were burning with a cold fire. Teddy stared at him round-eyed, not knowing him. Suddenly it registered on Davy that both of her hands were now visible on the table, and that neither of Freddy's were.

"They'll put us in the same Emergency Room," Freddy said dreamily. "You're a lot younger than I am. But I'm *still* faster. Leave this table."

Shortly Davy realized that his face was blank with shock, and hastily hung a sneer on it. "Hah." He got to his feet. "My pleasure." Standing beside them he was nearly at eye-level. "Just another couple of dumb Atlases." He left.

Freddy turned to his wife, found her gaping at him. The fire went out in him; he slumped again in his chair, and finished off his beer. "Stay here, darling," he said, his voice soft again. "I'll get us another round."

Her eyes followed him as he walked to the bar.

• • • • • •

Pop had two more beers waiting for him. "Thanks for the munchies, Pop. And the wink."

"My pleasure," Pop said, smiling.

"Can I buy you a drink, Pop?"

The old man's smile broadened. "Thank you." He punched himself up an apricot sour. "You're well shut of that one. Little vampire."

Freddy's eye was caught by graffiti crudely spray-painted on a nearby wall. It said: "TAKE OUT YOUR OWN FUCKIN GARBAGE." On the opposite wall a neater hand had thoughtfully misquoted, "HOW SHARPER THAN A SERPENT'S TOOTH IS A THANKLESS CHILD."

"Why is it that the word 'another' is the cruelest word in the language, Pop?"

"How d'ya mean?"

"Well, when he's alone with himself a man may get real honest and acknowledge—and accept—that he is a fool. But nobody wants to be 'just' *another* fool. 'Another couple of dumb Atlases,' he called us, and of all the things he said that hurt the most."

"Here now—easy! Here, use this here bar rag. Be right back." While Freddy wiped his eyes, the old man quickly filled a tray of orders for the waiter. By the time he returned Freddy was under control and had begun repairing his makeup with a hand mirror. "See here," Pop said, "if you're hip deep in used food, well, maybe you could climb out. But if you see a whole other bunch of people hip deep too, then the chances of you becoming the rare one to climb out seem to go down drastic. But you see, that's a kind of optical illusion. All those others don't affect *your* odds atall. What matters is how bad *you* want to get up out of the shit, and what purchase you can find for your feet."

Freddy took a sip of his new beer, and sighed. "Thanks, Pop. I think you're into something."

"Sure. Don't let that kid throw you. Did he tell you his parents divorced *him*? Mental cruelty, by the Jesus."

Freddy blinked, then roared with laughter.

"Now take that beer on back to your wife, she's looking kind o' shell-shocked. Oh, and I would recommend the redhead over in the corner, the funny-looking boy with the holes in his shoes. He's worth getting to know better, he's got some stuff."

Freddy stared at him, then raised his glass and drank deep. "Thanks again, Pop."

"Any time, son," the old man said easily, and went off to punch up two scotches and a chocolate ice cream soda.

*This is the story of how Dan and Uncle Joshua went to rescue
Leezie Johnson from monsters.*

*Debra Doyle and James D. Macdonald are the authors of many
works of SF fantasy, including the "Mageworlds" series of SF
adventure novels.*

Uncle Joshua and the Grooglemen
· ·
DEBRA DOYLE and JAMES D. MACDONALD

*"In the First Year came the Plague, and in the Tenth Year the
Burning, and afterwards came the Grooglemen out of the Dead
Lands. . . ."*

> —*A History of the New World From the Beginning to the
> Present Day* by Absolom Steerforth, Speaker of the Amity
> Crossroads Assembly

> *Groogleman, groogleman,*
> *Take one in three.*
> *Groogleman, groogleman,*
> *Don't take me.*

> —Children's counting-out rhyme, Foothills District

Daniel Henchard was sixteen and a bit, and Leezie Johnson
was almost fourteen when the grooglemen came down out of the
mountains into the new-settled country.

The grooglemen came between hay-making and harvesttime, on a moonless night when the lightning flashed and the thunder boomed across the hills. In the dawn a column of smoke rose from the Johnson homestead off to the east. Those of the Henchards who were eating breakfast in the kitchen saw the smoke and made up their minds to go have a look. They would see the trouble and help if they could, for the Henchards and the Johnsons were kin as well as neighbors.

The Johnson place was more than an hour away to run, and longer at a walk. It was midmorning before the farmhouse came into view, and what the Henchards saw then was as bad as could be. The whole house was burnt, and the ashes gone white from burning out without being quenched—the outbuildings, too, and never a sight of living man or beast.

The farmyard told the rest of the story: nine burned patches in a straight row, nine tidy black rectangles on the hard-packed earth, and in each rectangle a lump of burnt bone and blackened meat. Dan Henchard said later that you could tell which one was which, almost—the big one would have been Rafe, who was tall, and at the end of the row, the little patch no more than two feet long and half that wide, that one would have been the baby. Its bones were gone entirely.

"The grooglemen," said Aunt Min Henchard.

"There's only nine here," Sam Henchard said. He was the oldest of the Henchard brothers, and Dan's father. "There were ten Johnsons."

"Sometimes the grooglemen take one back with them to their castle," said Bartolmy Henchard—Aunt Min's husband and

Sam's brother. "There's worse things than being dead, and that's one of them. I hear sometimes the grooglemen get hungry."

"Who is it that's missing?" asked young Dan Henchard.

"Leezie," said Uncle Joshua. He'd been standing by, saying nothing, for that was his way. "I feared that if the grooglemen came, it's her that they'd take. And now, there's none of her size here," he said, nodding at the row.

Uncle Joshua wasn't anyone's blood uncle, but a wanderer who'd come by the Henchard farm one day two winters gone, traveling on foot from some place farther north. He wasn't much of a farmer, but when he went off into the woods for a day or a week at a time with his long flintlock rifle, he always came back with meat. He brought in more than enough food to earn his keep, and in the evenings by the fireside he told marvelous stories of distant lands.

So he stayed on and became a part of the family by courtesy if not in fact, for all he was much younger than any of Father's brothers. Aunt Min said he was only waiting for Leezie Johnson to grow old enough for a husband, and then they'd both be off to whatever foreign place it was whose accent still marked Joshua's speech. Dan Henchard had always hoped that Min was wrong, because Leezie had been like a sister to him while they were young, and he would miss her sorely if she grew up to marry an outlander and leave the settlement. But even that was better than being dead—or a prisoner of the grooglemen.

"We have to bury them," Sam Henchard said.

"You bury them," said Uncle Joshua. "I'm off to find the girl."

"You can't," Aunt Min told him. "You're a hunter, but the

grooglemen leave no footprints to trace. They fly through the air by night."

"Min's right," said Bartolmy. "The grooglemen see in the dark, and you can't hide from them. No one has ever been to their castle and come back down again."

"That's where you're wrong," said Uncle Joshua. The outlands accent was strong in his words. "One man at least has been to their stronghold and come back, for I've done it."

"Then there's never a man done it twice!" Bartolmy said. "And when they find where you've come from, they'll follow you back and kill us, too."

Uncle Joshua shook his head. "They'll not trace me."

"How can you say that?" said Aunt Min. "Everybody knows that when a groogleman asks you a question, you have to tell him the truth. Can't help yourself."

But Uncle Joshua only slung his rifle over his shoulder and said, "What's worse—being taken by the grooglemen or knowing that nobody will ever come to win you back?"

No one answered. Dan Henchard said afterward that his father, Sam, looked sad and ashamed, but Bartolmy and Aunt Min never so much as blinked an eye.

So Dan said to Uncle Joshua, "I'll come with you," because he understood what the answer to the question was. It was worse, far worse, to be abandoned.

Uncle Joshua frowned at him. "You don't know what you're saying. Stay home with your father."

"Walk beside you or follow behind you," said Dan, "it makes no difference to me. I'm no safer at home than on the road."

"As you will."

Uncle Joshua turned without a further word and walked off to the north, and Dan walked beside him.

The two walked a long way, over hills and through a mountain gap, past where Dan had ever heard of anyone going, or anyone coming from. For eight days they walked.

"Whatever was going to happen to Leezie has happened by now," Dan said. "She's dead for sure."

Uncle Joshua looked at him with an angry expression. "If you want to go home, go now and never let me see your face again. Tomorrow, or the next day at the last, we'll pass beyond the living lands, and then it will be too late to turn back."

They went on; but it was two more days, not one, before they crossed over the border into the dead lands.

Dan could see why the name was given. The ground here was jumbled and broken stone, and the trees were stunted and mis-shapen where they grew at all. The sounds of birds and tracks of beasts were left behind as well. The air itself smelled dead, like the taste of licking metal.

At the end of the first day Dan asked, "Is it like this much longer?"

"Don't talk," Uncle Joshua said. "The grooglemen can hear you."

They didn't light a fire in the dark that night, nor was there food beyond what was in their pouches, gathered in the days when they'd been walking through fertile country. The next morning they journeyed onward—but they walked warily, and if Uncle Joshua had moved like a hunter before, now he moved doubly so and at times vanished from Dan's sight altogether.

And then, without warning, a vast rushing sound filled the air. Dan looked about wildly for help, but Uncle Joshua was nowhere to be seen. Dan cowered beside a rock that rose slab-sided out of the barren dirt, and when he lifted his head again, a groogle-man stood before him.

The groogleman had a wrinkled skin all dirty white like fungus, and huge glistening eyes over a round and wrinkled mouth. It shuffled when it walked, and Dan could hear it breathing—a loud hissing noise like a teakettle on the hearth. The creature took Dan and bound him and carried him over hard and blackened fields to the castle of the grooglemen, where the great gate shut behind them.

Then the groogleman laid its misshapen hands on Dan's shoulders and looked him full in the face and spoke; and Dan couldn't understand a word of what it said.

The dungeon cells beneath the castle were carved each from a solid piece of stone, and the air was full of whispers of far-off voices speaking too low to be understood. The groogleman took Dan there and left him. Though he was not bound, he felt no desire to escape, and in the small part of his mind that was still his own he knew he was under a spell.

He didn't move, even when the groogleman put out a claw and tasted his blood, and he didn't try to run when the groogle-man left him and the door stayed open. Nor did he move when the groogleman returned and—in a voice that was harsh and strangely accented—asked him from where he came and why.

Dan tried to remain silent. But he answered every question

that was put to him, and told of Leezie, of Uncle Joshua, of the Henchard farm, of his family and his friends. Nothing was secret, and the groogleman was quiet except for its hissing and gurgling breath as it listened.

But what wasn't asked, the spell couldn't force Dan to betray. So the groogleman never asked or learned that Dan expected Uncle Joshua to come to Leezie's rescue, and to his.

The dungeon of the grooglemen was never dark—the light there was cold and unnatural, coming from torches that burned without smoke and never seemed to flicker or be diminished— but at last Dan slept. When he awoke, Uncle Joshua was standing at his feet.

"You've come," Dan said.

Uncle Joshua put his finger to his lips and helped Dan to stand. They went out of the cell into a corridor lit by the weird pale fires, going past open doors and closed doors and colored lines and paintings of black and yellow flowers. The wind sighed around them and brought to their ears the muttering of far-off voices.

"How did you find me?" Dan asked as they went.

"You've not been here long," Uncle Joshua whispered back. "Finding you was easy. It's Leezie will be hard to find. Did you see her—or did the groogleman tell of her?"

"No," said Dan.

"Then it's up to us to find her. Can you walk faster?"

Dan nodded.

"Come on, then," Uncle Joshua told him. "We'll live as long as we're not seen."

"Are we going home without Leezie?"

"No," said Uncle Joshua.

They went on deeper into the castle, with Uncle Joshua walking a little way ahead, watching in all directions. He carried his rifle in both hands across his chest, with the hammer back and the flint poised above the pan like a wild animal's sharp fang.

"Can grooglemen be killed?" Dan asked.

"We may yet find out," Uncle Joshua said. "Now hush and help me search for Leezie. If she lives, it will be our doing."

And so they walked for a long time, silent, through the maze of rooms and corridors and halls, up stairs and down ramps, in the castle of the grooglemen. Some doors were open, some were locked, and at last they came to a place where they heard a girl's voice weeping.

Uncle Joshua held up his hand to call a halt and began to step carefully forward. Slowly he looked around the corner of the passageway, then gestured for Dan to come join him. He'd found a door, and the weeping voice was on the other side. But the door was locked, and it had neither latch nor keyhole.

"What now?" Dan asked.

"We'll see," said Uncle Joshua, and cried out in a loud voice, "Leezie, is that you?"

The weeping stopped. "Who is it?" came a girl's voice from the other side of the door.

"It's us!" Dan called. "Dan Henchard and Uncle Joshua. We're here to bring you home."

"Get away!" Leezie shouted back. "Get away before it's too

late for you. It's too late for me already. The grooglemen can see me here. They'll see you, too, if you stay."

"Open the door!"

"I can't. There's a spell on it. Only a groogleman can pass through."

"The groogleman," Uncle Joshua muttered. "He'll let you out. Leezie—call the groogleman! Call him loud. Call him now."

"No!"

"Yes! He gave you words to say to bring him. Say them now."

"How do you know what the groogleman did?" Dan asked.

"I *know*," Uncle Joshua replied. "Come now."

He walked back to the corner and sat against the wall where he could look in both directions. There he waited, and Dan Henchard waited with him, until at length a shuffling noise sounded in the corridor.

Then the groogleman appeared, walking its slow and clumsy walk, its feet barely clearing the floor and its head moving from side to side as it looked about.

Uncle Joshua stood and raised his rifle to his shoulder. "Stand where you are!"

The groogleman seemed to see Uncle Joshua for the first time. It halted, and its massive head shook slowly from side to side. There was no expression in its blank eyes, and its tight, wrinkled mouth never moved. But the hissing of its breath stopped, and its hands, with their fat white fingers extended, rose up to the level of the groogleman's thick waist as if to push Uncle Joshua away.

Uncle Joshua jerked his head in the direction of the closed door. "Open it."

The groogleman shook its head again.

The rifle fired. A flash of white smoke rose up from the pan and a cloud of smoke came out of the barrel, and a noise like a thunderclap echoed in the cold stone hall. Uncle Joshua didn't pause. He slung the rifle back on his shoulder and dashed forward, even as the gunsmoke thinned and cleared, torn away by the castle's undying wind.

The groogleman lay splayed out on the floor, with a huge red stain all over the white hide of its torso. Uncle Joshua reached out and grabbed the groogleman under the shoulders to pull it upright.

"Help me!" he yelled at Dan.

Dan took the groogleman by the arm. The dead skin was cold and slimy to his touch and loose upon the bones beneath. He and Uncle Joshua carried the groogleman to Leezie's cell, and Uncle Joshua threw the body forward against the closed door.

Whatever spell had let the groogleman in and out still worked, and the door opened as the carcass touched it. The groogleman fell into the open doorway, and Dan saw that more blood ran from a hole in its wrinkled, gray-white back.

"Wait here," Uncle Joshua said, and entered the room. A moment later he reappeared carrying Leezie Johnson in his arms. Her eyes were closed, and she was trembling.

"Run," he said.

"But the groogleman is dead," said Dan.

"Run!"

A distant voice began to chant, echoing through the corridor, speaking words Dan couldn't understand. He ran, and Uncle Joshua ran with him, moving lightly in spite of Leezie's extra weight. Together they headed back the way they had come, through passages and rooms, while a keening sound echoed about them, as of inhuman things mourning, and the chanting voice never stopped.

Another groogleman appeared, coming around a corner and shambling toward them. Uncle Joshua did not slow but instead swung Leezie to the floor and in the same movement unslung his rifle and slammed the butt of the weapon into the side of the groogleman's head. The groogleman fell.

"They can't see much of anything to either side," Uncle Joshua muttered to Dan, but he didn't explain how he knew. "You take Leezie on ahead—a hundred paces, no more. Wait for me there."

"What will you do?"

Uncle Joshua had his knife out. "A hunter wears the skin of his prey to get closer to the herd. Now go."

He put the knife to the groogleman's throat and pushed it up until the red blood came.

"Go!"

Dan helped Leezie to her feet and supported her as they walked on, while the voices in the air mourned and chanted, and wet sounds came from behind them where Uncle Joshua worked.

Before they had gone the hundred paces, Uncle Joshua joined them again. As he had promised, he was dressed in the skin of the groogleman—with nothing to show he wasn't real except his face poking out of the wrinkled white neck, and a dribble of blood running along the loathsome hide. He carried the skin of the groogleman's head, still dripping, in his hand.

"Now we go," Uncle Joshua said. They walked on. Later he brought them to a halt again and said, "Don't look."

He moved out of sight behind them, and in a moment his breath began to hiss and bubble. Dan could guess what he had done: He'd pulled on the skin of the groogleman's head like a mask, enduring the blood and the foulness for the sake of the disguise. Dan and Leezie walked on, with Uncle Joshua shuffling clumsily behind them inside his stolen skin, until they came to the castle door.

Yet a third groogleman stood there, and the door was closed. Uncle Joshua called aloud, speaking a strange language in a harsh and hissing voice, and the groogleman turned away.

The door opened when Uncle Joshua touched it. Together, he and Dan and Leezie walked out of the grooglemen's castle into the night.

The three of them never went back to the Henchard farm. They buried the skin of the dead groogleman under a rock at the edge of the dead lands, then journeyed onward to the south, where there were towns and fishing villages all along the coast. Aunt Min had been right about one thing, at least: When Leezie grew a few years older, she married Uncle Joshua, and the two of them started their own clan.

Dan lived with them, and in time he brought home a wife from among the fisher folk. Later, when he was very old, he would sometimes tell children about his adventures in the castle of the groogleman, and how Uncle Joshua won back Leezie Johnson after she had been stolen out of the living lands.

But one thing he never did tell, that he'd learned by looking back over his shoulder when he should have been helping Leezie walk away: When you take the skin off a groogleman, what you see isn't blood and meat and pale blue bone.

What you see looks as human as you or me.

5. (TS) Implementation. Biologic Sampling and Sterilization Command [BSSC] is hereby established under direction of SECEC. Existence of this command shall be close-hold to avoid alarming of civilian population. Full biologic safety is a priority. Assigned personnel shall wear full anticontamination suits, to include boots, gloves, gas masks, and self-contained breathing apparatus, at all times when in contact with nonapproved environments.

—Annex K to ORDGEN 4B, TOP
SECRET NOFORN WINTEL,
distribution list Alfa only.

A letter that means one thing one year could mean something completely different a year later. The words are the same; it's the world that's changed.

Connie Willis is one of the most popular writers of science fiction today. Her novels include Doomsday Book and To Say Nothing of the Dog. "A Letter from the Clearys" won the Science Fiction Writers of America's Nebula Award for Best Short Story in 1982.

A Letter from the Clearys

CONNIE WILLIS

There was a letter from the Clearys at the post office. I put it in my backpack along with Mrs. Talbot's magazine and went outside to untie Stitch.

He had pulled his leash out as far as it would go and was sitting around the corner, half strangled, watching a robin. Stitch never barks, not even at birds. He didn't even yip when Dad stitched up his paw. He just sat there the way we found him on the front porch, shivering a little and holding his paw up for Dad to look at. Mrs. Talbot says he's a terrible watchdog, but I'm glad he doesn't bark. Rusty barked all the time and look where it got him.

I had to pull Stitch back around the corner to where I could get enough slack to untie him. That took some doing because he really liked that robin. "It's a sign of spring, isn't it, fella?" I said, trying to get at the knot with my fingernails. I didn't loosen the knot, but I managed to break one of my fingernails off to the quick. Great. Mom will demand to know if I've noticed any other fingernails breaking.

My hands are a real mess. This winter I've gotten about a hundred burns on the back of my hands from that stupid wood stove of ours. One spot, just above my wrist, I keep burning over and over so it never has a chance to heal. The stove isn't big enough and when I try to jam a log in that's too long the same spot hits the inside of the stove every time. My stupid brother David won't saw them off to the right length. I've asked him and asked him to please cut them shorter, but he doesn't pay any attention to me.

I asked Mom if she would please tell him not to saw the logs so long, but she didn't. She never criticizes David. As far as she's concerned he can't do anything wrong just because he's twenty-three and was married.

"He does it on purpose," I told her. "He's hoping I'll burn to death."

"Paranoia is the number one killer of fourteen-year-old girls," Mom said. She always says that. It makes me so mad I feel like killing her. "He doesn't do it on purpose. You need to be more careful with the stove, that's all," but all the time she was holding my hand and looking at the big burn that won't heal like it was a time bomb set to go off.

"We need a bigger stove," I said, and yanked my hand away. We do need a bigger one. Dad closed up the fireplace and put the woodstove in when the gas bill was getting out of sight, but it's just a little one because Mom didn't want one that would stick way out in the living room. Anyway, we were only going to use it in the evenings.

We won't get a new one. They are all too busy working on the stupid greenhouse. Maybe spring will come early, and my hand will have half a chance to heal. I know better. Last winter the snow kept up till the middle of June and this is only March. Stitch's robin is going to freeze his little tail if he doesn't head back south. Dad says that last year was unusual, that the weather will be back to normal this year, but he doesn't believe it either or he wouldn't be building the greenhouse.

As soon as I let go of Stitch's leash, he backed around the corner like a good boy and sat there waiting for me to stop sucking my finger and untie him. "We'd better get a move on," I told him. "Mom'll have a fit." I was supposed to go by the general store to try and get some tomato seeds, but the sun was already pretty far west, and I had at least a half hour's walk home. If I got home after dark I'd get sent to bed without supper and then I wouldn't get to read the letter. Besides, if I didn't go to the general store today they would have to let me go tomorrow and I wouldn't have to work on the stupid greenhouse.

Sometimes I feel like blowing it up. There's sawdust and mud on everything, and David dropped one of the pieces of plastic on the stove while they were cutting it and it melted onto the stove and stinks to high heaven. But nobody else even notices the mess, they're so busy talking about how wonderful it's going to be to have homegrown watermelon and corn and tomatoes next summer.

I don't see how it's going to be any different from last summer. The only things that came up at all were the lettuce and the potatoes. The lettuce was about as tall as my broken fingernail and the potatoes were as hard as rocks. Mrs. Talbot said it was the altitude, but Dad said it was the funny weather and this crummy Pike's Peak granite that passes for soil around here and he went up to the little library in the back of the general store and got a do-it-yourself book on greenhouses and started tearing everything up and now even Mrs. Talbot is crazy about the idea.

The other day I told them, "Paranoia is the number one killer of people at this *altitude*," but they were too busy cutting slats and stapling plastic to even pay any attention to me.

Stitch walked along ahead of me, straining at his leash, and as soon as we were across the highway, I took it off. He never runs away like Rusty used to. Anyway, it's impossible to keep him out of the road, and the times I've tried keeping him on his leash, he dragged me out into the middle and I got in trouble with Dad over leaving footprints. So I keep to the frozen edges of the road, and he moseys along, stopping to sniff at potholes, and when he gets behind I whistle at him and he comes running right up.

I walked pretty fast. It was getting chilly out, and I'd only worn my sweater. I stopped at the top of the hill and whistled at Stitch. We still had a mile to go. I could see the Peak from where I was standing. Maybe Dad is right about spring coming. There was hardly any snow on the Peak, and the burned part

didn't look quite as dark as it did last fall, like maybe the trees
are coming back.

Last year at this time the whole Peak was solid white. I remember because that was when Dad and David and Mr. Talbot
went hunting and it snowed every day and they didn't get back
for almost a month. Mom just about went crazy before they got
back. She kept going up to the road to watch for them even
though the snow was five feet deep and she was leaving footprints as big as the Abominable Snowman's. She took Rusty
with her even though he hated the snow about as much as Stitch
hates the dark. And she took a gun. One time she tripped over
a branch and fell down in the snow. She sprained her ankle and
was frozen stiff by the time she made it back to the house. I felt
like saying, "Paranoia is the number one killer of mothers," but
Mrs. Talbot butted in and said the next time I had to go with
her and how this was what happened when people were allowed
to go places by themselves, which meant me going to the post
office. And I said I could take care of myself and Mom told me
not to be rude to Mrs. Talbot and Mrs. Talbot was right, I should
go with her the next time.

She wouldn't wait till her ankle was better. She bandaged it
up and we went the very next day. She wouldn't say a word the
whole trip, just limped through the snow. She never even looked
up till we got to the road. The snow had stopped for a little
while and the clouds had lifted enough so you could see the
Peak. It was really neat, like a black-and-white photograph, the
gray sky and the black trees and the white mountain. The Peak
was completely covered with snow. You couldn't make out the

toll road at all. We were supposed to hike up the Peak with the Clearys.

When we got back to the house, I said, "The summer before last the Clearys never came."

Mom took off her mittens and stood by the stove, pulling off chunks of frozen snow. "Of course they didn't come, Lynn," she said.

Snow from my coat was dripping onto the stove and sizzling. "I didn't mean *that*," I said. "They were supposed to come the first week in June. Right after Rick graduated. So what happened? Did they just decide not to come or what?"

"I don't know," she said, pulling off her hat and shaking her hair out. Her bangs were all wet.

"Maybe they wrote to tell you they'd changed their plans," Mrs. Talbot said. "Maybe the post office lost the letter."

"It doesn't matter," Mom said.

"You'd think they'd have written or something," I said.

"Maybe the post office put the letter in somebody else's box," Mrs. Talbot said.

"It doesn't matter," Mom said, and went to hang her coat over the line in the kitchen. She wouldn't say another word about them. When Dad got home I asked him about the Clearys, too, but he was too busy telling about the trip to pay any attention to me.

Stitch didn't come. I whistled again and then started back after him. He was all the way at the bottom of the hill, his nose buried in something. "Come *on*," I said, and he turned around and then

I could see why he hadn't come. He'd gotten himself tangled up in one of the electric wires that was down. He'd managed to get the cable wound around his legs like he does his leash sometimes, and the harder he tried to get out, the more he got tangled up.

He was right in the middle of the road. I stood on the edge of the road, trying to figure out a way to get to him without leaving footprints. The road was pretty much frozen at the top of the hill, but down here snow was still melting and running across the road in big rivers. I put my toe out into the mud, and my sneaker sank in a good half inch, so I backed up, rubbed out the toe print with my hand, and wiped my hand on my jeans. I tried to think what to do. Dad is as paranoiac about footprints as Mom is about my hands, but he is even worse about my being out after dark. If I didn't make it back in time he might even tell me I couldn't go to the post office anymore.

Stitch was coming as close as he ever would to barking. He'd gotten the wire around his neck and was choking himself. "All right," I said, "I'm coming." I jumped out as far as I could into one of the rivers and then waded the rest of the way to Stitch, looking back a couple of times to make sure the water was washing away the footprints.

I unwound Stitch like you would a spool of thread, and threw the loose end of the wire over to the side of the road, where it dangled from the pole, all ready to hang Stitch next time he comes along.

"You stupid dog," I said. "Now hurry!" and I sprinted back to the side of the road and up the hill in my sopping wet sneakers. He ran about five steps and stopped to sniff at a tree. "Come on!" I said. "It's getting dark. Dark!"

He was past me like a shot and halfway down the hill. Stitch is afraid of the dark. I know, there's no such thing in dogs. But Stitch really is. Usually I tell him, "Paranoia is the number one killer of dogs," but right now I wanted him to hurry before my feet started to freeze. I started running, and we got to the bottom of the hill about the same time.

Stitch stopped at the driveway of the Talbots' house. Our house wasn't more than a few hundred feet from where I was standing, on the other side of the hill. Our house is down in kind of a well formed by hills on all sides. It's so deep and hidden you'd never even know it's there. You can't even see the smoke from our wood stove over the top of the Talbots' hill. There's a shortcut through the Talbots' property and down through the woods to our back door, but I don't take it anymore. "Dark, Stitch," I said sharply, and started running again. Stitch kept right at my heels.

The Peak was turning pink by the time I got to our driveway. Stitch peed on the spruce tree about a hundred times before I got it dragged back across the dirt driveway. It's a real big tree. Last summer Dad and David chopped it down and then made it look like it had fallen across the road. It completely covers up where the driveway meets the road, but the trunk is full of splinters, and I scraped my hand right in the same place as always. Great.

I made sure Stitch and I hadn't left any marks on the road (except for the marks he always leaves—another dog could find us in a minute. That's probably how Stitch showed up on our front porch, he smelled Rusty) and then got under cover of the hill as fast as I could. Stitch isn't the only one who gets nervous after dark. And besides, my feet were starting to hurt. Stitch was really paranoiac tonight. He didn't even take off running after we were in sight of the house.

David was outside, bringing in a load of wood. I could tell just by looking at it that they were all the wrong length. "Cutting it kind of close, aren't you?" he said. "Did you get the tomato seeds?"

"No," I said. "I brought you something else, though. I brought everybody something."

I went on in. Dad was rolling out plastic on the living room floor. Mrs. Talbot was holding one end for him. Mom was holding the card table, still folded up, waiting for them to finish so she could set it up in front of the stove for supper. Nobody even looked up. I unslung my backpack and took out Mrs. Talbot's magazine and the letter.

"There was a letter at the post office," I said. "From the Clearys."

They all looked up.

"Where did you find it?" Dad said.

"On the floor, mixed in with all the third-class stuff. I was looking for Mrs. Talbot a magazine."

Mom leaned the card table against the couch and sat down. Mrs. Talbot looked blank.

"The Clearys were our best friends," I said. "From Illinois. They were supposed to come see us the summer before last. We were going to hike up Pike's Peak and everything."

David banged in the door. He looked at Mom sitting on the couch and Dad and Mrs. Talbot still standing there holding the plastic like a couple of statues. "What's wrong?" he said.

"Lynn says she found a letter from the Clearys today," Dad said.

David dumped the logs on the hearth. One of them rolled onto the carpet and stopped at Mom's feet. Neither of them bent over to pick it up.

"Shall I read it out loud?" I said, looking at Mrs. Talbot. I was still holding her magazine. I opened up the envelope and took out the letter.

" 'Dear Janice and Todd and everybody,' " I read. " 'How are things in the glorious west? We're raring to come out and see you, though we may not make it quite as soon as we hoped. How are Carla and David and the baby? I can't wait to see little David. Is he walking yet? I bet Grandma Janice is so proud she's busting her britches. Is that right? Do you westerners wear britches or have you all gone to designer jeans?' "

David was standing by the fireplace. He put his head down across his arms on the mantelpiece.

" 'I'm sorry I haven't written, but we were very busy with Rick's graduation and anyway I thought we would beat the letter out to Colorado, but now it looks like there's going to be a slight change in plans. Rick has definitely decided to join the Army. Richard and I have talked ourselves blue in the face, but I guess we've just made matters worse. We can't even get him to wait to join until after the trip to Colorado. He says we'd spend the

whole trip trying to talk him out of it, which is true, I guess.
I'm just so worried about him. The Army! Rick says I worry
too much, which is true too, I guess, but what if there was a
war?' "

Mom bent over and picked up the log that David had dropped
and laid it on the couch beside her.

" 'If it's okay with you out there in the Golden West, we'll
wait until Rick is done with basic the first week in July and then
all come out. Please write and let us know if this is okay. I'm
sorry to switch plans on you like this at the last minute, but look
at it this way: you have a whole extra month to get into shape
for hiking up Pike's Peak. I don't know about you, but I sure
can use it.' "

Mrs. Talbot had dropped her end of the plastic. It didn't land
on the stove this time, but it was so close to it it was curling
from the heat. Dad just stood there watching it. He didn't even
try to pick it up.

" 'How are the girls? Sonja is growing like a weed. She's out
for track this year and bringing home lots of medals and dirty
sweat socks. And you should see her knees! They're so banged
up I almost took her to the doctor. She says she scrapes them
on the hurdles, and her coach says there's nothing to worry
about, but it does worry me a little. They just don't seem to heal.
Do you ever have problems like that with Lynn and Melissa?

" 'I know, I know. I worry too much. Sonja's fine. Rick's fine.
Nothing awful's going to happen between now and the first week
in July, and we'll see you then. Love, the Clearys. P.S. Has
anybody ever fallen off Pike's Peak?' "

Nobody said anything. I folded up the letter and put it back in the envelope.

"I should have written them," Mom said. "I should have told them, 'Come now.' Then they would have been here."

"And we would probably have climbed up Pike's Peak that day and gotten to see it all go blooie and us with it," David said, lifting his head up. He laughed and his voice caught on the laugh and kind of cracked. "I guess we should be glad they didn't come."

"Glad?" Mom said. She was rubbing her hands on the legs of her jeans. "I suppose we should be glad Carla took Melissa and the baby to Colorado Springs that day so we didn't have so many mouths to feed." She was rubbing her jeans so hard she was going to rub a hole right through them. "I suppose we should be glad those looters shot Mr. Talbot."

"No," Dad said. "But we should be glad the looters didn't shoot the rest of us. We should be glad they only took the canned goods and not the seeds. We should be glad the fires didn't get this far. We should be glad—"

"That we still have mail delivery?" David said. "Should we be glad about that too, Dad?" He went outside and shut the door behind him.

"When I didn't hear from them I should have called or something," Mom said.

Dad was still looking at the ruined plastic. I took the letter over to him. "Do you want to keep it or what?" I said.

"I think it's served its purpose," he said. He wadded it up, tossed it in the stove, and slammed the door shut. He didn't even get burned. "Come help me on the greenhouse, Lynn," he said.

It was pitch-dark outside and really getting cold. My sneakers were starting to get stiff. Dad held the flashlight and pulled the plastic tight over the wooden slats. I stapled the plastic every two inches all the way around the frame and my finger about every other time. After we finished one frame I asked Dad if I could go back in and put on my boots.

"Did you get the seeds for the tomatoes?" he said, like he hadn't even heard me. "Or were you too busy looking for the letter?"

"I didn't look for it," I said. "I found it. I thought you'd be glad to get the letter and know what happened to the Clearys."

Dad was pulling the plastic across the next frame, so hard it was getting little puckers in it. "We already knew," he said.

He handed me the flashlight and took the staple gun out of my hand. "You want me to say it?" he said. "You want me to tell you exactly what happened to them? All right. I would imagine they were close enough to Chicago to have been vaporized when the bombs hit. If they were, they were lucky. Because there aren't any mountains like ours around Chicago. So they got caught in the fire storm or they died of flash burns or radiation sickness or else some looter shot them."

"Or their own family," I said.

"Or their own family." He put the staple gun against the wood and pulled the trigger. "I have a theory about what happened the summer before last," he said. He moved the gun down and shot another staple into the wood. "I don't think the Russians started it or the United States either. I think it was some little terrorist group somewhere or maybe just one person. I don't think they had any idea what would happen when they dropped their bomb. I think they were just so hurt and angry and frightened by the way things were that they just lashed out. With a bomb." He stapled the frame clear to the bottom and straightened up to start on the other side. "What do you think of that theory, Lynn?"

"I told you," I said. "I found the letter while I was looking for Mrs. Talbot's magazine."

He turned and pointed the staple gun at me. "But whatever reason they did it for, they brought the whole world crashing down on their heads. Whether they meant it or not, they had to live with the consequences."

"If they lived," I said. "If somebody didn't shoot them."

"I can't let you go to the post office anymore," he said. "It's too dangerous."

"What about Mrs. Talbot's magazines?"

"Go check on the fire," he said.

I went back inside. David had come back and was standing by the fireplace again, looking at the wall. Mom had set up the card table and the folding chairs in front of the fireplace. Mrs. Talbot was in the kitchen cutting up potatoes, only it looked like it was onions the way she was crying.

The fire had practically gone out. I stuck a couple of wadded-up magazine pages in to get it going again. The fire flared up with a brilliant blue and green. I tossed a couple of pine cones and some sticks onto the burning paper. One of the pine cones rolled off to the side and lay there in the ashes. I grabbed for it and hit my hand on the door of the stove.

Right in the same place. Great. The blister would pull the old scab off and we could start all over again. And of course Mom was standing right there, holding the pan of potato soup. She put it on the top of the stove and grabbed up my hand like it was evidence in a crime or something. She didn't say anything, she just stood there holding it and blinking.

"I burned it," I said. "I just burned it."

She touched the edges of the old scab, like she was afraid of catching something.

"It's a burn!" I shouted, snatching my hand back and cramming David's stupid logs into the stove. "It isn't radiation sickness. It's a burn."

"Do you know where your father is, Lynn?" she said as if she hadn't even heard me.

"He's out on the back porch," I said, "building his fucking greenhouse."

"He's gone," she said. "He took Stitch with him."

"He can't have taken Stitch," I said. "He's afraid of the dark." She didn't say anything. "Do you *know* how dark it is out there?"

"Yes," she said, and went and looked out the window. "I know how dark it is."

I got my parka off the hook by the fireplace and started out the door.

David grabbed my arm. "Where the hell do you think you're going?"

I wrenched away from him. "To find Stitch. He's afraid of the dark."

"It's too dark," he said. "You'll get lost."

"So what? It's safer than hanging around this place," I said and slammed the door shut on his hand.

I made it halfway to the woodpile before he grabbed me again, this time with his other hand. I should have gotten them both with the door.

"Let me go," I said. "I'm leaving. I'm going to go find some other people to live with."

"There aren't any other people! For Christ's sake, we went all the way to South Park last winter. There wasn't anybody. We didn't even see those looters. And what if you run into them, the looters that shot Mr. Talbot?"

"What if I do? The worst they could do is shoot me. I've been shot at before."

"You're acting crazy, you know that, don't you?" he said. "Comin' in here out of the clear blue, taking potshots at everybody with that crazy letter!"

"Potshots!" I said, so mad I was afraid I was going to start crying. "Potshots! What about last summer? Who was taking potshots then?"

"You didn't have any business taking the shortcut," David said. "Dad told you never to come that way."

"Was that any reason to try and *shoot* me? Was that any reason to *kill* Rusty?"

David was squeezing my arm so hard I thought he was going to snap it right in two. "The looters had a dog with them. We found its tracks all around Mr. Talbot. When you took the shortcut and we heard Rusty barking, we thought you were the looters." He looked at me. "Mom's right. Paranoia's the number one killer. We were all a little crazy last summer. We're all a little crazy all the time, I guess, and then you pull a stunt like bringing that letter home, reminding everybody of everything that's happened, of everybody we've lost..." He let go of my arm and looked down at his hand like he didn't even know he'd practically broken my arm.

"I told you," I said. "I found it while I was looking for a magazine. I thought you'd all be glad I found it."

"Yeah," he said. "I'll bet."

He went inside and I stayed out a long time, waiting for Dad and Stitch. When I came in, nobody even looked up. Mom was still standing at the window. I could see a star over her head. Mrs. Talbot had stopped crying and was setting the table. Mom dished up the soup and we all sat down. While we were eating, Dad came in.

He had Stitch with him. And all the magazines. "I'm sorry, Mrs. Talbot," he said. "If you'd like, I'll put them under the house and you can send Lynn for them one at a time."

"It doesn't matter," she said. "I don't feel like reading them anymore."

Dad put the magazines on the couch and sat down at the card table. Mom dished him up a bowl of soup. "I got the seeds," he said. "The tomato seeds had gotten watersoaked, but the corn and squash were okay." He looked at me. "I had to board up the post office, Lynn," he said. "You understand that, don't you, that I can't let you go there anymore? It's just too dangerous."

"I told you," I said. "I found it. While I was looking for a magazine."

"The fire's going out," he said.

After they shot Rusty I wasn't allowed to go anywhere for a month for fear they'd shoot me when I came home, not even when I promised to take the long way around. But then Stitch showed up and nothing happened and they let me start going again. I went every day till the end of summer and after that whenever they'd let me. I must have looked through every pile of mail a hundred times before I found the letter from the Clearys. Mrs. Talbot was right about the post office. The letter was in somebody else's box.

It's amazing what people will do to avoid noticing the obvious.
Adults are no exception.

Will Shetterly is the author of several excellent SF and fantasy novels for younger and older readers, including Elsewhere *and* Dogland.

Brian and the Aliens

•••

WILL SHETTERLY

A boy and his dog were walking in the woods when they saw a spaceship land. Two space aliens came out of it. One alien was blue, and one was green, and they were both covered with scales, large red eyes, and long tentacles. Otherwise, there was nothing unusual about them.

The aliens walked into the middle of the clearing and jammed a flagpole into the ground. The flag had strange colors on it that hurt the boy's eyes, and odd lettering that looked like "We got here first. Nyah-nyah."

The boy whispered to his dog, "I'm not scared. You go first."

The dog said, "Rowf! Rowf!"

The boy thought the dog meant, "You are, too, scared. You can't fool me." So the boy said, "Am not," and he walked toward the aliens.

(What the dog really meant was, "If you'd throw a stick, I'd chew on it until it was soft and slimy, and then I'd bring it back so you could throw it again.")

The blue alien said, "Hello, native person. I am Miglick and this is my partner, Splortch. We have discovered your planet."

"Yep," said the green alien. "We did. It's ours."

"And we name it Miglick Planet," said Miglick.

"Yep," said Splortch. "We do. No, wait! We name it Splortch Planet."

The boy said, "It has a name. It's Earth."

Miglick told Splortch, "Perhaps we should name it for our home. We could call it New Veebilzania."

"Boring!" said Splortch.

"Everybody calls it Earth," said the boy.

"Rowf! Rowf!" said the dog.

Splortch said, "Are these Splortchians trying to tell us something?"

Miglick said, "The little Miglickian said 'Rowf!' I believe that means they'd like to give us all their gold." (What the dog really meant was, "Are these aliens friendly? Do they want to roll in some mud?")

"Um, we don't have any gold to give you," said the boy.

"That's too bad." All of Miglick's eyes squinted. "Then what were you saying, Miglickian?"

"My name's Brian. And I'm a human on Earth. This is Lucky. He's a dog."

"His name's Pry-on," Splortch told Miglick. "He's of the tribe of Splortchians called hummings. This clearing where we landed is called Urp. The little Splortchian is extremely fortunate. Its tribe are called ducks."

"I know that," said Miglick. "I heard everything the Miglickian said."

"No, you didn't," said Brian. "The entire planet is called *Earth*. The people who live on it are called *humans*. My name's *Brian*, his name's *Lucky*, and he's a *dog*. Okay?"

Most of Splortch's eyes squinted in a frown. "Excuse me. If you want to name things, discover your own planet."

"But humans were here first," said Brian.

"Okay," said Miglick. "Whenever we can't think of a better name for something, we'll use the old humming name. Isn't that fair?"

"That's fair," said Splortch, squatting on its tentacles to look at Lucky. "You don't have much to say, do you, fortunate duck?"

Brian said, "Ducks fly. They have wings. Lucky's a *dog*."

All of Splortch's eyes squinted in a frown. "I understand, Pryon. I'm not stupid." The alien leaned close to Lucky. "So, where are your wings, fortunate duck?"

Lucky licked Splortch's face.

Miglick said, "I think that means the duck would rather not fly just now, but it is grateful that we discovered Miglick Planet."

Splortch looked at Brian. "You may lick my face, too, Pryon."

Brian said, "No way!"

Miglick said, "The humming does not think it is worthy to lick your face."

Splortch said, "Ah, modest humming, you are indeed worthy to lick my face."

Brian shook his head. "Excuse me, but I don't want to lick anybody's face."

All of Splortch's eyes opened wide to stare at Brian. "Does that mean you aren't grateful that we discovered your planet?"

"Well," said Brian, "I always knew where it was."

Miglick sighed. "These Miglickians are so unreasonable. And to think I was sorry that they would all have to die."

"Have to what?" said Brian.

"Die," said Splortch. "You breathe oxygen, right?"

"Right," said Brian.

"Okay, then," said Miglick.

"Okay, then, what?" said Brian.

"Okay, then, you'll all die when we replace Earth's oxygen with methane," said Miglick. "Isn't that obvious?"

"Oh, dang," Brian said.

Splortch said, "Veebilzanians breathe methane. We took oxygen-breathing pills when we landed, but they don't last very long. And they taste terrible."

Brian said, "I don't want to seem rude or anything, but why do you have to replace our oxygen with methane?"

Splortch looked at Brian, then shrugged several tentacles and said, "What kind of rest stop would Splortch Planet be if Veebilzanians had to breathe oxygen? Can you imagine being cooped up in a spaceship for hours and hours and hours, and finally you come to a planet where you can get out and walk around, and there's no methane to breathe?"

Miglick looked at Splortch. "Inconceivable."

"But Earth isn't a rest stop," said Brian.

"Of course not," said Miglick. "Until we replace the oxygen."

"These Splortchians aren't very smart," said Splortch.

"No," said Miglick. "Well, let's start the methane-making machine."

"Wait!" shouted Brian. "You can't just kill everything on Earth."

"Sure we can." Splortch pointed at a control panel on the side of the spaceship. "We just press the red button. That starts the methane-making machine. Presto, Earth's a rest stop, and everyone's happy."

"But what about humans and dogs and everything that's already here?" asked Brian.

Miglick nodded. "The humming's right."

Splortch nodded, too. "Well, they won't be happy. They'll be dead." Splortch extended a tentacle toward the red button.

"Don't do that!" shouted Brian. "It's wrong!"

"It is?" Splortch drew its tentacle back to scratch its head. "It's not the green button, because that starts—"

"No," said Brian. "It's wrong to kill people."

"Hey, we know that." Miglick reached to press the red button.

"Don't!" shouted Brian. "Humans are people, too!"

"You are?" All of Splortch's eyes opened wide.

Brian nodded.

Splortch said. "Do you speak Veebilzanian?"

"Well, um, no," said Brian.

"Do you worship the great Hoozilgobbler?" said Miglick.

"Um, I don't think so," said Brian.

"You *don't* have tentacles," said Splortch.

"Well, no," Brian agreed. "But we're still people."

"Hmm," said Miglick. "Do you have spaceships that can travel between the stars?"

"We have space shuttles that can go around the Earth. And humans have been to the moon."

"Only to your moon?" Miglick laughed. "That's not a spaceship. That's a space *raft*."

"We're really people," said Brian. "If you got to know us, you'd see."

Splortch and Miglick glanced at each other. Miglick said, "This planet would make such a nice rest stop."

"True," said Splortch. "But hummings and ducks *might* be people."

"Quite right," said Miglick. "We'll have to find out."

"Whew!" said Brian, thinking the aliens would become someone else's problem now.

"Rowf!" Lucky said. (What Lucky meant was, "Does anyone want to go home and see if there's any brown glop in my food bowl? If there is, we can all get down on the floor and eat together.")

Splortch said, "You two Splortchians stand over there. We'd like to take your image."

"Our picture?" said Brian.

"I guess so," said Splortch.

Brian shrugged and led Lucky under a tree, where he stood looking at Splortch and Miglick, who were standing in front of the spaceship. Miglick said, "Perfect," and Brian smiled as the alien pressed the green button on the control panel.

In the next instant Brian was looking at a boy who looked exactly like himself and a dog who looked exactly like Lucky. The blue alien was standing beside Brian, and the green alien was missing. The tree was behind the boy and the dog, and the spaceship was behind Brian and the blue alien.

Brian said, "Hey! What happened?"

The blue alien said, "Rowf! Rowf!"

Brian raised a green tentacle to scratch his head, and then he stared at the tentacle.

The dog said, "Ret's go, Splortch. And you two hummings, be carefur in our bodies."

"Don't press any buttons while we're gone," said the boy. "You don't want to start the methane machine until we're back."

Brian stared, then shook his tentacles in frustration.

"Rowf!" The blue alien rubbed its head against Brian's tentacles until Brian patted it. "Rowf!"

"Rots o' things smell grr-reat!" said the dog.

"Come on, Miglick," said the boy. "The sooner we prove hummings aren't really people, the sooner we can start the methane-making machine."

"Rokay! See you rater!" The dog ran ahead of the boy to get a good whiff of a dead skunk. "Yo! That's grr-reat!"

"Dang!" Brian stomped his tentacles twice, and then he squatted and told the blue alien beside him, "It's okay, Lucky. We'll fix this. Um, somehow."

Just then, a woman behind him said, "All right, who's making a monster movie?"

Brian turned around. A tall police officer stood at the edge of the clearing with her hand on her holstered pistol.

Brian said, "I'm not a monster, I'm a space alien. I mean, I'm a kid, and this is my dog. No one's making a movie. Can you help?"

The police officer cocked her head to one side, then called, "Jack, what do you think?"

A fat police officer came out of the woods and walked toward the spaceship. He stared at it and said, "I think I don't know what I think, Sarge."

"It's simple," said Brian. "Only I can't explain it. And there's no time to try, 'cause we have to save Earth right away!"

"You're a kid?" The policewoman moved her hand away from her pistol and scratched her head.

"Sure," said Brian. "The aliens switched bodies with us by pushing that green button." He pointed at it with a tentacle.

"This one?" the policeman asked. And he pressed the green button.

Meanwhile, the alien who looked like Lucky and the alien who looked like Brian walked out of the woods. A girl called, "Brian!"

"Herro," said the dog.

"No, I think I'm Pry-on," said the boy. He called to the girl, "Who are you, humming from Urp?"

"What's the game?" said the girl.

"There's no game," said the boy. "I'm Splortch. This is Miglick. We're from Veebilzania. We must decide whether we should kill everyone on your planet by turning it into a rest stop for space travelers."

The dog nodded in agreement.

"Okay," said the girl. "I'm Captain Brandi of the Starship *Enterprise*."

"Glad to meet you, Captain Pran-dee."

The girl said, "I've got your spaceship locked in a tractor beam. You have to leave Earth alone, or I'll blow up your ship with my photon torpedoes."

"Oh, oh!" said the dog.

The girl said, "Is Lucky okay?"

The boy said, "Um, we have to go now."

"No way," said the girl. "Or I'll blow up your ship. Besides, Mom said you have to come in for lunch."

The boy said, "These Urp creatures are more clever than we suspected. Maybe they really are people."

"I don' know," said the dog.

The girl patted the dog's head. "Poor Lucky. Did you eat something you shouldn't have?"

A woman stepped out of a house and called, "Brian! Brandi! Lunch is ready!"

"Coming, Mom!" The girl grabbed the boy's hand and tugged him toward the house. The dog stared at them, then back at the woods, and then followed the girl and the boy inside.

At the kitchen table the girl sat in one chair, so the boy sat in another. The dog jumped into a third. The Mom looked at the dog and said, "Down, Lucky!"

"But he's hungry," said the boy.

"He has food." The Mom pointed at Lucky's dish, which was full of brown mush.

"Good!" said the dog as it jumped down.

"Lucky sure sounds strange," said the Mom.

"He can't speak as well as I can," said the boy. "And he can't pick up things in his hands." The boy pointed at his thumb. "I think it's because hummings have this special finger, and ducks don't. Tentacles are far more practical. And far more attractive."

The girl and the Mom laughed. The girl said, "Brian's a space alien. I always knew it."

The boy nodded proudly. "I am Splortch from Veebilzania. That is Miglick, my partner."

"Herro," said the dog, looking up from his dish.

"How do you like the duck food?" asked the boy.

"Good!" said the dog.

The Mom asked, "How'd you train Lucky to bark like that?"

"He di'n't," said the dog.

"I didn't," said the boy. "We learned your language from your television broadcasts."

The Mom put her hand on the boy's forehead. "I think you've been watching too much television, mister. Do you feel all right?"

Before the boy could answer, someone pressed the door buzzer. "I'll get it!" the girl said.

"Oh," said the boy in relief. "That's *not* the sound of you hummings blowing up our spaceship?"

The girl opened the front door, then said, "Mom? It's the police."

"No, it's not." A fat policeman walked into the room. "It's me, Brian."

"Rowf," said a tall policewoman, trotting in after the policeman.

"Oh, oh," said the boy.

"Ro, ro," said the dog.

"Mom!" said the policeman, pointing at the boy and the dog. "They're aliens and they want to kill everyone on Earth. We have to stop them!"

As the policewoman ran toward the dog dish, the policeman called, "Lucky! Come back here!" The policewoman barked sadly and returned to the policeman's side.

The Mom looked from the two police officers to the boy and the dog.

"It's me, really!" the policeman said. "The aliens switched bodies with Lucky and me. And when the police showed up, I got put into the policeman's body by mistake."

"That is not true," said the boy. "I'm Pry-on the humming, not Splortch from Veebilzania." He pointed at the dog. "This is a fortunate duck, not my partner Miglick. Send away those hummings in blue clothing and let us stay with you until we decide whether you're really people."

The Mom stared at the boy.

The boy added, "Please?"

"Brian?" the Mom asked the boy. "The joke's over now, understand?"

"It's not a joke!" said the policeman. "If you don't believe me, they'll turn all the oxygen into methane, and everyone will die!"

"Yes, they're playing a joke!" said the boy. "But not me! I'm really Pry-on! Make the joking people go away!"

The Mom said, "This isn't funny, Brian." She turned toward the police officers. "And you two should be ashamed of yourselves, playing some game like this—"

The policewoman whimpered. The policeman said, "Oh, dang."

The girl pointed to the policeman. "Mom, that's Brian."

The woman stared at the boy. "Then who're you?"

"Oh, all right," said the boy, sighing. "I'm Splortch. I traded bodies with Pry-on."

The dog said, "But where are our real bodies?"

"Right here," said someone at the door.

"Hey, great!" said Brandi. "Space aliens!"

The green alien pointed a tentacle at the policewoman, who was hiding behind the policeman. "Just don't let me eat dog food, okay?"

"Don't worry, Sergeant," said the policeman. "Lucky does everything I tell him to—except when he doesn't."

At that moment a man in cowboy boots walked in the front door and stared at the two aliens, the two police officers, the two children, the dog, and the Mom.

"Dad!" the policeman yelled, wrapping his arms around the

surprised man and giving him a big hug. "You're home early!"

"Uh—" began the Dad.

"Roo's he?" said the dog.

The policewoman started drinking water out of Lucky's water dish.

The boy said, "Please tell Captain Pran-dee not to destroy our spaceship. We could put our rest stop on another planet."

"I—" began the Dad.

"Do you live here?" said the blue alien. "Or are you another space alien?"

"Um—" began the Dad.

"Everything's under control," the green alien said. "But your son promised he wouldn't let me drink out of the dog dish, and look at me now." The alien pointed a tentacle at the police-woman, who was happily lapping up water from the dog dish.

"Oh, sorry." The policeman released the very confused Dad and called, "Lucky! Stop that." The policewoman looked up from the dog dish, then ran over and crouched beside the po-liceman.

The Dad said, "If I go outside and come back in again, will this make sense?"

"I doubt it," said the Mom. "But if it works, I'll try it, too."

"We only saw your television broadcasts," said the boy. "We didn't know you were intelligent beings."

"Rat's right," said the dog. "We won't take away your grr-oxygen now."

The girl gave the Dad a hug. "Isn't this great? Everyone's in the wrong bodies, except for you and me and Mom!"

The blue alien said, "Sarge, I sure hope you'll write the report on this case," and then coughed.

The green alien nodded and said, "Maybe we should say we fell aslee—" and then coughed, too.

The Dad scratched his head. "This is one of those TV shows where they trick people, right?"

"No time to explain, Dad!" said the policeman, running outside with the policewoman following behind him. "C'mon, everybody!"

"Hey, our bodies!" cried the space aliens, running after the police officers.

"Hey, our bodies!" cried the boy and the dog, running after the aliens.

"Hey, Brian and Lucky!" cried the Dad, running after the boy and the dog.

"Hey, Dad!" cried the girl, running after the Dad.

"Hey, everybody!" cried the Mom, not running after anyone. "Who's going to explain what's going on?"

"Not now, Mom!" said the policeman, stopping for a moment at the edge of the woods. "The aliens said their oxygen-breathing pills don't last very long!"

"Rat's right!" said the dog. "Grr-I forgot!"

"What oxygen-breathing pills?" asked the blue alien.

"I don't like the sound of this," said the green alien, and then it coughed again.

"Hurry!" said the girl, running back and grabbing the Mom's hand to lead her into the woods.

The Dad looked up into the trees as they ran. "They sure hide the video cameras well."

Just as everyone entered the clearing where the spaceship stood, the two aliens fell on the ground and began gasping desperately. The dog pressed a purple button on the spaceship's control panel, and two small yellow pills popped out. The dog gave them to the aliens. As soon as the aliens popped them into their mouths, they quit coughing.

After Splortch and Miglick used their machine to put everyone back into their proper bodies, Splortch said, "Thank you for not destroying our ship, Captain Pran-dee."

The girl shrugged. "Oh, that's all right."

Splortch said, "And thank you for remembering about the oxygen-breathing pills, Pry-on. You saved us from having to live the rest of our lives as hideous freaks. Um, nothing personal."

"I kind of liked being a duck," said Miglick.

"*I* kind of like being alive," said the policewoman. "You did good, kid."

Brian blushed and shrugged. "That's all right."

Splortch said, "After we build a rest stop on Pluto, you all have to come and visit us."

"That'd be nice," said the Mom.

"And bring some of that good duck food," called Miglick as the spaceship's door closed behind him.

"Goodbye!" everyone shouted as the spaceship took off. After it disappeared in the sky, the Dad said, "They use very long wires and a *really* big mirror, right?"

"Let's go finish our lunch," said the Mom.

Brian patted Lucky's head. "Glad to be a dog again?"

Lucky licked Brian's face and said "Rowf! Rowf!" And everyone knew that meant "Yes!" (Though it really meant "You smell that dead skunk? Let's all go roll on it!")

An unsettling story about some frightening mathematics and some very smart kids. Or, perhaps, vice versa.

David Langford has been a scientist, a computer consultant, a gossip columnist, a book reviewer, and the author of a diverse collection of fiction and nonfiction books. "Different Kinds of Darkness" won the Hugo Award in 2001.

Different Kinds of Darkness

DAVID LANGFORD

It was always dark outside the windows. Parents and teachers sometimes said vaguely that this was all because of Deep Green terrorists, but Jonathan thought there was more to the story. The other members of the Shudder Club agreed.

The dark beyond the window-glass at home, at school and on the school bus was the second kind of darkness. You could often see a little bit in the first kind, the ordinary kind, and of course you could slice through it with a torch. The second sort of darkness was utter black, and not even the brightest electric torch showed a visible beam or lit anything up. Whenever Jonathan watched his friends walk out through the school door ahead of him, it was as though they stepped into a solid black wall. But when he followed them and felt blindly along the handrail to where the homeward bus would be waiting, there was nothing around him but empty air. Black air.

Sometimes you found these super-dark places indoors. Right now Jonathan was edging his way down a black corridor, one of the school's no-go areas. Officially he was supposed to be outside, mucking around for a break period in the high-walled playground where (oddly enough) it wasn't dark at all and you could see the sky overhead. Of course, outdoors was no place for the dread secret initiations of the Shudder Club.

Jonathan stepped out on the far side of the corridor's inky-dark section, and quietly opened the door of the little storeroom they'd found two terms ago. Inside, the air was warm, dusty and stale. A bare light-bulb hung from the ceiling. The others were already there, sitting on boxes of paper and stacks of battered textbooks.

"You're late," chorused Gary, Julie and Khalid. The new candidate Heather just pushed back long blonde hair and smiled, a slightly strained smile.

"Someone has to be last," said Jonathan. The words had become part of the ritual, like a secret password that proved that the last one to arrive wasn't an outsider or a spy. Of course they all knew each other, but imagine a spy who was a master of disguise. . . .

Khalid solemnly held up an innocent-looking ring-binder. That was his privilege. The Club had been his idea, after he'd found the bogey picture that someone had left behind in the school photocopier. Maybe he'd read too many stories about ordeals and secret initiations. When you'd stumbled on such a splendid ordeal, you simply had to invent a secret society to use it.

"We are the Shudder Club," Khalid intoned. "We are the ones who can take it. Twenty seconds."

Jonathan's eyebrows went up. Twenty seconds was *serious*. Gary, the fat boy of the gang, just nodded and concentrated on his watch. Khalid opened the binder and stared at the thing inside. "One . . . two . . . three . . ."

He almost made it. It was past the seventeen-second mark when Khalid's hands started to twitch and shudder, and then his arms. He dropped the book, and Gary gave him a final count of eighteen. There was a pause while Khalid overcame the shakes and pulled himself together, and then they congratulated him on a new record.

Julie and Gary weren't feeling so ambitious, and opted for ten-second ordeals. They both got through, though by the count of ten she was terribly white in the face and he was sweating great drops. So Jonathan felt he had to say ten as well.

"You sure, Jon?" said Gary. "Last time you were on eight. No need to push it today."

Jonathan quoted the ritual words, "We are the ones who can take it," and took the ring-binder from Gary. "Ten."

In between times, you always forgot exactly what the bogey picture looked like. It always seemed new. It was an abstract black-and-white pattern, swirly and flickery like one of those old Op Art designs. The shape was almost pretty until the whole thing got into your head with a shock of connection like touching a high-voltage wire. It messed with your eyesight. It messed with your brain. Jonathan felt violent static behind his eyes . . . an electrical storm raging somewhere in there . . . instant fever singing through the blood . . . muscles locking and unlocking . . . and oh dear God had Gary only counted four?

He held on somehow, forcing himself to keep still when every part of him wanted to twitch in different directions. The dazzle of the bogey picture was fading behind a new kind of darkness, a shadow inside his eyes, and he knew with dreadful certainty that he was going to faint or be sick or both. He gave in and shut his eyes just as, unbelievably and after what had seemed like years, the count reached ten.

Jonathan felt too limp and drained to pay much attention as Heather came close—but not close enough—to the five seconds you needed to be a full member of the Club. She blotted her eyes with a violently trembling hand. She was sure she'd make it next time. And then Khalid closed the meeting with the quotation he'd found somewhere: "That which does not kill us, makes us stronger."

School was a place where mostly they taught you stuff that had nothing to do with the real world. Jonathan secretly reckoned that quadratic equations just didn't ever happen outside the classroom. So it came as a surprise to the Club when things started getting interesting in, of all places, a maths class.

Mr. Whitcutt was quite old, somewhere between grandfather and retirement age, and didn't mind straying away from the official maths course once in a while. You had to lure him with the right kind of question. Little Harry Steen—the chess and wargames fanatic of the class, and under consideration for the Club—scored a brilliant success by asking about a news item he'd heard at home. It was something to do with "mathwar," and terrorists using things called blits.

"I actually knew Vernon Berryman slightly," said Mr. Whitcutt, which didn't seem at all promising. But it got better. "He's the B in blit, you know: B-L-I-T, the Berryman Logical Imaging Technique, as he called it. Very advanced mathematics. Over your heads, probably. Back in the first half of the twentieth century, two great mathematicians called Gödel and Turing proved theorems which . . . um. Well, one way of looking at it is that mathematics is booby-trapped. For any computer at all, there are certain problems that will crash it and stop it dead."

Half the class nodded knowingly. Their home-made computer programs so often did exactly that.

"Berryman was another brilliant man, and an incredible idiot. Right at the end of the twentieth century, he said to himself, 'What if there are problems that crash the human brain?' And he went out and found one, and came up with his wretched "imaging technique" that makes it a problem you can't ignore. Just *looking* at a BLIT pattern, letting it in through your optic nerves, can stop your brain." A click of old knotty fingers. "Like that."

Jonathan and the Club looked sidelong at each other. They knew something about staring at strange images. It was Harry, delighted to have stolen all this time from boring old trig, who stuck his hand up first. "Er, did this Berryman look at his own pattern, then?"

Mr. Whitcutt gave a gloomy nod. "The story is that he did. By accident, and it killed him stone dead. It's ironic. For centuries, people had been writing ghost stories about things so awful that just looking at them makes you die of fright. And then a mathematician, working in the purest and most abstract of all the sciences, goes and brings the stories to life. . . ."

He grumbled on about BLIT terrorists like the Deep Greens, who didn't need guns and explosives—just a photocopier, or a stencil that let them spray deadly graffiti on walls. According to Whitcutt, TV broadcasts used to go out "live," not taped until the notorious activist Tee Zero broke into a BBC studio and showed the cameras a BLIT known as the Parrot. Millions had died. It wasn't safe to look at anything these days.

Jonathan had to ask. "So the, um, the special kind of dark outdoors is to stop people seeing stuff like that?"

"Well . . . yes, in effect that's quite right." The old teacher rubbed his chin for a moment. "They brief you about all that when you're a little older. It's a bit of a complicated issue . . . Ah, another question?"

It was Khalid who had his hand up. With an elaborate lack of interest that struck Jonathan as desperately unconvincing, he said, "Are all these BLIT things, er, really dangerous, or are there ones that just jolt you a bit?"

Mr. Whitcutt looked at him hard for very nearly the length of a beginner's ordeal. Then he turned to the whiteboard with its scrawled triangles. "Quite. As I was saying, the cosine of an angle is defined . . ."

The four members of the inner circle had drifted casually together in their special corner of the outdoor play area, by the dirty climbing frame that no one ever used. "So we're terrorists," said Julie cheerfully. "We should give ourselves up to the police."

"No, our picture's different," Gary said. "It doesn't kill people, it . . ."

A chorus of four voices: ". . . makes us stronger."

Jonathan said, "What do Deep Greens terrorize about? I mean, what don't they like?"

"I think it's biochips," Khalid said uncertainly. "Tiny computers for building into people's heads. They say it's unnatural, or something. There was a bit about it in one of those old issues of *New Scientist* in the lab."

"Be good for exams," Jonathan suggested. "But you can't take calculators into the exam room. 'Everyone with a biochip, please leave your head at the door.' "

They all laughed, but Jonathan felt a tiny shiver of uncertainty, as though he'd stepped on a stair that wasn't there. "Biochip" sounded very like something he'd overheard in one of his parents' rare shouting matches. And he was pretty sure he'd heard 'unnatural' too. *Please don't let Mum and Dad be tangled up with terrorists*, he thought suddenly. But it was too silly. They weren't like that. . . .

"There was something about control systems too," said Khalid. "You wouldn't want to be controlled, now."

As usual, the chatter soon went off in a new direction, or rather an old one: the walls of type-two darkness that the school used to mark off-limits areas like the corridor leading to the old storeroom. The Club were curious about how it worked, and had done some experiments. Some of the things they knew about the dark and had written down were:

Khalid's Visibility Theory, which had been proved by painful experiment. Dark zones were brilliant hiding places when it came to hiding from other kids, but teachers could spot you even through the blackness and tick you off something rotten for being where you shouldn't be. Probably they had some kind of special detector, but no one had ever seen one.

Jonathan's Bus Footnote to Khalid's discovery was simply that the driver of the school bus certainly *looked* as if he was seeing something through the black windscreen. Of course (this was Gary's idea) the bus might be computer-guided, with the steering wheel turning all by itself and the driver just pretending—but why should he bother?

Julie's Mirror was the weirdest thing of all. Even Julie hadn't believed it could work, but if you stood outside a type-two dark place and held a mirror just inside (so it looked as though your arm was cut off by the black wall), you could shine a torch at the place where you couldn't see the mirror, and the beam would come bouncing back out of the blackness to make a bright spot on your clothes or the wall. As Jonathan pointed out, this was how you could have bright patches of sunlight on the floor of a classroom whose windows all looked out into protecting darkness. It was a kind of dark that light could travel through but eyesight couldn't. None of the Optics textbooks said a word about it.

By now, Harry had had his Club invitation and was counting the minutes to his first meeting on Thursday, two days away.

Perhaps he would have some ideas for new experiments when he'd passed his ordeal and joined the Club. Harry was extra good at maths and physics.

"Which makes it sort of interesting," Gary said. "If our picture works by maths like those BLIT things . . . will Harry be able to take it for longer because his brain's built that way? Or will it be harder because it's coming on his own wavelength? Sort of thing?"

The Shudder Club reckoned that, although of course you shouldn't do experiments on people, this was a neat idea that you could argue either side of. And they did.

Thursday came, and after an eternity of history and double physics there was a free period that you were supposed to spend reading or in computer studies. Nobody knew it would be the Shudderers' last initiation, although Julie—who read heaps of fantasy novels—insisted later that she'd felt all doom-laden and could sense a powerful reek of wrongness. Julie tended to say things like that.

The session in the musty storeroom began pretty well, with Khalid reaching his twenty seconds at last, Jonathan sailing beyond the count of ten which only a few weeks ago had felt like an impossible Everest, and (to carefully muted clapping) Heather finally becoming a full member of the Club. Then the trouble began, as Harry the first-timer adjusted his little round glasses, set his shoulders, opened the tatty ritual ring-binder, and went rigid. Not twitchy or shuddery, but stiff. He made horrible grunts and pig-squeals, and fell sideways. Blood trickled from his mouth.

"He's bitten his tongue," said Heather. "Oh lord, what's first aid for biting your tongue?"

At this point the storeroom door opened and Mr. Whitcutt came in. He looked older and sadder. "I might have known it would be like this." Suddenly he turned his eyes sideways and shaded them with one hand, as though blinded by strong light. "Cover it up. Shut your eyes, Patel, don't look at it, and just cover that damned thing up."

Khalid did as he was told. They helped Harry to his feet: he kept saying "Sorry, sorry," in a thick voice, and dribbling like a vampire with awful table manners. The long march through the uncarpeted, echoey corridors to the school's little sickroom, and then onward to the Principal's office, seemed to go on for endless grim hours.

Ms. Fortmayne the Principal was an iron-gray woman who according to school rumors was kind to animals but could reduce any pupil to ashes with a few sharp sentences—a kind of human BLIT. She looked across her desk at the Shudder Club for one eternity of a moment, and said sharply: "Whose idea was it?"

Khalid slowly put up a brown hand, but no higher than his shoulder. Jonathan remembered the Three Musketeers' motto, *One for all and all for one*, and said, "It was all of us really." So Julie added, "That's right."

"I really don't know," said the Principal, tapping the closed ring-binder that lay in front of her. "The single most insidious weapon on Earth—the information-war equivalent of a neutron bomb—and you were *playing* with it. I don't often say that words fail me . . ."

"Someone left it in the photocopier. Here. Downstairs," Khalid pointed out.

"Yes. Mistakes do happen." Her face softened a little. "And I'm getting carried away, because we do actually use that BLIT image as part of a little talk I have with older children when they're about to leave school. They're exposed to it for just two seconds, with proper medical supervision. Its nickname is the Trembler, and some countries use big posters of it for riot control—but not Britain or America, naturally. Of course you couldn't have known that Harry Steen is a borderline epileptic or that the Trembler would give him a fit . . ."

"I should have guessed sooner," said Mr. Whitcutt's voice from behind the Club. "Young Patel blew the gaff by asking what was either a very intelligent question or a very incriminating one. But I'm an old fool who never got used to the idea of a school being a terrorist target."

The Principal gave him a sharp look. Jonathan felt suddenly dizzy, with thoughts clicking through his head like one of those workings in algebra where everything goes just right and you can almost see the answer waiting in the white space at the bottom of the page. What don't Deep Green terrorists like? Why are we a target?

Control systems. You wouldn't want to be controlled.

He blurted, "Biochips. We've got biochip control systems in our heads. All us kids. They make the darkness somehow. The special dark where grown-ups can still see."

There was a moment's frozen silence.

"Go to the top of the class," murmured old Whitcutt.

The Principal sighed and seemed to sag in her chair a little. "There had to be a first time," she said quietly. "This is what my little lecture to school-leavers is all about. How you're specially privileged children, how you've been protected all your lives by biochips in your optic nerves that edit what you can see. So it always seems dark in the streets and outside the windows, wherever there might be a BLIT image waiting to kill you. But that kind of darkness isn't real—except to you. Remember, your parents had a choice, and they agreed to this protection."

Mine didn't both agree, thought Jonathan, remembering an overheard quarrel.

"It's not fair," said Gary uncertainly. "It's doing experiments on people."

Khalid said, "And it's not just protection. There are corridors here indoors that are blacked out, just to keep us out of places. To control us."

Ms. Fortmayne chose not to hear them. Maybe she had a biochip of her own that stopped rebellious remarks from getting through. "When you leave school you are given full control over your biochips. You can choose whether to take risks . . . once you're old enough."

Jonathan could almost bet that all five Club members were thinking the same thing: *What the hell, we took our risks with the Trembler and we got away with it.*

Apparently they had indeed got away with it, since when the

Principal said "You can go now," she'd still mentioned nothing about punishment. As slowly as they dared, the Club headed back to the classroom. Whenever they passed side-turnings which were filled with solid darkness, Jonathan cringed to think that a chip behind his eyes was stealing the light and with different programming could make him blind to everything, everywhere.

The seriously nasty thing happened at going-home time, when the caretaker unlocked the school's side door as usual while a crowd of pupils jostled behind him. Jonathan and the Club had pushed their way almost to the front of the mob. The heavy wooden door swung inward. As usual it opened on the second kind of darkness, but something bad from the dark came in with it, a large sheet of paper fixed with a drawing-pin to the door's outer surface and hanging slightly askew. The caretaker glanced at it, and toppled like a man struck by lightning.

Jonathan didn't stop to think. He shoved past some smaller kid and grabbed the paper, crumpling it up frantically. It was already too late. He'd seen the image there, completely unlike the Trembler yet very clearly from the same terrible family, a slanted dark shape like the profile of a perched bird, but with complications, twirly bits, patterns like fractals, and it hung there blazing in his mind's eye and wouldn't go away—

—something hard and horrible smashing like a runaway express into his brain—

—burning falling burning falling—

—BLIT.

• • • • • •

After long and evil dreams of bird-shapes that stalked him in darkness, Jonathan found himself lying on a couch, no, a bed in the school sickroom. It was a surprise to be anywhere at all, after feeling his whole life crashing into that enormous full stop. He was still limp all over, too tired to do more than stare at the white ceiling.

Mr. Whitcutt's face came slowly into his field of vision. "Hello? Hello? Anyone in there?" He sounded worried.

"Yes . . . I'm fine," said Jonathan, not quite truthfully.

"Thank heaven for that. Nurse Baker was amazed you were alive. Alive and sane seemed like too much to hope for. Well, I'm here to warn you that you're a hero. Plucky Boy Saves Fellow-Pupils. You'll be surprised how quickly you can get sick of being called plucky."

"What was it, on the door?"

"One of the very bad ones. Called the Parrot, for some reason. Poor old George the caretaker was dead before he hit the ground. The anti-terrorist squad that came to dispose of that BLIT paper couldn't believe you'd survived. Neither could I."

Jonathan smiled. "I've had practice."

"Yes. It didn't take *that* long to realize Lucy—that is, Ms. Fortmayne—failed to ask you young hooligans enough questions. So I had another word with your friend Khalid Patel. God in heaven, that boy can outstare the Trembler for twenty seconds! Adult crowds fall over in convulsions once they've properly, what d'you call it, registered the sight, let it lock in. . . ."

"My record's ten and a half. Nearly eleven really."

The old man shook his head wonderingly. "I wish I could say I didn't believe you. They'll be re-assessing the whole biochip protection program. No one ever thought of training young, flexible minds to resist BLIT attack by a sort of vaccination process. If they'd thought of it, they still wouldn't have dared try it. . . . Anyway, Lucy and I had a talk, and we have a little present for you. They can reprogram those biochips by radio in no time at all, and so—"

He pointed. Jonathan made an effort and turned his head. Through the window, where he'd expected to see only artificial darkness, there was a complication of rosy light and glory that at first his eyes couldn't take in. A little at a time, assembling itself like some kind of healing opposite to those deadly patterns, the abstract brilliance of heaven became a town roofscape glowing in a rose-red sunset. Even the chimney-pots and satellite dishes looked beautiful. He'd seen sunsets on video, of course, but it wasn't the same, it was the aching difference between live flame and an electric fire's dull glare: like so much of the adult world, the TV screen lied by what it didn't tell you.

"The other present is from your pals. They said they're sorry there wasn't time to get anything better."

It was a small, somewhat bent bar of chocolate (Gary always had a few tucked away), with a card written in Julie's careful left-sloping script and signed by all the Shudder Club. The inscription was, of course: *That which does not kill us, makes us stronger.*

Here's a story that starts out in the voice of an illustrated children's book, and then goes somewhere entirely unexpected.

Greg van Eekhout's work has appeared in Fantasy and Science Fiction, Starlight, *and elsewhere. He is working on his first novel.*

Will You Be an Astronaut?

· ·

GREG VAN EEKHOUT

Astronauts are people who ride rockets into space. They must train for a very long time before they go. Astronauts must be brave and smart.

Will you be an astronaut?

The biggest rocket ever was the *Saturn V*. On the launch pad it was taller than a thirty-story building. Today's rockets are smaller and lighter. Today's rockets can be launched more than once. They have wings and can come back to Earth and land like airplanes.

When a rocket engine blasts out flame and smoke, it is so loud that windows rattle and the ground shakes. Everybody knows when astronauts are traveling to space.

Antonio is strapped into his seat. He is about to ride to a space station. Because there is no air in space, Antonio must wear a space suit. In the suit, Antonio can breathe and talk over radio.

He wears a helmet with a special faceplate that protects him from the sun. The fingers of his gloves have tiny claws that help him work with small objects.

The rocket is about to take off. There go the engines. 5-4-3-2-1! Lift off!

Astronauts come from many countries. Antonio is from Mexico. Other astronauts come from Ecuador, Colombia, Brazil, the North American Diaspora, El Salvador, and other countries. Astronauts must be able to work well with others. They also must be good at math, computer science, and engineering.

In space, astronauts speak Spanish. No matter what language you speak at home, you must learn Spanish if you want to be an astronaut.

¿Habla español?

Mercury was America's first manned spacecraft. It was smaller than a car and could hold just one man, all scrunched up. *Gemini* was more roomy and could take two men into orbit. And the *Apollo* spacecraft was even larger. It could take three men to the Moon and back.

On July 20, 1969, *Apollo 11* brought the first astronauts to walk on the Moon. There are no plants or animals on the Moon. There is no water to drink or air to breathe. Astronauts Neil Armstrong and Buzz Aldrin conducted experiments and talked to people on Earth. They collected many Moon rocks, but their spacecraft was lost while returning to Earth. Space exploration is dangerous.

Astronauts must be very brave. Neil Armstrong and Buzz Aldrin made one giant leap for mankind.

Will you be an astronaut?

Antonio's rocket docks with *Space Station Vigilancia*. The space station circles 19,000 kilometers above the Earth. It also has rockets to help it move out of orbit. In some ways, the space station is like a spaceship. It is shaped like a big donut with a needle through the center. Antonio's rocket links up with the space station at the bottom of the needle. He rides an elevator up to *Vigilancia*'s living quarters.

The living quarters are small but comfortable. Antonio cooks some of his own food in a kitchen and grows some of it in garden-bubbles. He sleeps in a hammock and exercises with weights and a bicycle. When he's not working, sleeping or exercising, he watches movies and plays games, just like you do at home.

Antonio replaces another astronaut. The old astronaut will ride back to Earth in the rocket that brought Antonio. Antonio will remain on *Space Station Vigilancia* for nine months. During that time, he will finally get to put all his training to use. He will use telescopes and other instruments to watch for incoming Asps. If he sees an Asp, he will track it with radio waves, and if it gets close enough he will blast it with the space station's proton guns. Antonio has practiced doing this on Earth for a long time. He is very good at it. It is a great responsibility to be an astronaut, protecting Earth from Asps.

If even a single Asp gets through, millions of people could die.

How did Antonio become an astronaut? Astronauts come from all kinds of places. They come from big cities and small cities, from mountains and jungles, from farms and refugee camps.

Asps destroyed Mexico City, the place where Antonio's parents lived. They had to move to the refugee camp where Antonio was born.

Here is Antonio in the refugee camp. He is standing in line at the depot. At the depot he is given a box with food in it. It is enough food to feed Antonio for a week. Antonio eats bean cakes and fruit paste and crackers with peanut butter.

Every time Antonio picks up a box of food, the people at the depot ask him questions.

"How do you spell *rocket?*" asks a man.

"R-O-C-K-E-T," says Antonio.

"Very good," says the man. The man is from Africa and works for the United Nations. He writes something in his notepad and asks Antonio another question.

Antonio can spell many words.

P-R-O-T-E-C-T.

E-A-R-T-H.

H-U-M-A-N-I-T-Y.

L-O-Y-A-L.

Not all the questions are about spelling. Some are about math. Antonio can answer those easily.

And some questions are very different. They are "pretend" questions.

"Antonio, pretend your best friend is hungry. He has already eaten his crackers. When you go to the clinic to get your shot, you see a food box that someone has left by the door. The person who left it there must not be hungry, since they were so careless. Your stomach is rumbling. Do you eat the crackers, or do you give them to your best friend?"

Antonio says, "I tell the nurse there is a food box by the door."

The man says, "Very good, Antonio."

All Antonio's answers are entered in the notepad. After a while, people know that Antonio is very smart. When he is twelve years old he is chosen to attend astronaut school in Rio de Janeiro. It is a great honor to be picked for astronaut school. It is important to study hard. Always speak intelligently to adults. Don't be afraid of big words.

Antonio has to leave his parents in the refugee camp, and he is very sad.

His father hugs him. "Be good," says his father.

"You will make us proud," says his mother.

Antonio flies to astronaut school in an airplane.

He will miss his parents when he is at astronaut school, but he knows he is learning how to protect them from Asps.

It is okay to be sad when you help other people.

The Earth is beautiful. When Antonio has free time he looks through one of the space station's windows. Antonio learned geography at school in the refugee camp, and he learned even more at astronaut school. He sleeps with a picture of Earth over his hammock. The Earth is the most important thing there is.

Antonio sees blue ocean beneath the white clouds. The Gobi Desert is the color of a camel. The tip of Cape Horn is white like a polar bear. North America is green and brown, but parts of it are ash gray. Across Europe is a patch of ash gray. Across China is a patch of ash gray.

The gray parts are where Asps have touched down. More than two billion people used to live where the patches are. But nobody lives there now. There are no people, no animals, and no plants in the patches. Over two billion people have died in the patches since man started going into space. Many more have died because the people in the patches grew food for others to eat, all over the world. Now their farms are gone.

People like your parents have died. People like your brothers or sisters have died. People like your teachers and friends at school have died. Dogs and cats and fishes and hamsters have died.

Do you have a pet?

An astronaut's most important job is to prevent people and animals from dying. An astronaut will do anything to save a life.

On the space station, Antonio controls the guns. Here he is at work. He sits in a special chair. Doesn't it look like a dentist's chair? Antonio's chair has a gyroscope inside it. If something hits the space station, Antonio will remain steady. That's the gyroscope's job. An astronaut must be able to concentrate on his job no matter what.

From his chair, Antonio controls twenty guns at once. The guns are satellites with little rockets that control their movements. Each gun is as big as a tram car. Some of the guns are very far away. Some are out beyond the Moon. Antonio aims and fires his guns with radio signals.

Some astronauts will spend their entire time in space without ever firing a shot. But they're still working. Firefighters are working even when there is no fire. Police officers are working even when nobody is committing a crime. Cleaners are working even when there is no quarantine. Working means always paying attention, even when not much is going on around you.

But now there is an alarm!

Robot detectors have picked up something. Antonio checks the computer. The computer can do math very quickly. It can figure out the size of an object, and its speed, and where it's headed, and even what it's made of.

An Asp is headed toward Earth.

Antonio is ready. He is very brave.

He waits for the incoming Asp to come close to his first gun battery. If he fires at the Asp and misses, the Asp will change course. Then it will be even harder to hit.

Asps are like pieces of string. They can be kilometers long, but only a few meters thick. They are like giant worms. They are disgusting.

Sitting in his gunner's seat, Antonio stares at his computer screen. He sees the Asp as a bright purple line. He tries to line up a red circle over the purple line. When the red circle is in the right place, Antonio can tell his guns to fire. The Asp moves quickly though, and it is hard to aim. It is important to hit the Asp in the correct place. Antonio wants to shoot it in a soft spot so it will break up into parts so tiny they'll burn away as they fall to Earth. But if he shoots the Asp in the wrong place, in one of its hard joints, it will break up into several Asp segments and will be harder to kill.

The red circle is on the purple line. Antonio squeezes the trigger. A signal is sent to his guns and they fire.

Oh, no! The Asp wriggles! It is not a clean hit!

Now there are four Asps.

Antonio's job is harder now, but he does not give up. Being an astronaut means never giving up. He sends radio signals to his guns. He tries to line up four red circles over four purple lines.

Number one is lined up. Antonio fires. It's a hit! The Asp segment breaks up into many tiny bits. He doesn't have to worry about them.

Number two is lined up. Antonio fires. Right on the mark!

Number three is lined up. Antonio fires. It's a bull's-eye!

Now number four is lined up. But only for a second. The red circle drifts away from the purple line. Antonio tries to aim his guns again, but he can't move the red circle at all. He hears a voice inside his head.

We have descrambled your code, the voice says. *We now control your guns. Thank you.*

Asps know how to send signals to Earth. They know how to speak over our radios and televisions. They can interrupt our shows. Recently, they learned how to talk directly to people inside their heads. This kind of communication is called telepathy. Asps may have talked to you. What did they say?

Asps want Earth to stop going into space. They want us to stop broadcasting radio and television. They want us to shut down our factories. They want us to stop drilling for oil. They want us to stop using metals. They want us to stop breeding animals. They want us to stop growing food on our farms.

When the Asps talk to you, it is very easy to want the same things they want. Some people have listened to them. They have started living the way the Asps want all of us to live. You may have heard your parents or teachers talking about "worms." Worms look like normal people, but they are not normal. Worms are people who do what the Asps want. How can you tell who is a worm and who is normal? Worms sometimes say strange things. They may say that machines are wrong or evil. They may complain about pollution. They may make their own clothes.

If you think someone is a worm, you should tell three grownups. You could tell your mother or father, and your teacher, and a police officer.

Remember, worms can be anybody. Worms look like normal people.

Even your parents could be worms.

That is why you must tell *three* grownups.

The Asp is coming toward Earth. If it gets through, everything where it lands will die. It will kill all the people and all the plants and all the animals.

Antonio's guns no longer work. The Asp has taken control of them. What can he do?

Antonio has an idea.

The Asp speaks again: *Your name is Antonio. Your favorite color is blue. Don't use your machines. Be happy, Antonio. Be soft. Hello.*

Antonio unstraps himself from the gunner's seat and floats to the space station's navigation controls. The space station has rocket engines that allow it to change its orbit. If it has to, it can even go to the Moon.

Metals are poison. Chemicals are poison. We will keep you warm. Antonio. We love you. Your favorite color is blue. Thank you.

Antonio wants to listen to the Asp. It has a nice voice. It is a little like his mother's. He wants to shut down the space station's power. He believes the Asp will make him soft and warm. The Asp loves him.

Don't be scratchy, Antonio. Call home. Tell them they can be alive and soft. We can make them alive and soft. Death is scratchy, Antonio. Hello.

Sometimes it is hard to do the right thing.

Antonio fires some of the space station's engines. He switches them on and off to steer the station. The space station moves into the Asp's path.

The Asp knows how to avoid beams from guns, but it does not know that the space station itself is a threat.

Through the window, Antonio watches the Asp come closer and closer. He thinks about his friends in the astronaut corps.

He thinks about his mother and father back in the refugee camp. He would like to talk to them on the radio. He would like to be alive and soft with them.

The Asp is moving in fast. It is huge. Antonio is afraid. But it is just a purple line, he tells himself.

It is just a purple line, and I am a red circle.

He puts his hands behind his back.

The Earth is so pretty from space.

Astronauts are the smartest and bravest people there are. There is nothing an astronaut won't do to help people.

Sometimes schools are named after astronauts who sacrifice their lives to protect our planet.

What is your school's name?

Will you be an astronaut?

This is a story about a woman who changed the world, only that was a long time ago. It is a story she tells to someone who will change the world again. And it's about a world where "to grieve" and "to remember" are almost the same word.

Jane Yolen is the author of more than two hundred books, ranging from picture books like Owl Moon to novels for older readers like Briar Rose. A great deal of her work is fantasy. Despite what it looks like at first, this story is science fiction.

Cards of Grief
• •
JANE YOLEN

You have Come to See Me about the cards? You have left your calling until it is almost too late. My voice is so weak these days, I can scarcely sing an elegy without coughing, though there are those who would tell you that singing was never my strong point. And that is true enough. While some in the Halls of Grief could bring in lines of mourners by the power of their singing, and others by the eloquence of their mouths, such was not my way. But many, many have come to watch me draw grief pictures on paper and board. Even now, when my hand, which had once been called an old hand on a young arm, is ancient beyond its years, I still can call mourners with the power in my fingertips. Oh, I try to sing as I draw, in that strange, high, fluting voice that one critic likened to "a slightly demented turtledove." But I have always known it is the pictures, not the singing, that bring mourners to our table.

That was how she found me, you know, singing and drawing at a minor, minor Hall for one of my dying great-aunts, a sister to my mother's mother. In those days, our mother lines were quite defined. We were a family of swineherds and had always been so. I found it easier to talk to pigs than people and had never played at any Hall games, having no brothers or sisters, only pigs. Once, though, I had made up a threnody of sow lines. I think I could recall it still—if I tried.

No matter. The irony is that I can remember the look of my favorite sow's face, but the great-aunt I mourned for—her face is lost to me forever. Though, of course, I know her lines: Grendi, of Grendinna, of Grenesta, and so forth.

The Gray Wanderer (she was still called that by backwater folk like us) had been on a late pilgrimage. She often went back to country Halls. "Touching true grief," she liked to call it, though I wonder how *true* that grief really was. We tried to ape the cities and city folk, and we copied our dirges from the voice boxes the new men had brought. Many of my first drawings were tracings of tracings. How could I, a pigkeeper, know otherwise?

But she saw me at a Hall so minor that both pillars and capitals were barren of carvings, though there was an ill-conceived painting of a weeping woman decorating one wall. Its only value was its age. Paint flaked off it like colorful scabs. The arms were stiff, the pose awkward. I know that now.

"The girl, let me take her," the Gray Wanderer said.

My mother and her sisters did not want to let me go. It was not love that bound us, but greed. I worked hard, and the pigs would suffer from my going. Besides, I had become quite a success as a griever in our little town. They could not see beyond our sties to the outside world.

But the Gray Wanderer pointed out, rightfully, that they had no means to educate me beyond this minor Hall. "Let her come with me and learn," the Gray Wanderer said. "And I will give you gold besides, to find another pigkeeper."

They hesitated.

"She will bring mourners to Halls all over the land to know the names of your lines. To remember you."

I will never know which argument decided them. But they gave me into her hands.

"You will not see her again," the Gray Wanderer told them. "Except from afar. But her name will still be your name. And I promise you that she will not forget her lines."

And so it was.

No, do not rush me. I will get to the cards. But this, this must all come first. So that you will understand.

I was sixteen summers then. Not as young as the Wanderer herself had been when she had been chosen. But young enough. Yet I left home without a backward glance, my hand on her robe. I did not even paint my face with tears for the leaving. It was such a small grief. I left them counting the gold, greedier than their own swine, who sensed my going and mourned the only way they could, by refusing a meal. Later, I heard, my mother and one of her sisters had come and asked for more gold. They were given it—along with a beating.

"If you come again," the warning had been set, "she will have more names to add to the lines of grief. And they will be your own."

Well, no one likes to be called to the cave before her time. They did not set foot in the city again.

I became, in effect, the Gray Wanderer's child. I would have taken her family name, had she let me. But she had promised I would retain my own. So I did. But in all else I was hers. I learned as much as she could teach—and more. For even when she did not teach, I learned. By watching. By listening. By loving.

But she was already old, and so all of our time added together was still short. Excuse my tears. Crying, she used to say, does not become a griever. But of course, I am not a griever now. Those who come after will grieve me. But I am as near the cave as makes no difference.

So I come to the part you wish to hear. About the cards. But first I must touch upon *her* death, for it was that which inspired the cards of grief. It is many, many years ago, but as you can see, I have not left off my grieving.

I remember it as if it were yesterday. Here, let me paint it for you and tell the pictures aloud. My paints are over there, in the corner, in the round wooden box. Yes, that is it, the one with the picture of tears that look like flowers on the top. Bring it to me.

First I will sketch the cave. It was back in the mountains above the palace, one of the many rock outcroppings in the lower hills. We were three days finding it, though it was only a walk of a day. She knew where it was, but she had a palsy, a halting gait, which made walking slow. We camped at night and watched the stars together. She told me their names; strange names they were, in a language not our own. She knew tales about many of them. Does that surprise you? It should not. The Gray Wanderer remembered everything she ever heard from you starfolk. And used it, too.

Just as you say in your language, *"I see,"* when you understand something, we say, *"I hear."* And of course the Gray Wanderer's hearing was better than anyone's.

This then is the cave. The entrance was hidden behind evergreen branches, so cleverly concealed that only she knew of it. She had discovered it when she had first come to be the Queen's own griever. Often, she told me, in that first year she had run off into the hills for quiet. She was terribly homesick. Not I. I had not ever been happy until I left my home. I would have been sick only at the thought of returning there. If I regretted anything, it was leaving my poor pigs to the mercy of my kin.

In the cave was a bed, a cot really, constructed of that same evergreen wood with weaving strung from side to side. I packed a new mattress for her each day of sweet-smelling rushes, grasses, and sharp-scented boughs. I set candles at the head and foot of the bed. There was a natural chimney in the cave, and the smoke from the candles was drawn up it and out in a thin thread. Once I fancied it was the Gray Wanderer's essence slowly unwinding from her, unwinding and threading its way out of the cave. Here, I'll draw it like that. Do you see?

She knew she was dying, of course. It was why we were there. She set me the task of retelling all I remembered of the history of grieving, to set it for good in my memory. Since she had taught me every day I had been with her, I had many, many hours of recounting to do. But when I had told nearly all I knew, she added a new story, one I had heard only from others. It was her own tale. I still remember every word of it, as if it had been told to me just this morning.

Then she bade me bring her the Cup of Sleep, putting her hand out to me, thus. I can scarcely draw her fingers as thin and gnarled as they were. It makes me ache to see them again, but it is not that which stops me. It requires a delicacy that, alas, my own hands have forgot. But as thin and as pale and as drawn up as she was, her hair was still the vigorous dark color it had been when she was a child. I bound it up for her as she instructed, with red trillium for life, and blue-black elderberry for death. I twined green boughs around the bed for the passage between.

Then she smiled at me, and comforted me when she saw I would weep—I who never wept for anything in my life before.

I stood here, with the cup in my hands. Does the figure look strange to you? A bit cramped? Well, it should. My back and neck hurt from the tension of wanting to give the cup to her to ease her pain, and yet not wanting to because, though her pain would be over then, mine would go on and on alone. But in the end I gave it to her and left as she bid. I left, and went outside and waited two days. I sang all the grief songs I knew to keep from crying again, but I never ate. Nor did I draw.

At the end of that time, I went back into the cave. I had to cut the boughs away again, so quickly had they grown over the entrance.

She was lying there as I had left her, her face composed, her hands laced together. It surprised me to see her look so young and so peaceful.

I brought her husk out and put it on the pyre and pylons we had built together outside, though in truth she had only watched, her hand pressed against her side, while I did the work of the building. I sat another day, still as a stone, until the first birds came and settled on her, and one, a blackbird with wild white eyes, took the first bite.

Then I fled down the mountainside where I was sick several times, though I had sat pyrewatch before and had never blanched. It is funny how one can be sick with nothing in the stomach but bile and tears.

I went directly to the queen's own room and knelt and said, "The Gray Wanderer is gone."

"You will make them remember her?" she asked. She was always a cold woman, rigid. It was the proper response, but I had wanted more. I knew she had loved the Wanderer in her own way.

"Your Majesty," I said, giving her back ice for ice, "I will."

"May your lines of grieving be long," she said.

I turned and left. She knew that I had left out the last line of the ritual. I would not give her the satisfaction of my words. She would not hear "May your time of dying be short." I did not care if hers was short or long. The only one I cared about had already had too long a time of dying, too short a time of living.

I went to the rooms we had shared and wept again. Then I dried my tears with one of the many towels the Wanderer had collected in her years of grieving in Halls. I pinched my cheeks for color and sat down with a harp to compose a small dirge, a threnody, a lament. But nothing would come. Even the Gray Wanderer's own words could not contain my feelings.

I stared at my reflection in the glass. Real tears marked a passage down my cheeks. I could paint over them with tear lines in any color I wanted. But I could not just paint my face and let her go.

I spoke to her under my breath. *Forgive me, Gray*, I said. *Forgive my excess of sorrow*. She would have shuddered at the ocean of my tears. But though I was no girl of her lines, I was her true apprentice. She was dearer to me than a line mother, and I had to do more to honor her. She would have long, long lines of mourners to remember her. I would give her immortality for sure.

So all that night in the royal Hall of Grief, with mourners passing in and out, speaking their ritual parts with as much sincerity as they could manage, I began to devise the cards of grief.

I was silent while I worked, and it may be that it was my silence that first called the mourners in, for if I had any reputation at all as a young griever, it was not for silence. But if it was the silence that drew them in, it was the cards of grief that brought them back.

It took a week of days and sleepless nights before I was done with the painting of them. And then I slept for another week, hardly knowing who I was or what I was or where it was I was sleeping. My hands were so stained with paint that it was months before they were clean again. The clothes I had worn for that week I burned. I do not think I ever truly recovered my health. But I brought her a line of grievers as had never been seen before, long solemn rows of mourners; young and old, men as well as women. Even the starfarers came, borne in by curiosity I am sure, but staying to weep with the rest. And each time the cards are seen, another griever is added to her line. Oh, the Gray Wanderer is an immortal for sure.

The cards? I have not forgotten. Here, put the paints away. The painting? It is nothing, a quick sketch. Certainly you may keep it. And each time you see it, you will remember the Gray Wanderer.

You would have liked her? I see you know our rituals. So I will answer you in kind. She would have grown by your friendship. And *that* is quite true. Though she eschewed the ways of your people, she did not forget to grow in her art by understanding.

And now the cards. You see, I have not forgotten. Now is the time to show you.

That first pack was an eleven, not the more ornate thirteen plus thirteen that gamesters now use. I drew the cards on a heavy paper that I made of pressed reeds. I drew lightly so that only I could see the outline. Then I colored them in with the paints and chalks I should have used for my grief mask. That is why the colors are so basic: not the wider palette of art but the mono-chromatic range of the body's grief paints. The red? That color has been so remarked upon. Here is the truth of it. It was not paint at all. It was my own blood. I drew it from the soft inside of my left elbow, the turning closest to the heart. You can still see the scar. It is no more than a raised pinprick now.

To this day, the original thirteen is called the Prime Pack. Does that confuse you? You are counting on your fingers. There were eleven done at the Hall of Grief. And then, after my week of sleep, I rose and painted two more. The Prime Pack is kept on velvet in the Queen's Museum, under glass. They are arranged at each month's turning in a new order. As if the order mattered now.

That first pack spoke directly to my need. There was no arcane symbology. The Seven Grievers were one for each of the great families. The Cave That Is Fed By No Light—the darkest card— is of course the death card. For as we come from the womb cave, so we go to that other cave in the end. And, of course, my beloved Wanderer came to her end in a real cave. The picture on the card is an exact rendering of her last resting.

The Queen of Shadows is the major card, for the Wanderer was always loyal to the queen on the throne. And the Singer of Dirges is the minor card. The moving card, the card that goes with ease from high place to low, was the card I called after my master, the Gray Wanderer. Its face is her face, and the dark hair under the cloak of gray is twined with flowers. But it is the Wanderer as she was when she was young, not crabbed with age and in pain, but when her face was unlined and she had a prince for a lover.

Seven Grievers. The Cave. The Queen. The Singer. And the

Gray Wanderer. Eleven cards in all. And after my sleep I added two: the Man Without Tears and the Cup.

I sometimes think it was only a sentimental gesture. Gray often told me I must not confuse true sentiment with sentimentality. I wonder what she would have thought of it. But I meant it for her, I meant it as all true grievers mean the poems and scriptings and songs they make. Those are the old, slow ways, but for all that they were old and slow, they were about life and death and the small passage between.

I did not have to explain the cards to the many lines of mourners who came to honor my master. Not the way I have to explain them today. Over and over, to those like you who have come from the far stars with voice boxes and light boxes and faulty memories, who say "I see" even when you see nothing at all. And over and over to those of my own people who now ape grief with comic songs and dances and who turn even the cards of grief into a game.

But I will do it once more. One final time. I will tell the Prime Pack. Forgive me if the telling is one whose parts you have heard before. And this time I will tell it with infinite care, for there have been times that I, even I, have told them as a rota, a list, without meaning. This time I will unwind the thread of honest grief. For the Gray Wanderer. And for myself. For the story must be told.

I lay out the cards, one by one. Listen well. Do not rely on your boxes. Use your eyes. Use your ears. Memory is the daughter of the eye and ear.

Here are the Seven Grievers.

The figure on each card is dressed as one of the great families. There is not a person in our world who cannot trace connection to them. I am myself of Lands. And all who work the soil—farmers and stockmen, harrowers and pigkeepers—are here. So it is the Number One card because it is mine. We Lands were first before all the rest, and will remain when all the rest lie forgotten. In the Prime Pack, Lands wears the brown tunic and trews of our family and rides astride a white sow because that is, in a sense, how I was found.

The Number Two card is Moon, those who know the seasons' turning and can reckon the changes—the seers and priestesses, dressed in white. Three, Arcs and Bows: the warrior-hunters. Four, Waters and all who plow there. Five, Rocks who wrest gemstones from the mountain face and craft them. Six, Stars, who carry our world's knowledge and script that knowledge into books. And Seven, the queen's own, the Royals, the smallest family of all.

Seven Grievers, seven families, all who were touched by and who touched my master.

Then the Cave card. The Queen of Shadows. The Gray Wanderer. The Singer of Dirges. I have spoken of them already. The Cup of Sleep and the Man Without Tears.

The first thirteen were known as the Cards of Dark, for all the faces on the original pack were dark since I drew them in in my grief. The thirteen cards added later by the gamesters are called the Cards of Light, and all the figures grin, their whitened faces set in a rictus, a parody of all we hold sacred.

Here, you can see the difference even in this pack. In my

drawing of the Man Without Tears, he wears a landing suit and holds his hands outstretched by his sides, the light streaming through a teardrop in each palm. But his face cannot be seen, obscured as it is by the blackened bubble of his headgear. Yet in the gamesters' thirteen, he wears a different uniform, one with stars and bars on the shoulders. And though his hands are still outstretched, with the light reflecting through the palms, his face is drawn as plain as any griever's, and he smiles a painful, sad grimace.

You can see the difference also in the Queen of Shadows card. In my pack, she is dressed in red and black, and her picture was a dark portrait of the queen then on the throne. But the packs today are no-faced and every-faced, the features as bland as the mash one feeds a child. There is no meaning there. *My* queen wore a real face, but the card looked back to an even older tale. You know it, of course? The queen mourning for her dead consort who went into the cave at the center of the world. She wore a red dress and a black cloak and carried a bag of her most precious jewels to purchase his release from Death. In those days Death was thought to live in a great stone palace in the world's center surrounded by circles of unmourned folk who had to grieve for themselves.

The queen followed the twisting, winding cave for miles, learning to see in the dark land with a night sight as keen as that she had used to see with in the day. Many long night-days passed, and at last she stopped by a pool and knelt down to drink. She saw, first, the dartings of phosphorescent fish, as numerous as stars. Then she saw, staring up from the pool, her own reflection, with shining night-eyes, big and luminous. She did not recognize herself, so changed was she from her journey. But she fell in love with the image, a queen from the dark sky, she thought. And she stayed by the poolside, weeping her diamonds and pearls into it, begging the jewel-eyed star woman to come up to her.

After thirteen days of weeping, her grief for her consort was forgotten and her precious gems were all gone. She returned home empty-handed. But her eyes remained wide and dark-seeing; she had become a visionary and seeress who spoke in riddles and read signs in the stars and was never again quite sane. She was called Queen of Shadows.

You do not understand the other cards in my deck? The Singer of Dirges? It is named after the simple singer who first brought my master into her fame. He was of no great importance otherwise—a helper, a pointer of ways. And so the Singer card within the deck simply helps the other cards along, leading them from place to place within the pattern, being nothing in itself, only indicating the path to take.

And the Cup of Sleep? It is the changer. If it precedes a card, it changes the card and the pattern. If it follows a card, it does no harm. And the only card it cannot change is the Cave.

There, now you know the deck as well as I. Are you a player with the cards? Do you use them to tell you what will be, waiting on the message before you make a choice? Neither? Good. Only a fool uses them thus. They are grief cards, to help you understand your own grieving, as they helped me with mine.

We are each a card, you know. I am like the Singer card, a

pointer of ways. I point back to the old ways of the Wanderer, and forward to what will come.

And you, starfarer, bring change. You and your people are like cups of sleep. Without changing yourselves, you deal out death to our ways. The Wanderer knew this, but she could do nothing to stop it. And neither can I. I can but tell you what you do, force you to look backward and forward. That was the real reason I said that you could come and capture me in your boxes. But you, yourself, starfarer, who are a woman and might have been a griever or a queen, listen to me well. Forget your boxes, and hear my words in your heart and bones. Do you mean to be a death card? Do you know what it is you do?

So much telling. My mouth is dry. Hand me that cup, the one on the table. Yes, it is a lovely thing. The engravings are quite old. From the third kingdom, I believe. I need to moisten my tongue. That is good.

What do the writings mean? I will read them to you. "Here is the Cup. Take it willingly. May your time of dying be short."

Do not look so startled. I know what I do. And now you know, too. Remember, there is no penalty in our world for giving a peaceful death. Tell your people that. Mine already know.

But you can do something for me. Grieve for me. Grieve for all of us in this quiet, dying land. You owe us that immortality at least.

Now go, for I feel sleep coming on me. The time of dying will, indeed, be short. I hope my lines of mourning will be very, very long, for I want to see my beloved Gray Wanderer again in the cave beyond all stars.

And sometimes it's the outsiders who see truth the most clearly.

Greg Bear is the author of some of the best SF of the last twenty years, including novels such as Blood Music, Eon, *and* Moving Mars. *"Tangents" won the Nebula Award in 1986 and the Hugo Award in 1987.*

Tangents

. . . .

GREG BEAR

The nut-brown boy stood in the California field, his Asian face shadowed by a hardhat, his short stocky frame clothed in a T-shirt and a pair of brown shorts. He squinted across the hip-high grass at the spraddled old two-story ranch house, whistling a few bars from a Haydn piano sonata.

Out of the upper floor of the house came a man's high, frustrated "Bloody hell!" and the sound of a fist slamming on a solid surface. Silence for a minute. Then, more softly, a woman's question, "Not going well?"

"No. I'm swimming in it, but I don't see it."

"The encryption?" the woman asked timidly.

"The tesseract. If it doesn't gel, it isn't aspic."

The boy squatted in the grass and listened.

"And?" the woman encouraged.

"Ah, Lauren, it's still cold broth."

The boy lay back in the grass. He had crept over the split-rail and brick-pylon fence from the new housing project across the road. School was out for the summer and his mother—adoptive mother—did not like him around the house all day. Or at all.

Behind his closed eyes, a huge piano keyboard appeared, with him dancing on the keys. He loved music.

He opened his eyes and saw a thin, graying lady in a tweed suit leaning over him, staring. "You're on private land," she said, brows knit.

He scrambled up and brushed grass from his pants. "Sorry."

"I thought I saw someone out here. What's your name?"

"Pal," he replied.

"Is that a name?" she asked querulously.

"Pal Tremont. It's not my real name. I'm Korean."

"Then what's your real name?"

"My folks told me not to use it any more. I'm adopted. Who are you?"

The gray woman looked him up and down. "My name is Lauren Davies," she said. "You live near here?"

He pointed across the fields at the close-packed tract homes.

"I sold the land for those homes ten years ago," she said. She seemed to be considering something. "I don't normally enjoy children trespassing."

"Sorry," Pal said.

"Have you had lunch?"

"No."

"Will a grilled cheese sandwich do?"

He squinted at her and nodded.

In the broad, red-brick and tile kitchen, sitting at an oak table with his shoulders barely rising above the top, he ate the slightly charred sandwich and watched Lauren Davies watching him.

"I'm trying to write about a child," she said. "It's difficult. I'm a spinster and I don't know children well."

"You're a writer?" he asked, taking a swallow of milk.

She sniffed. "Not that anyone would know."

"Is that your brother, upstairs?"

"No," she said. "That's Peter. We've been living together for twenty years."

"But you said you're a spinster . . . isn't that someone who's never married, or never loved?" Pal asked.

"Never married. And never you mind. Peter's relationship to me is none of your concern." She placed a bowl of soup and a tuna salad sandwich on a lacquer tray. "His lunch," she said. Without being asked, Pal trailed up the stairs after her.

"This is where Peter works," Lauren explained. Pal stood in the doorway, eyes wide. The room was filled with electronics gear, computer terminals and bookcases with odd cardboard sculptures sharing each shelf with books and circuit boards. She rested the tray precariously on a pile of floppy disks atop a rolling cart.

"Time for a break," she told a thin man seated with his back toward them.

The man turned around on his swivel chair, glanced briefly at Pal and the tray and shook his head. The hair on top of his head was a rich, glossy black; on the close-cut sides, the color changed abruptly to a startling white. He had a small thin nose and a large green eyes. On the desk before him was a high-resolution computer monitor. "We haven't been introduced," he said, pointing to Pal.

"This is Pal Tremont, a neighborhood visitor. Pal, this is Peter Tuthy. Pal's going to help me with that character we discussed this morning."

Pal looked at the monitor curiously. Red and green lines shadowed each other through some incomprehensible transformation on the screen, then repeated.

"What's a 'tesseract'?" Pal asked, remembering what he had heard as he stood in the field.

"It's a four-dimensional analog of a cube. I'm trying to find a way to teach myself to see it in my mind's eye," Tuthy said. "Have you ever tried that?"

"No," Pal admitted.

"Here," Tuthy said, handing him the spectacles. "As in the movies."

Pal donned the spectacles and stared at the screen. "So?" he said. "It folds and unfolds. It's pretty—it sticks out at you, and then it goes away." He looked around the workshop. "Oh, wow!" The boy ran to a yard-long black music keyboard propped in one corner. "A Tronclavier! With all the switches! My mother had me take piano lessons, but I'd rather play this. Can you play it?"

"I toy with it," Tuthy said, exasperated. "I toy with all sorts of electronic things. But what did you see on the screen?" He glanced up at Lauren, blinking. "I'll eat the food, I'll eat it. Now please don't bother us."

"He's supposed to be helping *me*," Lauren complained.

Peter smiled at her. "Yes, of course. I'll send him downstairs in a little while."

When Pal descended an hour later, he came into the kitchen to thank Lauren for lunch. "Peter's a real flake," he said confidentially. "He's trying to learn to see certain directions."

"I know," Lauren said, sighing.

"I'm going home now," Pal said. "I'll be back, though . . . if it's all right with you. Peter invited me."

"I'm sure it will be fine," Lauren said dubiously.

"He's going to let me learn the Tronclavier." With that, Pal smiled radiantly and exited through the kitchen door, just as he had come in.

When she retrieved the tray, she found Peter leaning back in his chair, eyes closed. The figures on the screen were still folding and unfolding.

"What about Hockrum's work?" she asked.

"I'm on it," Peter replied, eyes still closed.

Lauren called Pal's foster mother on the second day to apprise them of their son's location, and the woman assured her it was quite all right. "Sometimes he's a little pest. Send him home if he causes trouble . . . but not right away! Give me a rest," she said, then laughed nervously.

Lauren drew her lips together tightly, thanked the woman and hung up.

Peter and the boy had come downstairs to sit in the kitchen, filling up paper with line-drawings. "Peter's teaching me how to use his program," Pal said.

"Did you know," Tuthy said, assuming his highest Cambridge professorial tone, "that a cube, intersecting a flat plane, can be cut through a number of geometrically different cross-sections?"

Pal squinted at the sketch Tuthy had made. "Sure," he said.

"If shoved through the plane the cube can appear, to a two-dimensional creature living on the plane—let's call him a 'Flatlander'—to be either a triangle, a rectangle, a trapezoid, a rhombus, a square, even a hexagon or a pentagon, depending on the depth of penetration and the angle of incidence. If the two-dimensional being observes the cube being pushed through all the way, what he sees is one or more of these objects growing larger, changing shape suddenly, shrinking, and disappearing."

"Sure," Pal said, tapping his sneakered toe. "That's easy. Like in that book you showed me."

"And a sphere pushed through a plane would appear, to the hapless flatlander, first as an 'invisible' point (the two-dimensional surface touching the sphere, tangential), then as a circle. The circle would grow in size, then shrink back to a point and disappear again." He sketched two-dimensional stick figures looking in awe at such an intrusion.

"Got it," Pal said. "Can I play with the Tronclavier now?"

"In a moment. Be patient. So what would a tesseract look like, coming into our three-dimensional space? Remember the program, now . . . the pictures on the monitor."

Pal looked up at the ceiling. "I don't know," he said, seeming bored.

"Try to think," Tuthy urged him.

"It would . . ." Pal held his hands out to shape an angular object. "It would like like one of those Egyptian things, but with three sides . . . or like a box. It would look like a weird-shaped box, too, not square. And if *you* were to fall through a flat-land . . ."

"Yes, that would look very funny," Peter acknowledged with a smile. "Cross-sections of arms and legs and body, all covered with skin . . ."

"And a head!" Pal enthused. "With eyes and a nose."

The doorbell rang. Pal jumped off the kitchen chair. "Is that my mom?" he asked, looking worried.

"I don't think so," Lauren said. "More likely it's Hockrum." She went to the front door to answer. She returned a moment later with a small, pale man behind her. Tuthy stood and shook the man's hand. "Pal Tremont, this is Irving Hockrum," he introduced, waving his hand between them. Hockrum glanced at Pal and blinked a long, not-very-mammalian blink.

"How's the work coming?" he asked Tuthy.

"It's finished," Tuthy said. "It's upstairs. Looks like your savants are barking up the wrong logic tree." He retrieved a folder of papers and print-outs and handed them to Hockrum.

Hockrum leafed through the print-outs. "I can't say this makes me happy. Still, I can't find fault. Looks like the work is up to your usual brilliant standards. Here's your check." He handed Tuthy an envelope.

"I just wish you'd had it to us sooner. It would have saved me some grief—and the company quite a bit of money."

"Sorry," Tuthy said.

"Now I have an important bit of work for you . . ." And Hockrum outlined another problem. Tuthy thought it over for several minutes and shook his head.

"Most difficult, Irving. Pioneering work there. Take at least a month to see if it's even feasible."

"That's all I need to know for now—whether it's feasible. A lot's riding on this, Peter." Hockrum clasped his hands together in front of him, looking even more pale and worn than when he had entered the kitchen. "You'll let me know soon?"

"I'll get right on it," Tuthy said.

"Protégé?" he asked, pointing to Pal. There was a speculative expression on his face, not quite a leer.

"No, a young friend. He's interested in music," Tuthy said. "Damned good at Mozart, in fact."

"I help with his tesseracts," Pal asserted.

"I hope you don't interrupt Peter's work. Peter's work is important."

Pal shook his head solemnly. "Good," Hockrum said, and then left the house with the folder under his arm.

Tuthy returned to his office, Pal in train. Lauren tried to work in the kitchen, sitting with fountain pen and pad of paper, but the words wouldn't come. Hockrum always worried her. She climbed the stairs and stood in the open doorway of the office. She often did that; her presence did not disturb Tuthy, who could work under all sorts of adverse conditions.

"Who was that man?" Pal was asking Tuthy.

"I work for him." Tuthy said. "He's employed by a big electronics firm. He loans me most of the equipment I use. The computers, the high-resolution monitors. He brings me problems and then takes my solutions or answers back to his bosses and claims he did the work."

"That sounds stupid," Pal said. "What kind of problems?"

"Codes, encryptions. Computer security. That was my expertise, once."

"You mean, like fencerail, that sort of thing?" Pal asked, face brightening. "We learned some of that in school."

"Much more complicated, I'm afraid," Tuthy said, grinning. "Did you ever hear of the German 'Enigma,' or the 'Ultra' project?"

Pal shook his head.

"I thought not. Don't worry about it. Let's try another figure on the screen now." He called up another routine on the four-space program and sat Pal before the screen. "So what would a hypersphere look like if it intruded into our space?"

Pal thought a moment. "Kind of weird," he said.

"Not really. You've been watching the visualizations."

"Oh, in *our* space. That's easy. It just looks like a balloon, blowing up from nothing and then shrinking again. It's harder to see what a hypersphere looks like when it's real. Reft of us, I mean."

"Reft?" Tuthy said.

"Sure. Reft and light. Dup and owwen. Whatever the directions are called."

Tuthy stared at the boy. Neither of them had noticed Lauren

in the doorway. "The proper terms are *ana* and *kata*," Tuthy said. "What does it look like?"

Pal gestured, making two wide swings with his arms. "It's like a ball and it's like a horseshoe, depending on how you look at it. Like a balloon stung by bees, I guess, but it's smooth all over, not lumpy."

Tuthy continued to stare, then asked quietly. "You actually see it?"

"Sure," Pal said. "Isn't that what your program is supposed to do—make you see things like that?"

Tuthy nodded, flabbergasted.

"Can I play the Tronclavier now?"

Lauren backed out of the doorway. She felt she had eavesdropped on something momentous, but beyond her. Tuthy came downstairs an hour later, leaving Pal to pick out Telemann on the synthesizer. He sat at the kitchen table with her. "The program works," he said. "It doesn't work for me, but it works for him. I've just been showing him reverse-shadow figures. He caught on right away, and then he went off and played Haydn. He's gone through all my sheet music. The kid's a genius."

"Musical, you mean?"

He glanced directly at her and frowned. "Yes, I suppose he's remarkable at that, too. But spacial relations—coordinates and motion in higher dimensions. . . . Did you know that if you take a three-dimensional object and rotate it in the fourth dimension, it will come back with left-right reversed? So if I were to take my hand—" he held up his right hand—"and lift it *dup*—" he enunciated the word clearly, *dup*—"or drop it *owwen*, it would come back like this?" He held his left hand over his right, balled the right up into a fist and snuck it away behind his back.

"I didn't know that," Lauren said. "What are *dup* and *owwen*?"

"That's what Pal calls movement along the fourth dimension. *Ana* and *kata* to purists. Like up and down to a flatlander, who only comprehends left and right, back and forth." She thought about the hands for a moment. "I still can't see it," she said.

"I've tried, but neither can I," Tuthy admitted. "Our circuits are just too hard-wired, I suppose."

Upstairs, Pal had switched the Tronclavier to a cathedral organ and steel guitar combination and was playing variations on Pergolesi.

"Are you going to keep working for Hockrum?" Lauren asked. Tuthy didn't seem to hear her.

"It's remarkable," he murmured. "The boy just walked in here. You brought him in by accident. Remarkable."

"Can you show me the direction, point it out to me?" Tuthy asked the boy three days later.

"None of my muscles move that way," the boy replied. "I can see it, in my head, but . . ."

"What is it like, seeing that direction?"

Pal squinted. "It's a lot bigger. We're sort of stacked up with other places. It makes me feel lonely."

"Why?"

"Because I'm stuck here. Nobody out there pays any attention to us."

Tuthy's mouth worked. "I thought you were just intuiting

those directions in your head. Are you telling me . . . you're actually *seeing* out there?"

"Yeah. There's people out there, too. Well, not people, exactly. But it isn't my eyes that see them. Eyes are like muscles—they can't point those ways. But the head—the brain, I guess—can."

"Bloody hell," Tuthy said. He blinked and recovered. "Excuse me. That's rude. Can you show me the people . . . on the screen?"

"Shadows, like we were talking about," Pal said.

"Fine. Then draw the shadows for me."

Pal sat down before the terminal, fingers pausing over the keys. "I can show you, but you have to help me with something."

"Help you with what?"

"I'd like to play music for them . . . out there. So they'll notice us."

"The people?"

"Yeah. They really look weird. They stand on us, sort of. They have hooks in our world. But they're tall . . . high dup. They don't notice us because we're so small, compared to them."

"Lord, Pal, I haven't the slightest idea how we'd send music out to them . . . I'm not even sure I believe they exist."

"I'm not lying," Pal said, eyes narrowing. He turned his chair to face a mouse on a black ruled pad and began sketching shapes on the monitor. "Remember, these are just shadows of what they look like. Next I'll draw the dup and owwen lines to connect the shadows."

The boy shaded the shapes he drew to make them look solid,

smiling at his trick but explaining it was necessary because the projection of a four-dimensional in normal space was, of course, three-dimensional.

"They look like you take the plants in a garden, flowers and such, and giving them lots of arms and fingers . . . and it's kind of like seeing things in an aquarium," Pal explained.

After a time, Tuthy suspended his disbelief and stared in open-mouthed wonder at what the boy was re-creating on the monitor.

"I think you're wasting your time, that's what I think," Hockrum said. "I needed that feasibility judgment by today." He paced around the living room before falling as heavily as his light frame permitted into a chair.

"I *have* been distracted," Tuthy admitted.

"By that boy?"

"Yes, actually. Quite a talented fellow—"

"Listen, this is going to mean a lot of trouble for me. I guaranteed the study would be finished by today. It'll make me look bad." Hockrum screwed his face up in frustration. "What in hell are you doing with that boy?"

"Teaching him, actually. Or rather, he's teaching me. Right now, we're building a four-dimensional cone, part of a speaker system. The cone is three-dimensional, the material part, but the magnetic field forms a fourth-dimensional extension—"

"Do you ever think how it looks, Peter?" Hockrum asked.

"It looks very strange on the monitor, I grant you—"

"I'm talking about you and the boy."

Tuthy's bright, interested expression fell into long, deep-lined dismay. "I don't know what you mean."

"I know a lot about you, Peter. Where you come from, why you had to leave. . . . It just doesn't look good."

Tuthy's face flushed crimson.

"Keep him away from here," Hockrum advised.

Tuthy stood. "I want you out of this house," he said quietly. "Our relationship is at an end."

"I swear," Hockrum said, his voice low and calm, staring up at Tuthy from under his brows, "I'll tell the boy's parents. Do you think they'd want their kid hanging around an old . . . pardon the expression . . . queer? I'll tell them if you don't get the feasibility judgment made. I think you can do it by the end of this week—two days. Don't you?"

"No, I don't think so," Tuthy said. "Please leave."

"I know you're here illegally. There's no record of you entering the country. With the problems you had in England, you're certainly not a desirable alien. I'll pass word to the INS. You'll be deported."

"There isn't time to do the work," Tuthy said.

"Make time. Instead of 'educating' that kid."

"Get out of here."

"Two days, Peter."

Over dinner that evening, Tuthy explained to Lauren the exchange he had had with Hockrum. "He thinks I'm buggering Pal. Unspeakable bastard. I will never work for him again."

"I'd better talk to a lawyer, then," Lauren said. "You're sure you can't make him . . . happy, stop all this trouble?"

"I could solve his little problem for him in just a few hours. But I don't want to see him or speak to him again."

"He'll take your equipment away."

Tuthy blinked and waved one hand through the air helplessly. "Then we'll just have to work fast, won't we? Ah, Lauren, you were a fool to bring me here. You should have left me to rot."

"They ignored everything you did for them," Lauren said bitterly. "You saved their hides during the war, and then. . . . They would have shut you up in prison." She stared through the kitchen window at the overcast sky and woods outside.

The cone lay on the table near the window, bathed in morning sun, connected to both the mini-computer and the Tronclavier. Pal arranged the score he had composed on a music stand before the synthesizer. "It's like Bach," he said, "but it'll play better for them. It has a kind of over-rhythm that I'll play on the dup part of the speaker."

"Why are we doing this, Pal?" Tuthy asked as the boy sat down to the keyboard.

"You don't belong here, really, do you, Peter?" Pal asked. Tuthy stared at him.

"I mean, Miss Davies and you get along okay—but do you belong *here*, now?"

"What makes you think I don't belong?"

"I read some books in the school library. About the war and everything. I looked up 'Enigma' and 'Ultra.' I found a fellow named Peter Thornton. His picture looked like you. The books made him seem like a hero."

Tuthy smiled wanly.

"But there was this note in one book. You disappeared in 1965. You were being prosecuted for something. They didn't say what you were being prosecuted for."

"I'm a homosexual," Tuthy said quietly.

"Oh. So what?"

"Lauren and I met in England in 1964. We became good friends. They were going to put me in prison, Pal. She smuggled me into the U.S. through Canada."

"But you said you're a homosexual. They don't like women."

"Not at all true, Pal. Lauren and I like each other very much. We could talk. She told me about her dreams of being a writer, and I talked to her about mathematics, and about the war. I nearly died during the war."

"Why? Were you wounded?"

"No. I worked too hard. I burned myself out and had a nervous breakdown. My lover . . . a man . . . kept me alive throughout the forties. Things were bad in England after the war. But he died in 1963. His parents came in to settle the estate, and when I contested the settlement in court, I was arrested. So I suppose you're right, Pal. I don't really belong here."

"I don't, either. My folks don't care much. I don't have too many friends. I wasn't even born here, and I don't know anything about Korea."

"Play," Tuthy said, his face stony. "Let's see if they'll listen."

"Oh, they'll listen," Pal said. "It's like the way they talk to each other."

The boy ran his fingers over the keys on the Tronclavier. The cone, connected with the keyboard through the mini-computer, vibrated tinnily.

For an hour, Pal paged back and forth through his composition, repeating and trying variations. Tuthy sat in a corner, chin in hand, listening to the mousy squeaks and squeals produced by the cone. *How much more difficult to interpret a four-dimensional sound*, he thought. *Not even visual clues . . .*

Finally the boy stopped and wrung his hands, then stretched his arms. "They must have heard. We'll just have to wait and see." He switched the Tronclavier to automatic playback and pushed the chair away from the keyboard.

Pal stayed until dusk, then reluctantly went home. Tuthy sat in the office until midnight, listening to the tinny sounds issuing from the speaker cone.

All night long, the Tronclavier played through its pre-programmed selection of Pal's compositions. Tuthy lay in bed in his room, two doors down from Lauren's room, watching a shaft of moonlight slide across the wall. *How far would a four-dimensional being have to travel to get here?*

How far have I come to get here?

Without realizing he was asleep, he dreamed, and in his dream a wavering image of Pal appeared, gesturing with both arms as if swimming, eyes wide. *I'm okay*, the boy said without moving his lips. *Don't worry about me . . . I'm okay. I've been back to*

Korea to see what it's like. It's not bad, but I like it better here . . .

Tuthy awoke sweating. The moon had gone down and the room was pitch-black. In the office, the hyper-cone continued its distant, mouse-squeak broadcast.

Pal returned early in the morning, repetitively whistling a few bars from Mozart's Fourth Violin Concerto. Lauren let him in and he joined Tuthy upstairs. Tuthy sat before the monitor, replaying Pal's sketch of the four-dimensional beings.

"Do you see anything?" he asked the boy.

Pal nodded. "They're coming closer. They're interested. Maybe we should get things ready, you know . . . be prepared." He squinted. "Did you ever think what a four-dimensional footprint would look like?"

Tuthy considered for a moment. "That would be most interesting," he said. "It would be solid."

On the first floor, Lauren screamed.

Pal and Tuthy almost tumbled over each other getting downstairs. Lauren stood in the living room with her arms crossed above her bosom, one hand clamped over her mouth. The first intrusion had taken out a section of the living room floor and the east wall.

"Really clumsy," Pal said. "One of them must have bumped it."

"The music," Tuthy said.

"What in HELL is going on?" Lauren demanded, her voice starting as a screech and ending as a roar.

"Better turn the music off," Tuthy elaborated.

"Why?" Pal asked, face wreathed in an excited smile.

"Maybe they don't like it."

A bright filmy blue blob rapidly expanded to a yard in diameter just beside Tuthy. The blob turned red, wriggled, froze, and then just as rapidly vanished.

"That was like an elbow," Pal explained. "One of its arms. I think it's listening. Trying to find out where the music is coming from. I'll go upstairs."

"Turn it off!" Tuthy demanded.

"I'll play something else." The boy ran up the stairs. From the kitchen came a hideous hollow crashing, then the sound of vacuum being filled—a reverse-pop, ending in a hiss—followed by a low-frequency vibration that set their teeth on edge . . .

The vibration caused by a four-dimensional creature *scraping* across its "floor," their own three-dimensional space. Tuthy's hands shook with excitement.

"Peter—" Lauren bellowed, all dignity gone. She unwrapped her arms and held clenched fists out as if she were about to start exercising, or boxing.

"Pal's attracted visitors," Tuthy explained.

He turned toward the stairs. The first four steps and a section of floor spun and vanished. The rush of air nearly drew him down the hole. Regaining his balance, he kneeled to feel the precisely cut, concave edge. Below was the dark basement.

"Pal!" Tuthy called out.

"I'm playing something original for them," Pal shouted back. "I think they like it."

The phone rang. Tuthy was closest to the extension at the bottom of the stairs and instinctively reached out to answer it. Hockrum was on the other end, screaming.

"I can't talk now—" Tuthy said. Hockrum screamed again, loud enough for Lauren to hear. Tuthy abruptly hung up. "He's been fired, I gather," he said. "He seemed angry." He stalked back three paces and turned, then ran forward and leaped the gap to the first intact step. "Can't talk." He stumbled and scrambled up the stairs, stopping on the landing. "Jesus," he said, as if something had suddenly occured to him.

"He'll call the government," Lauren warned.

Tuthy waved that off. "I know what's happening. They're knocking chunks out of three-space, into the fourth. The fourth dimension. Like Pal says: clumsy brutes. They could kill us!"

Sitting before the Tronclavier, Pal happily played a new melody. Tuthy approached and was abruptly blocked by a thick green column, as solid as rock and with a similar texture. It vibrated and ascribed an arc in the air. A section of the ceiling four feet wide was kicked out of three-space. Tuthy's hair lifted in the rush of wind. The column shrank to a broomstick and hairs sprouted all over it, writhing like snakes.

Tuthy edged around the hairy broomstick and pulled the plug on the Tronclavier. A cage of zeppelin-shaped brown sausages encircled the computer, spun, elongated to reach the ceiling, the floor and the top of the monitor's table, and then pipped down to tiny strings and was gone.

"They can't see too clearly here," Pal said, undisturbed that his concert was over. Lauren had climbed the outside stairs and stood behind Tuthy. "Gee, I'm sorry about the damage."

In one smooth curling motion, the Tronclavier and cone and all the wiring associated with them were peeled away as if they had been stick-on labels hastily removed from a flat surface.

"Gee," Pal said, his face suddenly registering alarm.

Then it was the boy's turn. He was removed with greater care. The last thing to vanish was his head, which hung suspended in the air for several seconds.

"I think they liked the music," he said, grinning.

Head, grin and all, dropped away in a direction impossible for Tuthy or Lauren to follow. The air in the room sighed.

Lauren stood her ground for several minutes, while Tuthy wandered through what was left of the office, passing his hand through mussed hair.

"Perhaps he'll be back," Tuthy said. "I don't even know . . ." But he didn't finish. Could a three-dimensional boy survive in a four-dimensional void, or whatever lay dup . . . or owwen?

Tuthy did not object when Lauren took it upon herself to call the boy's foster parents and the police. When the police arrived, he endured the questions and accusations stoically, face immobile, and told them as much as he knew. He was not believed; nobody knew quite what to believe. Photographs were taken. The police left.

It was only a matter of time, Lauren told him, until one or the other or both of them were arrested. "Then we'll make up a story," he said. "You'll tell them it was my fault."

"I will *not*," Lauren said. "But where *is* he?"

"I'm not positive," Tuthy said. "I think's he's all right, however."

"How do you *know*?"

He told her about the dream.

"But that was before," she said.

"Perfectly allowable in the fourth dimension," he explained. He pointed vaguely up, then down, then shrugged.

On the last day, Tuthy spent the early morning hours bundled in an overcoat and bathrobe in the drafty office, playing his program again and again, trying to visualize *ana* and *kata*. He closed his eyes and squinted and twisted his head, intertwined his fingers and drew odd little graphs on the monitors, but it was no use. His brain was hard-wired.

Over breakfast, he reiterated to Lauren that she must put all the blame on him.

"Maybe it will all blow over," she said. "They haven't got a case. No evidence . . . nothing."

"All blow *over*," he mused, passing his hand over his head and grinning ironically. "How *over*, they'll never know."

The doorbell rang. Tuthy went to answer it, and Lauren followed a few steps behind.

Tuthy opened the door. Three men in gray suits, one with a briefcase, stood on the porch. "Mr. Peter Thornton?" the tallest asked.

"Yes," Tuthy acknowledged.

A chunk of the doorframe and wall above the door vanished with a roar and a hissing pop. The three men looked up at the gap. Ignoring what was impossible, the tallest man returned his attention to Tuthy and continued, "We have information that you are in this country illegally."

"Oh?" Tuthy said.

Beside him, an irregular filmy blue cylinder grew to a length of four feet and hung in the air, vibrating. The three men backed away on the porch. In the middle of the cylinder, Pal's head emerged, and below that, his extended arm and hand.

"It's fun here," Pal said. "They're friendly."

"I believe you," Tuthy said.

"Mr. Thornton," the tallest man continued valiantly.

"Won't you come with me?" Pal asked.

Tuthy glanced back at Lauren. She gave him a small fraction of a nod, barely understanding what she was assenting to, and he took Pal's hand. "Tell them it was all my fault," he said.

From his feet to his head, Peter Tuthy was peeled out of this world. Air rushed in. Half of the brass lamp to one side of the door disappeared.

The INS men returned to their car without any further questions, with damp pants and embarrassed, deeply worried expressions. They drove away, leaving Lauren to contemplate the quiet. They did not return.

She did not sleep for three nights, and when she did sleep, Tuthy and Pal visited her, and put the question to her.

Thank you, but I prefer it here, she replied.

It's a lot of fun, the boy insisted. *They like music.*

Lauren shook her head on the pillow and awoke. Not very far

away, there was a whistling, tinny kind of sound, followed by a deep vibration.

To her, it sounded like applause.

She took a deep breath and got out of bed to retrieve her notebook.

Treat your fellow creatures well. You never know who might be watching.

Philip K. Dick was one of the great SF writers of the twentieth century. Since his death in 1982, his work has grown in popularity and been the basis for several successful Hollywood films, beginning with Blade Runner. Among his best-known novels are The Man in the High Castle, Martian Time-Slip, and Ubik.

The Alien Mind

PHILIP K. DICK

Inert within the depths of his Theta Chamber he heard the faint tone and then the synthovoice. "Five minutes."

"Okay," he said, and struggled out of his deep sleep. He had five minutes to adjust the course of his ship; something had gone wrong with the autocontrol system. An error on his part? Not likely; he never made errors. Jason Bedford make errors? Hardly.

As he made his way unsteadily to the control module, he saw that Norman, who had been sent with him to amuse him, was also awake. The cat floated slowly in circles, batting at a pen that somehow had gotten loose. Strange, Bedford thought.

"I thought you were unconscious with me." He examined the read-out of the ship's course. Impossible! A fifth-parsec off in the direction of Sirius. It would add a week to his journey. With grim precision he reset the controls, then sent out an alert signal to Meknos III, his destination.

"Troubles?" the Meknosian operator answered. The voice was dry and cold, the calculating monotone of something that always made Bedford think of snakes.

He explained his situation.

"We need the vaccine," the Meknosian said. "Try to stay on course."

Norman the cat floated majestically by the control module, reached out a paw and jabbed at random; two activated buttons sounded faint *bleeps* and the ship altered course.

"So you did it," Bedford said. "You humiliated me in the eyes of an alien. You have reduced me to idiocy vis-á-vis the alien mind." He grabbed the cat. And squeezed.

"What was that strange sound?" the Meknosian operator asked. "A kind of lament."

Bedford said quietly, "There's nothing left to lament. Forget you heard it." He shut off the radio, carried the cat's body to the trash sphincter and ejected it.

A moment later he had returned to his Theta Chamber and, once more, dozed. This time there would be no tampering with his controls. He dozed in peace.

When his ship docked at Meknos III, the senior member of the alien medical team greeted him with an odd request. "We would like to see your pet."

"I have no pet," Bedford said. Certainly it was true.

"According to the manifest filed with us in advance—"

"It is really none of your business," Bedford said. "You have your vaccine; I'll be taking off."

The Meknosian said, "The safety of any life form is our business. We will inspect your ship."

"For a cat that doesn't exist," Bedford said.

Their search proved futile. Impatiently, Bedford watched the alien creatures scrutinize every storage locker and passage-way on his ship. Unfortunately, the Meknosian found ten sacks of dry cat-kibble. A lengthy discussion ensued among them, in their own language.

"Do I have permission," Bedford said harshly, "to return to Earth now? I'm on a tight schedule." What the aliens were thinking and saying was of no importance to him; he wished only to return to his silent Theta Chamber and profound sleep.

"You'll have to go through decontamination procedure A," the senior Meknosian medical officer said. "So that no spore or virus from—"

"I realize that," Bedford said. "Let's get it done."

Later, when decontamination had been completed and he was back in his ship starting up the drive, his radio came on. It was one or another of the Meknosians; to Bedford they all looked alike. "What was the cat's name?" the Meknosian asked.

"Norman," Bedford said, and jabbed the ignite switch. His ship shot upward and he smiled.

He did not smile, however, when he found the power supply to his Theta Chamber missing. Nor did he smile when the back-up unit could also not be located. Did I forget to bring it? he asked himself. No, he decided; I wouldn't do that. They took it.

Two years before he reached Terra. Two years of full consciousness on his part, deprived of theta sleep; two years of sitting or floating or—as he had seen in military-preparedness training holofilms—curled up in a corner totally psychotic.

He punched out a radio request to return to Meknos III. No response. Well, so much for that.

Seated at his control module, he snapped on the little inboard computer and said, "My Theta Chamber won't function; it's been sabotaged. What do you suggest I do for two years?"

THERE ARE EMERGENCY ENTERTAINING TAPES

"Right," he said. He would have remembered. "Thank you." Pressing the proper button, he caused the door of the tape compartment to slide open.

No tapes. Only a cat toy—a miniature punching bag—that had been included for Norman; he had never gotten around to giving it to him. Otherwise . . . bare shelves.

The alien mind, Bedford thought. Mysterious and cruel.

Setting the ship's audio recorder going, he said calmly and with as much conviction as possible, "What I will do is build my next two years around the daily routine. First, there are meals. I will spend as much time as possible planning, fixing, eating and enjoying delicious repasts. During the time ahead of me I will try out every combination of victuals possible." Unsteadily, he rose and made his way to the massive food-storage locker.

As he stood gazing into the tightly packed locker—tightly

packed with row upon row of identical snacks—he thought, On the other hand there's not much you can do with a two-year supply of cat-kibble. In the way of variety. Are they all the same flavor?

They were all the same flavor.

A tale of aliens: the kind from out there, and the kind from right here.

Nancy Kress is the author of many excellent SF novels, including the Beggars trilogy: Beggars in Spain, Beggars and Choosers, and Beggars Ride. "Out of All Them Bright Stars" won the Nebula Award in 1985.

Out of All Them Bright Stars

● ●

NANCY KRESS

So I'm filling the catsup bottles at the end of the night, and I'm listening to the radio Charlie has stuck up on top of the movable panel in the ceiling, when the door opens and one of them walks in. I know right away it's one of them—no chance to make a mistake about *that*—even though it's got on a nice-cut suit and a brim hat like Humphrey Bogart used to wear in *Casablanca*. But there's nobody with it, no professor from the college or government men like on the TV show from the college or even any students. It's all alone. And we're a long way out on the highway from the college.

It stands in the doorway, blinking a little, with rain dripping off its hat. Kathy, who's supposed to be cleaning the coffee machine behind the counter freezes and stares with one hand still holding the used filter up in the air like she's never going to move again. Just then Charlie calls out from the kitchen, "Hey, Kathy, you ask anybody who won the trifecta?" and she doesn't even answer him. Just goes on staring with her mouth open like she's thinking of screaming but forgot how. And the old couple in the corner booth, the only ones left from the crowd after the movie got out, stop chewing their chocolate cream pie and stare, too. Kathy closes her mouth and opens it again, and a noise comes out like "Uh—errrgh. . . ."

Well, that made me annoyed. Maybe she tried to say "ugh" and maybe she didn't, but here it is standing in the doorway with rain falling around it in little drops and we're staring like it's a clothes dummy and not a customer. So I think that's not right and maybe we're even making it feel a little bad. I wouldn't like Kathy staring at me like that, and I dry my hands on my towel and go over.

"Yes, sir, can I help you?" I say.

"Table for one," it says, like Charlie's was some nice steak house in town. But I suppose that's the kind of place the government people mostly take them to. And besides, its voice is polite and easy to understand, with a sort of accent but not as bad as some we get from the college. I can tell what it's saying. I lead him to a booth in the corner opposite the old couple, who come in every Friday night and haven't left a tip yet.

He sits down slowly. I notice he keeps his hands on his lap, but I can't tell if that's because he doesn't know what to do with them or because he thinks I won't want to see them. But I've seen the closeups on TV—they don't look so weird to me like they do to some. Charlie says they make his stomach turn, but

I can't see it. You'd think he'd of seen worse meat in Vietnam. He talks enough like he did, on and on, and sometimes we even believe him.

I say, "Coffee, sir?"

He makes a sort of movement with his eyes. I can't tell what the movement means, but he says in that polite voice, "No, thank you. I am unable to drink coffee," and I think that's a good thing, because I suddenly remember that Kathy's got the filter out. But then he says, "May I have a green salad, please? With no dressing, please."

The rain is still dripping off his hat. I figure the government people never told him to take off his hat in a restaurant, and for some reason that tickles me and makes me feel real bold. This polite blue guy isn't going to bother anybody, and that fool Charlie was just spouting off his mouth again.

"The salad's not too fresh, sir," I say, experimental-like, just to see what he'll say next. And it's the truth—the salad is left over from yesterday. But the guy answers like I asked him something else.

"What is your name?" he says, so polite I know he's curious and not starting anything. And what could he start anyway, blue and with those hands? Still, you never know.

"Sally," I say. "Sally Gourley."

"I am John," he says, and makes that movement with his eyes again. All of a sudden it tickles me—"John!" For this blue guy! So I laugh, and right away I feel sorry, like I might have hurt his feelings or something. How could you tell?

"Hey, I'm sorry," I say, and he takes off his hat. He does it real slow, like taking off the hat is important and means some-thing, but all there is underneath is a bald blue head. Nothing weird like with the hands.

"Do not apologize," John says. "I have another name, of course, but in my own language."

"What is it?" I say, bold as brass, because all of a sudden I picture myself telling all this to my sister Mary Ellen and her listening real hard.

John makes some noise with his mouth, and I feel my own mouth open because it's not like a word he says at all, it's a beautiful sound—like a birdcall, only sadder. It's just that I wasn't expecting it, that beautiful sound right here in Charlie's diner. It surprised me, coming out of that bald blue head. That's all it was: surprise.

I don't say anything. John looks at me and says, "It has a meaning that can be translated. It means—" But before he can say what it means, Charlie comes charging out of the kitchen, Kathy right behind him. He's still got the racing form in one hand, like he's been studying the trifecta, and he pushes right up against the booth and looks red and furious. Then I see the old couple scuttling out the door, their jackets clutched to their fronts, and the chocolate cream pie not half-eaten on their plates. I see they're going to stiff me for the check, but before I can stop them, Charlie grabs my arm and squeezes so hard his nails slice into my skin.

"What the hell do you think you're doing?" he says right to me. Not so much as a look at John, but Kathy can't stop looking and her fist is pushed up to her mouth.

I drag my arm away and rub it. Once I saw Charlie push his wife so hard she went down and hit her head and had to have four stitches. It was me that drove her to the emergency room.

Charlie says again, "What the hell do you think you're doing?"

"I'm serving my table. He wants a salad. Large." I can't remember if John'd said a large or a small salad, but I figure a large order would make Charlie feel better. But Charlie doesn't want to feel better.

"You get him out of here," Charlie hisses. He still doesn't look at John. "You hear me, Sally? You get him *out*. The government says I gotta serve spiks and niggers, but it don't say I gotta serve *him*!"

I look at John. He's putting on his hat, ramming it onto his bald head, and half-standing in the booth. He can't get out because Charlie and me are both in the way. I expect John to look mad or upset, but except that he's holding the muscles in his face in some different way, I can't see any change of expression. But I figure he's got to feel something bad, and all of a sudden I'm mad at Charlie, who's a bully and who's got the feelings of a scumbag. I open my mouth to tell him so, plus one or two other little things I been saving up, when the door flies open and in burst four men, and damn if they aren't *all* wearing hats like Humphrey Bogart in *Casablanca*. As soon as the first guy sees John, his walk changes and he comes over slower but more purposeful-like, and he's talking to John and to Charlie in a sincere voice like a TV anchorman giving out the news.

I see the situation now belongs to him, so I go back to the

catsup bottles. I'm still plenty burned, though, about Charlie manhandling me and about Kathy rushing so stupid into the kitchen to get Charlie. She's a flake and always has been.

Charlie is scowling and nodding. The harder he scowls, the nicer the government guy's voice gets. Pretty soon the government man is smiling sweet as pie. Charlie slinks back into the kitchen, and the four men move toward the door with John in the middle of them like some high school football huddle. Next to the real men, he looks stranger than he did before, and I see how really flat his face is. But then when the huddle's right opposite the table with my catsup bottles, John breaks away and comes over to me.

"I am sorry, Sally Gourley," he says. And then: "I seldom have the chance to show our friendliness to an ordinary Earth person. I make so little difference!"

Well, that throws me. His voice sounds so sad, and besides, I never thought of myself as an ordinary Earth person. Who would? So I just shrug and wipe off a catsup bottle with my towel. But then John does a weird thing. He just touches my arm where Charlie squeezed it, just touches it with the palm of those hands. And the palm's not slimy at all—dry, and sort of cool, and I don't jump or anything. Instead, I remember that beautiful noise when he said his other name. Then he goes out with three of the men, and the door bangs behind them on a gust of rain because Charlie never fixed the air-stop from when some kids horsing around broke it last spring.

The fourth man stays and questions me: What did the alien say, what did I say. I tell him, but then he starts asking the same exact questions all over again, like he didn't believe me the first time, and that gets me mad. Also, he has this snotty voice, and I see how his eyebrows move when I slip once and accidentally say, "he don't." I might not know what John's muscles mean, but I sure the hell can read those eyebrows. So I get miffed, and pretty soon he leaves and the door bangs behind him.

I finish the catsup and mustard bottles, and Kathy finishes the coffee machine. The radio in the ceiling plays something instrumental, no words, real sad. Kathy and me start to wash down the booths with disinfectant, and because we're doing the same work together and nobody comes in, I finally say to her, "It's funny."

She says, "What's funny?"

"Charlie called that guy 'him' right off. 'I don't got to serve him,' he said. And I thought of him as 'it' at first, least until I had a name to use. But Charlie's the one who threw him out."

Kathy swipes at the back of her booth. "And Charlie's right. That thing scared me half to death, coming in here like that. And where there's food being served, too." She snorts and sprays on more disinfectant.

Well, she's a flake. Always has been.

"*The National Enquirer*," Kathy goes on, "told how they have all this firepower up there in the big ship that hasn't landed yet. My husband says they could blow us all to smithereens, they're so powerful. I don't know why they even came here. *We* don't want them. I don't even know why they came, all that way."

"They want to make a difference," I say, but Kathy barrels on ahead, not listening.

"The Pentagon will hold them off, it doesn't matter what weapons they got up there or how much they insist on seeing about our defenses, the Pentagon won't let them get any toeholds on Earth. That's what my husband says. Blue bastards."

I say, "Will you please shut up?"

She gives me a dirty look and flounces off. I don't care. None of it is anything to me. Only, standing there with the disinfectant in my hand, looking at the dark windows and listening to the music wordless and slow on the radio, I remember that touch on my arm, so light and cool. And I think they didn't come here with any firepower to blow us all to smithereens. I just don't believe it. But then why did they come? Why come all that way from another star to walk into Charlie's diner and order a green salad with no dressing from an ordinary Earth person?

Charlie comes out with his keys to unlock the cash register and go over the tapes. I remember the old couple who stiffed me and I curse to myself. Only pie and coffee, but it still comes off my salary. The radio in the ceiling starts playing something else, not the sad song, but nothing snappy neither. It's a love song, about some guy giving and giving and getting treated like dirt. I don't like it.

"Charlie," I say, "what did those government men say to you?"

He looks up from his tapes and scowls. "What do you care?"

"I just want to know."

"And maybe I don't want you to know," he says, and smiles nasty-like. Me asking him has put him in a better mood, the creep. All of a sudden I remember what his wife said when she got the stitches, "The only way to get something from Charlie is to let him smack me around a little, and then ask him when I'm down. He'll give me anything when I'm down. He gives me shit if he thinks I'm on top."

I do the rest of the cleanup without saying anything. Charlie swears at the night's take—I know from my tips that it's not much. Kathy teases her hair in front of the mirror behind the doughnuts and pies, and I put down the breakfast menus. But all the time I'm thinking, and I don't much like my thoughts.

Charlie locks up and we all leave. Ouside it's stopped raining, but it's still misty and soft, real pretty but too cold. I pull my sweater around myself and in the parking lot, after Kathy's gone, I say, "Charlie."

He stops walking toward his truck. "Yeah?"

I lick my lips. They're all of a sudden dry. It's an experiment, like, what I'm going to say. It's an experiment.

"Charlie. What if those government guys hadn't come just then and the . . . blue guy hadn't been willing to leave? What would you have done?"

"What do you care?"

I shrug. "I don't care. Just curious. It's *your* place."

"Damn right it's my place!" I could see him scowl, through the mist. "I'd of squashed him flat!"

"And then what? After you squashed him flat, what if the men came then and made a stink?"

"Too bad. It'd be too late by then, huh?" He laughs, and I can see how he's seeing it: the blue guy bleeding on the linoleum, and Charlie standing over him, dusting his hands together.

Charlie laughs again and goes off to his truck, whistling. He has a little bounce to his step. He's still seeing it all, almost like it really *had* happened. Over his shoulder he calls to me, "They're built like wimps. Or girls. All bone, no muscle. Even *you* must of seen that," and his voice is cheerful. It doesn't have any more anger in it, or hatred, or anything but a sort of friendliness. I hear him whistle some more, until the truck engine starts up and he peels out of the parking lot, laying rubber like a kid.

I unlock my Chevy. But before I get in, I look up at the sky. Which is really stupid because of course I can't see anything, with all the mists and clouds. No stars.

Maybe Kathy's husband is right. Maybe they do want to blow us all to smithereens. I don't think so, but what the hell difference does it ever make what I think? And all at once I'm furious at John, furiously mad, as furious as I've ever been in my life.

Why does he have to come here, with his birdcalls and his politeness? Why can't they all go someplace else besides here? There must be lots of other places they can go, out of all them bright stars up there behind the clouds. They don't need to come here, here where I need this job and that means I need Charlie. He's a bully, but I want to look at him and see nothing else but a bully. Nothing else but that. That's all I want to see in Charlie, in the government men—just small-time bullies, nothing special, not a mirror of anything, not a future of anything. Just Charlie. That's all. I won't see anything else.

I won't.

"I make so little difference," he says.

Yeah. Sure.

The American Civil War is the focus of many "alternate history" tales—SF stories set in timelines where historical events turned out differently. Here's one of the best ever.

Maureen F. McHugh burst on the scene in the early 1990s with a clutch of strong SF stories and a remarkable first novel, China Mountain Zhang. *Her latest novel is* Nekropolis. *"The Lincoln Train" won the Hugo Award in 1996.*

The Lincoln Train

MAUREEN F. MCHUGH

Soldiers of the G.A.R. stand alongside the tracks. They are General Dodge's soldiers, keeping the tracks maintained for the Lincoln Train. If I stand right, the edges of my bonnet are like blinders and I can't see the soldiers at all. It is a spring evening. At the house the lilacs are blooming. My mother wears a sprig pinned to her dress under her cameo. I can smell it, even in the crush of these people all waiting for the train. I can smell the lilac, and the smell of too many people crowded together, and a faint taste of cinders on the air. I want to go home but that house is not ours anymore. I smooth my black dress. On the train platform we are all in mourning.

The train will take us to St. Louis, from whence we will leave for the Oklahoma territories. They say we will walk, but I don't know how my mother will do that. She has been poorly since the winter of '62. I check my bag with our water and provisions.

"Julia Adelaide," my mother says, "I think we should go home."

"We've come to catch the train," I say, very sharp.

I'm Clara, my sister Julia is eleven years older than me. Julia is married and living in Tennessee. My mother blinks and touches her sprig of lilac uncertainly. If I am not sharp with her, she will keep on it.

I wait. When I was younger I used to try to school my unruly self in Christian charity. God sends us nothing we cannot bear. Now I only try to keep it from my face, try to keep my outer self disciplined. There is a feeling inside me, an anger, that I can't even speak. Something is being bent, like a bow, bending and bending and bending—

"When are we going home?" my mother says.

"Soon," I say because it is easy.

But she won't remember and in a moment she'll ask again. And again and again, through this long long train ride to St. Louis. I am trying to be a Christian daughter, and I remind myself that it is not her fault that the war turned her into an old woman, or that her mind is full of holes and everything new drains out. But it's not my fault, either. I don't even try to curb my feelings and I know that they rise up to my face. The only way to be true is to be true from the inside and I am not. I am full of unchristian feelings. My mother's infirmity is her trial, and it is also mine.

I wish I were someone else.

The train comes down the track, chuffing, coming slow. It is an old, badly used thing, but I can see that once it was a model of chaste and beautiful workmanship. Under the dust it is a dark claret in color. It is said that the engine was built to be used by President Lincoln, but since the assassination attempt he is too infirm to travel. People begin to push to the edge of the platform, hauling their bags and worldly goods. I don't know how I will get our valise on. If Zeke could have come I could have at least insured that it was loaded on, but the Negroes are free now and they are not to help. The notice said no family Negroes could come to the station, although I see their faces here and there through the crowd.

The train stops outside the station to take on water.

"Is it your father?" my mother says diffidently. "Do you see him on the train?"

"No, Mother," I say. "We are taking the train."

"Are we going to see your father?" she asks.

It doesn't matter what I say to her, she'll forget it in a few minutes, but I cannot say yes to her. I cannot say that we will see my father even to give her a few moments of joy.

"Are we going to see your father?" she asks again.

"No," I say.

"Where are we going?"

I have carefully explained it all to her and she cried, every time I did. People are pushing down the platform toward the train, and I am trying to decide if I should move my valise toward the front of the platform. Why are they in such a hurry to get on the train? It is taking us all away.

"Where are we going? Julia Adelaide, you will answer me this moment," my mother says, her voice too full of quaver to quite sound like her own.

"I'm Clara," I say. "We're going to St. Louis."

"St. Louis," she says. "We don't need to go to St. Louis. We can't get through the lines, Julia, and I . . . I am quite indisposed. Let's go back home now, this is foolish."

We cannot go back home. General Dodge has made it clear that if we did not show up at the train platform this morning and get our names checked off the list, he would arrest every man in town, and then he would shoot every tenth man. The town knows to believe him. General Dodge was put in charge of the trains into Washington, and he did the same thing then. He arrested men and held them and every time the train was fired upon he hanged a man.

There is a shout and I can only see the crowd moving like a wave, pouring off the edge of the platform. Everyone is afraid there will not be room. I grab the valise and I grab my mother's arm and pull them both. The valise is so heavy that my fingers hurt, and the weight of our water and food is heavy on my arm. My mother is small and when I put her in bed at night she is all tiny like a child, but now she refuses to move, pulling against me and opening her mouth wide, her mouth pink inside and wet and open in a wail I can just barely hear over the shouting crowd. I don't know if I should let go of the valise to pull her, letting someone else get her on the train and finding her later.

A man in the crowd shoves her hard from behind. His face is twisted in wrath. What is he so angry at? My mother falls into me, and the crowd pushes us. I am trying to hold on to the valise, but my gloves are slippery, and I can only hold on with my right hand, with my left I am trying to hold up my mother. The crowd is pushing all around us, trying to push us toward the edge of the platform.

The train toots as if it were moving. There is shouting all around us. My mother is fallen against me, her face pressed against my bosom, turned up toward me. She is so frightened. Her face is pressed against me in improper intimacy, as if she were my child. My mother as my child. I am filled with revulsion and horror. The pressure against us begins to lessen. I still have a hold of the valise. We'll be all right. Let the others push around, I'll wait and get the valise on somehow. They won't leave us to travel without anything.

My mother's eyes close. Her wrinkled face looks up, the skin under her eyes making little pouches, as if it were a second blind eyelid. Everything is so grotesque. I am having a spell. I wish I could be somewhere where I could get away and close the windows. I have had these spells since they told us that my father was dead, where everything is full of horror and strangeness.

The person behind me is crowding into my back and I want to tell them to give way, but I cannot. People around us are crying out. I cannot see anything but the people pushed against me. People are still pushing, but now they are not pushing toward the side of the platform but toward the front, where the train will be when we are allowed to board.

Wait, I call out, but there's no way for me to tell if I've really called out or not. I can't hear anything until the train whistles.

The train has moved? They brought the train into the station? I can't tell, not without letting go of my mother and the valise. My mother is being pulled down into this mass. I feel her sliding against me. Her eyes are closed. She is a huge doll, limp in my arms. She is not even trying to hold herself up. She has given up to this moment.

I can't hold on to my mother and the valise. So I let go of the valise.

O merciful God.

I do not know how I will get through this moment.

The crowd around me is a thing that presses me and pushes me up, pulls me down. I cannot breathe for the pressure. I see specks in front of my eyes, white sparks, too bright, like metal and like light. My feet aren't under me. I am buoyed by the crowd and my feet are behind me. I am unable to stand, unable to fall. I think my mother is against me, but I can't tell, and in this mass I don't know how she can breathe.

I think I am going to die.

All the noise around me does not seem like noise anymore. It is something else, some element, like water or something, surrounding me and overpowering me.

It is like that for a long time, until finally I have my feet under me, and I'm leaning against people. I feel myself sink, but I can't stop myself. The platform is solid. My whole body feels bruised and roughly used.

My mother is not with me. My mother is a bundle of black on the ground, and I crawl to her. I wish I could say that as I crawl to her I feel concern for her condition, but at this moment

I am no more than base animal nature and I crawl to her because she is mine and there is nothing else in the world I can identify as mine. Her skirt is rucked up so that her ankles and calves are showing. Her face is black. At first I think it something about her clothes, but it is her face, so full of blood that it is black.

People are still getting on the train, but there are people on the platform around us, left behind. And other things. A surprising number of shoes, all badly used. Wraps, too. Bags. Bundles and people.

I try raising her arms above her head, to force breath into her lungs. Her arms are thin, but they don't go the way I want them to. I read in the newspaper that when President Lincoln was shot, he stopped breathing, and his personal physician started him breathing again. But maybe the newspaper was wrong, or maybe it is more complicated than I understand, or maybe it doesn't always work. She doesn't breathe.

I sit on the platform and try to think of what to do next. My head is empty of useful thoughts. Empty of prayers.

"Ma'am?"

It's a soldier of the G.A.R.

"Yes sir?" I say. It is difficult to look up at him, to look up into the sun.

He hunkers down but does not touch her. At least he doesn't touch her. "Do you have anyone staying behind?"

Like cousins or something? Someone who is not "reluctant" in their handling of their Negroes? "Not in town," I say.

"Did she worship?" he asks, in his northern way.

"Yes sir," I say, "she did. She was a Methodist, and you

should contact the preacher. The Reverend Robert Ewald, sir."

"I'll see to it, ma'am. Now you'll have to get on the train."

"And leave her?" I say.

"Yes ma'am, the train will be leaving. I'm sorry, ma'am."

"But I can't," I say.

He takes my elbow and helps me stand. And I let him.

"We are not really recalcitrant," I say. "Where were Zeke and Rachel supposed to go? Were we supposed to throw them out?"

He helps me climb onto the train. People stare at me as I get on, and I realize I must be all in disarray. I stand under all their gazes, trying to get my bonnet on straight and smoothing my dress. I do not know what to do with my eyes or hands.

There are no seats. Will I have to stand until St. Louis? I grab a seat back to hold myself up. It is suddenly warm and everything is distant and I think I am about to faint. My stomach turns. I breathe through my mouth, not even sure that I am holding on to the seat back.

But I don't fall, thank Jesus.

"It's not Lincoln," someone is saying, a man's voice, rich and baritone, and I fasten on the words as a lifeline, drawing myself back to the train car, to the world. "It's Seward. Lincoln no longer has the capacity to govern."

The train smells of bodies and warm sweaty wool. It is a smell that threatens to undo me, so I must concentrate on breathing through my mouth. I breathe in little pants, like a dog. The heat lies against my skin. It is airless.

"Of course Lincoln can no longer govern, but that damned actor made him a saint when he shot him," says a second voice, "and now no one dare oppose him. It doesn't matter if his policies make sense or not."

"You're wrong," says the first. "Seward is governing through him. Lincoln is an imbecile. He can't govern, look at the way he handled the war."

The second snorts. "He won."

"No," says the first, "we *lost*, there is a difference, sir. We lost even though the North never could find a competent general." I know the type of the first one. He's the one who thinks he is brilliant, who always knew what President Davis should have done. If they are looking for a recalcitrant southerner, they have found one.

"Grant was competent. Just not brilliant. Any military man who is not Alexander the Great is going to look inadequate in comparison with General Lee."

"Grant was a drinker," the first one says. "It was his subordinates. They'd been through years of war. They knew what to do."

It is so hot on the train. I wonder how long until the train leaves.

I wonder if the Reverend will write my sister in Tennessee and tell her about our mother. I wish the train were going east toward Tennessee instead of north and west toward St. Louis.

My valise. All I have. It is on the platform. I turn and go to the door. It is closed and I try the handle, but it is too stiff for me. I look around for help.

"It's locked," says a woman in gray. She doesn't look unkind.

"My things, I left them on the platform," I say.

"Oh, honey," she says. "they aren't going to let you back out there. They don't let anyone off the train."

I look out the window but I can't see the valise. I can see some of the soldiers, so I beat on the window. One of them glances up at me, frowning, but then he ignores me.

The train blows that it is going to leave, and I beat harder on the glass. If I could shatter that glass. They don't understand, they would help me if they understood. The train lurches and I stagger. It is out there, somewhere, on that platform. Clothes for my mother and me, blankets, things we will need. Things I will need.

The train pulls out of the station and I feel so terrible I sit down on the floor in all the dirt from people's feet and sob.

The train creeps slowly at first, but then picks up speed. The *clack-clack-clack-clack* rocks me. It is improper, but I allow it to rock me. I am in others' hands now and there is nothing to do but be patient. I am good at that. So it has been all my life. I have tried to be dutiful, but something in me has not bent right, and I have never been able to maintain a Christian frame of mind, but like a chicken in a yard, I have always kept my eyes on the small things. I have tended to what was in front of me, first the house, then my mother. When we could not get sugar, I learned to cook with molasses and honey. Now I sit and let my mind go empty and let the train rock me.

"Child," someone says. "Child."

The woman in gray has been trying to get my attention for a while, but I have been sitting and letting myself be rocked.

"Child," she says again, "would you like some water?"

Yes, I realize, I would. She has a jar and she gives it to me to sip out of. "Thank you," I say. "We brought water, but we lost it in the crush on the platform."

"You have someone with you?" she asks.

"My mother," I say, and start crying again. "She is old, and there was such a press on the platform, and she fell and was trampled."

"What's your name?" the woman says.

"Clara Corbett," I say.

"I'm Elizabeth Loudon," the woman says. "And you are welcome to travel with me." There is something about her, a simple pleasantness, that makes me trust her. She is a small woman, with a small nose and eyes as gray as her dress. She is younger than I first thought, maybe only in her thirties? "How old are you? Do you have family?" she asks.

"I am seventeen. I have a sister, Julia. But she doesn't live in Mississippi anymore."

"Where does she live?" the woman asks.

"In Beech Bluff, near Jackson, Tennessee."

She shakes her head. "I don't know it. Is it good country?"

"I think so," I say. "In her letters it sounds like good country. But I haven't seen her for seven years." Of course no one could travel during the war. She has three children in Tennessee. My sister is twenty-eight, almost as old as this woman. It is hard to imagine.

"Were you close?" she asks.

I don't know that we were close. But she is my sister. She is all I have now. I hope that the Reverend will write her about my mother, but I don't know that he knows where she is. I will have to write her. She will think I should have taken better care.

"Are you traveling alone?"

"My companion is a few seats farther in front. He and I could not find seats together."

Her companion is a man? Not her husband, maybe her brother? But she would say her brother if that's who she meant. A woman traveling with a man. An adventuress, I think. There are stories of women traveling, hoping to find unattached girls like myself. They befriend the young girls and then deliver them to the brothels of New Orleans.

For a moment Elizabeth takes on a sinister cast. But this is a train full of recalcitrant southerners, there is no opportunity to kidnap anyone. Elizabeth is like me, a woman who has lost her home.

It takes the rest of the day and a night to get to St. Louis, and Elizabeth and I talk. It's as if we talk in ciphers, instead of talking about home we talk about gardening, and I can see the garden at home, lazy with bees. She is a quilter. I don't quilt, but I used to do petit pointe, so we can talk sewing and about how hard it has been to get colors. And we talk about mending and making do, we have all been making do for so long.

When it gets dark, since I have no seat, I stay where I am sitting by the door of the train. I am so tired, but in the darkness all I can think of is my mother's face in the crowd and her hopeless open mouth. I don't want to think of my mother, but I am in a delirium of fatigue, surrounded by the dark and the rumble of the train and the distant murmur of voices. I sleep sitting by the door of the train, fitful and rocked. I have dreams like fever dreams. In my dream I am in a strange house, but it is supposed to be my own house, but nothing is where it should be, and I begin to believe that I have actually entered a stranger's house, and that they'll return and find me here. When I wake up and go back to sleep, I am back in this strange house, looking through things.

I wake before dawn, only a little rested. My shoulders and hips and back all ache from the way I am leaning, but I have no energy to get up. I have no energy to do anything but endure. Elizabeth nods, sometimes awake, sometimes asleep, but neither of us speak.

Finally the train slows. We come in through a town, but the town seems to go on and on. It must be St. Louis. We stop and sit. The sun comes up and heats the car like an oven. There is no movement of the air. There are so many buildings in St. Louis, and so many of them are tall, two stories, that I wonder if they cut off the wind and that is why it's so still. But finally the train lurches and we crawl into the station.

I am one of the first off the train by virtue of my position near the door. A soldier unlocks it and shouts for all of us to disembark, but he need not have bothered for there is a rush. I am borne ahead at its beginning but I can stop at the back of the platform. I am afraid that I have lost Elizabeth, but I see her in the crowd. She is on the arm of a younger man in a bowler. There is something about his air that marks him as different— he is sprightly and apparently fresh even after the long ride.

I almost let them pass, but the prospect of being alone makes me reach out and touch her shoulder.

"There you are," she says.

We join a queue of people waiting to use a trench. The smell is appalling, ammonia acrid and eye-watering. There is a wall to separate the men from the women, but the women are all together. I crouch, trying not to notice anyone and trying to keep my skirts out of the filth. It is so awful. It's worse than anything. I feel so awful.

What if my mother were here? What would I do? I think maybe it was better, maybe it was God's hand. But that is an awful thought, too.

"Child," Elizabeth says when I come out, "what's the matter?"

"It's so awful," I say. I shouldn't cry, but I just want to be home and clean. I want to go to bed and sleep.

She offers me a biscuit.

"You should save your food," I say.

"Don't worry," Elizabeth says, "We have enough."

I shouldn't accept it, but I am so hungry. And when I have a little to eat, I feel a little better.

I try to imagine what the fort will be like where we will be going. Will we have a place to sleep, or will it be barracks? Or worse yet, tents? Although after the night I spent on the train I can't imagine anything that could be worse. I imagine if I have to stay awhile in a tent then I'll make the best of it.

"I think this being in limbo is perhaps worse than anything we can expect at the end," I say to Elizabeth. She smiles.

She introduces her companion, Michael. He is enough like her to be her brother, but I don't think that they are. I am resolved not to ask, if they want to tell me they can.

We are standing together, not saying anything, when there is some commotion farther up the platform. It is a woman, her black dress is like smoke. She is running down the platform, coming toward us. There are all of these people and yet it is as if there is no obstacle for her. "NO NO NO NO, DON'T TOUCH ME! FILTHY HANDS! DON'T LET THEM TOUCH YOU! DON'T GET ON THE TRAINS!"

People are getting out of her way. Where are the soldiers? The fabric of her dress is so threadbare it is rotten and torn at the seams. Her skirt is greasy black and matted and stained. Her face is so thin. "ANIMALS! THERE IS NOTHING OUT THERE! PEOPLE DON'T HAVE FOOD! THERE IS NOTHING THERE BUT INDIANS! THEY SENT US OUT TO SETTLE BUT THERE WAS NOTHING THERE!"

I expect she will run past me but she grabs my arm and stops and looks into my face. She has light eyes, pale eyes in her dark face. She is mad.

"WE WERE ALL STARVING, SO WE WENT TO THE FORT BUT THE FORT HAD NOTHING. YOU WILL ALL STARVE, THE WAY THEY ARE STARVING THE INDIANS! THEY WILL LET US ALL DIE! THEY DON'T CARE!" She is screaming in my face, and her spittle sprays me, warm as her breath. Her hand is all tendons and twigs, but she's so strong I can't escape.

The soldiers grab her and yank her away from me. My arm aches where she was holding it. I can't stand up.

Elizabeth pulls me upright. "Stay close to me," she says and starts to walk the other way down the platform. People are looking up following the screaming woman.

She pulls me along with her. I keep thinking of the woman's hand and wrist turned black with grime. I remember my mother's face was black when she lay on the platform. Black like something rotted.

"Here," Elizabeth says at an old door, painted green but now weathered. The door opens and we pass inside.

"What?" I say. My eyes are accustomed to the morning brightness and I can't see.

"Her name is Clara," Elizabeth says. "She has people in Tennessee."

"Come with me," says another woman. She sounds older. "Step this way. Where are her things?"

I am being kidnapped. O merciful God, I'll die. I let out a moan.

"Her things were lost, her mother was killed in a crush on the platform."

The woman in the dark clucks sympathetically. "Poor dear. Does Michael have his passenger yet?"

"In a moment," Elizabeth says. "We were lucky for the commotion."

I am beginning to be able to see. It is a storage room, full of abandoned things. The woman holding my arm is older. There are some broken chairs and a stool. She sits me in the chair. Is Elizabeth some kind of adventuress?

"Who are you?" I ask.

"We are friends," Elizabeth says. "We will help you get to your sister."

I don't believe them. I will end up in New Orleans. Elizabeth is some kind of adventuress.

After a moment the door opens and this time it is Michael with a young man. "This is Andrew," he says.

A man? What do they want with a man? That is what stops me from saying "Run!" Andrew is blinded by the change in light, and I can see the astonishment working on his face, the way it must be working on mine. "What is this?" he asks.

"You are with Friends," Michael says, and maybe he has said it differently than Elizabeth, or maybe it is just that this time I have had the wit to hear it.

"Quakers?" Andrew says. "Abolitionists?"

Michael smiles, I can see his teeth white in the darkness. "Just Friends," he says.

Abolitionists. Crazy people who steal slaves to set them free. Have they come to kidnap us? We are recalcitrant southerners, I have never heard of Quakers seeking revenge, but everyone knows the Abolitionists are crazy and they are liable to do anything.

"We'll have to wait here until they begin to move people out, it will be evening before we can leave," says the older woman.

I am so frightened, I just want to be home. Maybe I should try to break free and run out to the platform, there are northern soldiers out there. Would they protect me? And then what, go to a fort in Oklahoma?

The older woman asks Michael how they could get past the

guards so early and he tells her about the madwoman. A "refugee," he calls her.

"They'll just take her back," Elizabeth says, sighing.

Take her back, do they mean that she really came from Oklahoma? They talk about how bad it will be this winter. Michael says there are Wisconsin Indians resettled down there, but they've got no food, and they've been starving on government handouts for a couple of years. Now there will be more people. They're not prepared for winter.

There can't have been much handout during the war. It was hard enough to feed the armies.

They explain to Andrew and to me that we will sneak out of the train station this evening, after dark. We will spend a day with a Quaker family in St. Louis, and then they will send us on to the next family. And so we will be passed hand to hand, like a bucket in a brigade, until we get to our families.

They call it the underground railroad.

But we are slave owners.

"Wrong is wrong," says Elizabeth. "Some of us can't stand and watch people starve."

"But only two out of the whole train," Andrew says.

Michael sighs.

The old woman nods. "It isn't right."

Elizabeth picked me because my mother died. If my mother had not died, I would be out there, on my way to starve with the rest of them.

I can't help it but I start to cry. I should not profit from my mother's death. I should have kept her safe.

"Hush, now," says Elizabeth. "Hush, you'll be okay."

"It's not right," I whisper. I'm trying not to be loud, we mustn't be discovered.

"What, child?"

"You shouldn't have picked me," I say. But I am crying so hard I don't think they can understand me. Elizabeth strokes my hair and wipes my face. It may be the last time someone will do these things for me. My sister has three children of her own, and she won't need another child. I'll have to work hard to make up my keep.

There are blankets there and we lie down on the hard floor, all except Michael, who sits in a chair and sleeps. I sleep this time with fewer dreams. But when I wake up, although I can't remember what they were, I have the feeling that I have been dreaming restless dreams.

The stars are bright when we finally creep out of the station. A night full of stars. The stars will be the same in Tennessee. The platform is empty, the train and the people are gone. The Lincoln Train has gone back south while we slept, to take more people out of Mississippi.

"Will you come back and save more people?" I ask Elizabeth.

The stars are a banner behind her quiet head. "We will save what we can," she says.

It isn't fair that I was picked. "I want to help," I tell her.

She is silent for a moment. "We only work with our own," she says. There is something in her voice that has not been there before. A sharpness.

"What do you mean?" I ask.

"There are no slavers in our ranks," she says, and her voice is cold.

I feel as if I have had a fever: tired, but clear of mind. I have never walked so far and not walked beyond a town. The streets of St. Louis are empty. There are few lights. Far off a woman is singing, and her voice is clear and carries easily in the night. A beautiful voice.

"Elizabeth," Michael says, "she is just a girl."

"She needs to know," Elizabeth says.

"Why did you save me then?" I ask.

"One does not fight evil with evil," Elizabeth says.

"I'm not evil!" I say.

But no one answers.

Of course we'll play baseball on Mars. Low gravity, nearer horizons: how could we resist?

Kim Stanley Robinson has been thinking and writing about the human settlement of Mars for many years. His best-known SF is his Mars trilogy: Red Mars, Green Mars, and Blue Mars. He has also written a number of shorter works about Martian colonization, of which this is one.

Arthur Sternbach Brings the Curveball to Mars

· ·

KIM STANLEY ROBINSON

He was a tall skinny Martian kid, shy and stooping. Gangly as a puppy. Why they had him playing third base I have no idea. Then again they had me playing short stop and I'm left-handed. And can't field grounders. But I'm American so there I was. That's what learning a sport by video will do. Some things are so obvious people never think to mention them. Like never put a lefty at shortstop. But on Mars they were making it all new. Some people there had fallen in love with baseball, and ordered the equipment and rolled some fields, and off they went.

So there we were, me and this kid Gregor, butchering the left side of the infield. He looked so young I asked him how old he was, and he said eight and I thought Jeez you're not *that* young, but realized he meant Martian years of course, so he was about sixteen or seventeen, but he seemed younger. He had recently moved to Argyre from somewhere else, and was staying at the local house of his co-op with relatives or friends, I never got that straight, but he seemed pretty lonely to me. He never missed practice even though he was the worst of a terrible team, and clearly he got frustrated at all his errors and strike-outs. I used to wonder why he came out at all. And so shy; and that stoop; and the acne; and the tripping over his own feet; the blushing, the mumbling—he was a classic.

English wasn't his first language, either. It was Armenian, or Moravian, something like that. Something no one else spoke, anyway, except for an elderly couple in his co-op. So he mumbled what passes for English on Mars, and sometimes even used a translation box, but basically tried never to be in a situation where he had to speak. And made error after error. We must have made quite a sight—me about waist-high to him, and both of us letting grounders pass through us like we were a magic show. Or else knocking them down and chasing them around, then winging them past the first baseman. We very seldom made an out. It would have been conspicuous except everyone else was the same way. Baseball on Mars was a high scoring game.

But beautiful anyway. It was like a dream, really. First of all the horizon, when you're on a flat plain like Argyre, is only three miles away rather than six. It's very noticeable to a Terran eye. Then their diamonds have just over normal-sized infields, but the outfields have to be huge. At my team's ballpark it was nine hundred feet to dead center, seven hundred down the lines.

Standing at the plate the outfield fence was like a little green line off in the distance, under a purple sky, pretty near the horizon itself—what I'm telling you is that the baseball diamond about covered *the entire visible world*. It was so great.

They played with four outfielders, like in softball, and still the alleys between fielders were wide. And the air was about as thin as at Everest base camp, and the gravity itself only bats .380, so to speak. So when you hit the ball solid it flies like a golf ball hit by a big driver. Even as big as the fields were, there were still a number of home runs every game. Not many shut-outs on Mars. Not till I got there anyway.

I went there after I climbed Olympus Mons, to help them establish a new soil sciences institute. They had the sense not to try that by video. At first I climbed in the Charitums in my time off, but after I got hooked into baseball it took up most of my spare time. Fine, I'll play, I said when they asked me. But I won't coach. I don't like telling people what to do.

So I'd go out and start by doing soccer exercises with the rest of them, warming up all the muscles we would never use. Then Werner would start hitting infield practice, and Gregor and I would start flailing. We were like matadors. Occasionally we'd snag one and whale it over to first, and occasionally the first baseman, who was well over two meters tall and built like a tank, would catch our throws, and we'd slap our gloves together. Doing this day after day Gregor got a little less shy with me, though not much. And I saw that he threw the ball pretty damned hard. His arm was as long as my whole body, and boneless it seemed, like something pulled off a squid, so loose-wristed that he got some real pop on the ball. Of course sometimes it would still be rising when it passed ten meters over the first baseman's head, but it was moving, no doubt about it. I began to see that maybe the reason he came out to play, beyond just being around people he didn't have to talk to, was the chance to throw things really hard. I saw too that he wasn't so much shy as he was surly. Or both.

Anyway our fielding was a joke. Hitting went a bit better. Gregor learned to chop down on the ball and hit grounders up the middle; it was pretty effective. And I began to get my timing together. Coming to it from years of slow-pitch softball, I had started by swinging at everything a week late, and between that and my short-stopping I'm sure my teammates figured they had gotten a defective American. And once they had a rule limiting each team to only two Terrans, no doubt they were disappointed by that. But slowly I adjusted my timing, and after that I hit pretty well. The thing was their pitchers had no breaking stuff. These big guys would rear back and throw as hard as they could, like Gregor, but it took everything in their power just to throw strikes. It was a little scary because they often threw right at you by accident. But if they got it down the pipe then all you had to do was time it. And If you hit one, how the ball flew! Every time I connected it was like a miracle. It felt like you could put one into orbit if you hit it right, in fact that was one of their nicknames for a home run, Oh that's orbital they would say, watching one leave the park headed for the horizon. They had a little bell, like a ship's bell, attached to the backstop, and every time someone hit one out they would ring that bell while you rounded the bases. A very nice local custom.

So I enjoyed it. It's a beautiful game even when you're butchering it. My sorest muscles after practice were in my stomach from laughing so hard. I even began to have some success at short. When I caught balls going to my right I twirled around backwards to throw to first or second. People were impressed though of course it was ridiculous. It was a case of the one-eyed man in the country of the blind. Not that they weren't good athletes, you understand, but none of them had played as kids, and so they had no baseball instincts. They just liked to play. And I could see why— but there on a green field as big as the world, under a purple sky, with the yellow-green balls flying around—it was beautiful. We had a good time.

I started to give a few tips to Gregor, too, though I had sworn to myself not to get into coaching. I don't like trying to tell people what to do. The game's too hard for that. But I'd be hitting flies to the outfielders, and it was hard not to tell them to watch the ball and run under it and then put the glove up and catch it, rather than run all the way with their arms stuck up like the Statue of Liberty's. Or when they took turns hitting flies (it's harder than it looks) giving them batting tips. And Gregor and I played catch all the time during warm-ups, so just watching me—and trying to throw to such a short target—he got better. He definitely threw hard. And I saw there was a whole lot of movement in his throws. They'd come tailing in to me every which way, no surprise given how loose-wristed he was. I had to look sharp or I'd miss. He was out of control, but he had potential.

And the truth was, our pitchers were bad. I loved the guys, but they couldn't throw strikes if you paid them. They'd regularly walk ten or twenty batters every game, and these were five-inning games. Werner would watch Thomas walk ten, then he'd take over in relief and walk ten more himself. Sometimes they'd go through this twice. Gregor and I would stand there while the other team's runners walked by as in a parade, or a line at the grocery store. When Werner went to the mound I'd stand by Gregor and say, You know Gregor you could pitch better than these guys. You've got a good arm. And he would look at me horrified, muttering. No no no no, not possible.

But then one time warming up he broke off a really mean curve and I caught it on my wrist. While I was rubbing it down I walked over to him. Did you see the way that ball curved? I said.

Yes, he said, looking away. I'm sorry.

Don't be sorry, That's called a curve ball, Gregor. It can be a useful throw. You twisted your hand at the last moment and the ball came over the top of it, like this, see? Here, try it again.

So we slowly got into it. I was all-state in Connecticut my senior year in high school, and it was all from throwing junk-curve, slider, split-finger, change. I could see Gregor throwing most of those just by accident, but to keep from confusing him I just worked on a straight curve. I told him Just throw it to me like you did that first time.

I thought you weren't to coach us, he said.

I'm not coaching you! Just throw it like that. Then in the games throw it straight. As straight as possible.

He mumbled a bit at me in Moravian, and didn't look me in the eye. But he did it. And after a while he worked up a good curve. Of course the thinner air on Mars meant there was little for the balls to bite on. But I noticed that the blue dot balls they played with had higher stitching than the red dot balls. They played with both of them as if there was no difference, but there was. So I filed that away and kept working with Gregor.

We practiced a lot. I showed him how to throw from the stretch, figuring that a wind-up from Gregor was likely to end up in knots. And by mid-season he threw a mean curve from the stretch. We had not mentioned it to anyone else. He was wild with it, but it hooked hard; I had to be really sharp to catch some of them. It made me better at shortstop too. Although finally in one game, behind twenty to nothing as usual, a batter hit a towering pop fly and I took off running back on it, and the wind kept carrying it and I kept following it, until when I got it I was out there sprawled between our startled center fielders.

Maybe you should play outfield, Werner said.

I said Thank God.

So after that I played left center or right center, and I spent the games chasing line drives to the fence and throwing them back in to the cut-off man. Or more likely, standing there and watching the other team take their walks. I called in my usual chatter, and only then did I notice that no one on Mars ever yelled anything at these games. It was like playing in a league of deaf-mutes. I had to provide the chatter for the whole team from two hundred yards away in center field, including of course criticism of the plate umpires' calls. My view of the plate was miniaturized but I still did a better job than they did, and they knew it too. It was fun. People would walk by and say, Hey there must be an American out there.

One day after one of our home losses, 28 to 12 I think it was, everyone went to get something to eat, and Gregor was just standing there looking off into the distance. You want to come along? I asked him, gesturing after the others, but he shook his head. He had to get back home and work. I was going back to work myself, so I walked with him into town, a place like you'd see in the Texas panhandle. I stopped outside his co-op, which was a big house or little apartment complex, I could never tell which was which on Mars. There he stood like a lamppost, and I was about to leave when an old woman came out and invited me in. Gregor had told her about me, she said in stiff English. So I was introduced to the people in the kitchen there, most of them incredibly tall. Gregor seemed really embarrassed, he didn't want me being there, so I left as soon as I could get away. The old woman had a husband, and they seemed like Gregor's grandparents. There was a young girl there too, about his age, looking at both of us like a hawk. Gregor never met her eye.

Next time at practice, I said, Gregor, were those your grand-parents?

Like my grandparents.

And that girl, who was she?

No answer.

Like a cousin or something?

Yes.

Gregor, what about your parents? Where are they?

He just shrugged and started throwing me the ball.

I got the impression they lived in another branch of his co-op somewhere else, but I never found out for sure. A lot of what I saw on Mars I liked—the way they run their businesses together in co-ops takes a lot of pressure off them, and they live pretty relaxed lives compared to us on Earth. But some of their parenting systems—kids brought up by groups, or by one parent, or whatever—I wasn't so sure about those. It makes for problems if you ask me. Bunch of teenage boys ready to slug somebody. Maybe that happens no matter what you do.

Anyway we finally got to the end of the season, and I was going to go back to Earth after it. Our team's record was three and fifteen, and we came in last place in the regular season standings. But they held a final weekend tournament for all the teams in the Argyre Basin, a bunch of three-inning games, as there were a lot to get through. Immediately we lost the first game and were in the loser's bracket. Then we were losing the next one too, and all because of walks, mostly. Werner relieved Thomas for a time, then when that didn't work out Thomas went back to the mound to re-relieve Werner. When that happened I ran all the way in from center to join them on the mound. I said Look you guys, let Gregor pitch.

Gregor! they both said. No way!

He'll be even worse than us, Werner said.

How could he be? I said. You guys just walked eleven batters in a row. Night will fall before Gregor could do that.

So they agreed to it. They were both discouraged at that point, as you might expect. So I went over to Gregor and said Okay, Gregor, you give it a try now.

Oh no, no no no no no no no. He was pretty set against it. He glanced up into the stands where we had a couple hundred spectators, mostly friends and family and some curious passersby, and I saw then that his like-grandparents and his girl something-or-other were up there watching. Gregor was getting more hangdog and sullen every second.

Come on Gregor, I said, putting the ball in his glove. Tell you what, I'll catch you. It'll be just like warming up. Just keep throwing your curve ball. And I dragged him over to the mound.

So Werner warmed him up while I went over and got on the catcher's gear, moving a box of blue dot balls to the front of the ump's supply area while I was at it. I could see Gregor was nervous, and so was I. I had never caught before, and he had never pitched, and bases were loaded and no one was out. It was an unusual baseball moment.

Finally I was geared up and I clanked on out to him. Don't worry about throwing too hard, I said. Just put the curve ball right in my glove. Ignore the batter. I'll give you the sign before every pitch; two fingers for curve, one for fastball.

Fastball? he says.

That's where you throw the ball fast. Don't worry about that. We're just going to throw curves anyway.

And you said you weren't to coach, he said bitterly.

I'm not coaching, I said, I'm catching.

So I went back and got set behind the plate. Be looking for

curve balls, I said to the ump. Curve ball? he said.

So we started up. Gregor stood crouched on the mound like a big praying mantis, red-faced and grim. He threw the first pitch right over our heads to the backstop. Two guys scored while I retrieved it, but I threw out the runner going from first to third. I went out to Gregor. Okay, I said, the bases are cleared and we got an out. Let's just throw now. Right into the glove. Just like last time, but lower.

So he did. He threw the ball at the batter, and the batter bailed, and the ball cut right down into my glove. The umpire was speechless. I turned around and showed him the ball in my glove. That was a strike, I told him.

Strike! he hollered. He grinned at me. That was a curve ball, wasn't it.

Damn right it was.

Hey, the batter said. What was that?

We'll show you again, I said.

And after that Gregor began to mow them down. I kept putting down two fingers, and he kept throwing curve balls. By no means were they all strikes, but enough were to keep him from walking too many batters. All the balls were blue dot. The ump began to get into it.

And between two batters I looked behind me and saw that the entire crowd of spectators, and all the teams not playing at that moment, had congregated behind the backstop to watch Gregor pitch. No one on Mars had ever seen a curve ball before, and now they were crammed back there to get the best view of it, gasping and chattering at every hook. The batter would bail or take a weak swing and then look back at the crowd with a big grin, as if to say Did you see that? That was a curve ball!

So we came back and won that game, and we kept Gregor pitching, and we won the next three games as well. The third game he threw exactly twenty-seven pitches, striking out all nine batters with three pitches each. Walter Feller once struck out all twenty-seven batters in a high school game; it was like that.

The crowd was loving it. Gregor's face was less red. He was standing straighter in the box. He still refused to look anywhere but at my glove, but his look of grim terror had shifted to one of ferocious concentration. He may have been skinny, but he was tall. Out there on the mound he began to look pretty damned formidable.

So we climbed back up into the winner's bracket, then into a semi-final. Crowds of people were coming up to Gregor between games to get him to sign their baseballs. Mostly he looked dazed, but at one point I saw him glance up at his co-op family in the stands and wave at them, with a brief smile.

How's your arm holding out? I asked him.

What do you mean? he said.

Okay, I said. Now look, I want to play outfield again this game. Can you pitch to Werner? Because there were a couple of Americans on the team we played next, Ernie and Caesar, who I suspected could hit a curve. I just had a hunch.

Gregor nodded, and I could see that as long as there was a glove to throw at, nothing else mattered. So I arranged it with Werner, and in the semifinals I was back out in right-center field. We were playing under the lights by this time, the field like green velvet under a purple twilight sky. Looking in from center field it was all tiny, like something in a dream.

And it must have been a good hunch I had, because I made one catch charging in on a liner from Ernie, sliding to snag it, and then another running across the middle for what seemed like thirty seconds, before I got under a towering Texas leaguer from Caesar. Gregor even came up and congratulated me between innings.

And you know that old thing about how a good play in the field leads to a good at-bat. Already in the day's games I had hit well, but now in this semifinal I came up and hit a high fastball so solid it felt like I didn't hit it at all, and off it flew. Home run over the center field fence, out into the dusk. I lost sight of it before it came down.

Then in the finals I did it again in the first inning, back-to-back with Thomas—his to left, mine again to center. That was two in a row for me, and we were winning, and Gregor was mowing them down. So when I came up again the next inning I was feeling good, and people were calling out for another homer, and the other team's pitcher had a real determined look. He was a really big guy, as tall as Gregor but massive-chested as so many Martians are, and he reared back and threw the first one right at my head. Not on purpose, he was out of control. Then I barely fouled several pitches off, swinging very late, and dodging his inside heat, until it was a full count, and I was thinking to myself Well heck, it doesn't really matter if you strike out here, at least you hit two in a row.

Then I heard Gregor shouting Come on, Coach, you can do

it! Hang in there! Keep your focus! All doing a passable imitation of me, I guess, as the rest of the team was laughing its head off. I suppose I had said all those things to them before, though of course it was just the stuff you always say automatically at a ball game, I never meant anything by it, I didn't even know people heard me. But I definitely heard Gregor, needling me, and I stepped back into the box thinking Look I don't even like to coach, I played ten games at shortstop trying not to coach you guys, and I was so irritated I was barely aware of the pitch, but hammered it anyway out over the it right field fence, higher and deeper even than my first two. Knee-high fastball, inside. As Ernie said to me afterwards, You *drove* that baby. My teammates rang the little ship's bell all the way around the bases, and I slapped hands with every one of them on the way from third to home, feeling the grin on my face. Afterwards I sat on the bench and felt the hit in my hands. I can still see it flying out.

So we were ahead 4–0 in the final inning, and the other team came up determined to catch us. Gregor was tiring at last, and he walked a couple, then hung a curve and their big pitcher got into it and clocked it far over my head. Now I do okay charging liners, but the minute a ball is hit over me I'm totally lost. So I turned my back on this one and ran for the fence, figuring either it goes out or I collect it against the fence, but that I'd never see it again in the air. But running on Mars is so weird. You get going too fast and then you're pinwheeling along trying to keep from doing a faceplant. That's what I was doing when I saw the warning track, and looked back up and spotted the ball coming down, so I jumped, trying to jump straight up, you know, but I had a lot of momentum, and had completely forgotten about the gravity, so I shot up and caught the ball, amazing, but found myself *flying right over the fence.*

I came down and rolled in the dust and sand, and the ball stayed stuck in my glove. I hopped back over the fence holding the ball up to show everyone I had it. But they gave the other pitcher a home run anyway, because you have to stay inside the park when you catch one, it's a local rule. I didn't care. The whole point of playing games is to make you do things like that anyway. And it was good that that pitcher got one too.

So we started up again and Gregor struck out the side, and we won the tournament. We were mobbed, Gregor especially. He was the hero of the hour. Everyone wanted him to sign something. He didn't say much, but he wasn't stooping either. He looked surprised. Afterward Werner took two balls and everyone signed them, to make kind-of trophies for Gregor and me. Later I saw half the names on my trophy were jokes, "Mickey Mantel" and other names like that. Gregor had written on it "Hi Coach Arthur, Regards Greg." I have the ball still, on my desk at home.

Be careful what you demand of those around you. They may just give it to you.

Orson Scott Card is the author of Ender's Game, *quite possibly the most popular SF novel of the last twenty years. "Salvage" is from a cycle of stories set in and around Utah in a future following a great calamity that affects the whole United States. These stories are collected in* The Folk of the Fringe.

Salvage

• •

ORSON SCOTT CARD

The road began to climb steeply right from the ferry, so the truck couldn't build up any speed. Deaver just kept shifting down, wincing as he listened to the grinding of the gears. Sounded like the transmission was chewing itself to gravel. He'd been nursing it all the way across Nevada, and if the Wendover ferry hadn't carried him these last miles over the Mormon Sea, he would have had a nice long hike. Lucky. It was a good sign. Things were going to go Deaver's way for a while.

The mechanic frowned at him when he rattled in to the loading dock. "You been ridin the clutch, boy?"

Deaver got down from the cab. "Clutch? What's a clutch?"

The mechanic didn't smile. "Couldn't you hear the transmission was shot?"

"I had mechanics all the way across Nevada askin to fix it for me, but I told em I was savin it for you."

The mechanic looked at him like he was crazy. "There ain't no mechanics in Nevada."

If you wasn't dumb as your thumb, thought Deaver, you'd know I was joking. These old Mormons were so straight they couldn't sit down, some of them. But Deaver didn't say anything. Just smiled.

"This truck's gonna stay here a few days," said the mechanic.

Fine with me, thought Deaver. I got plans. "How many days you figure?"

"Take three for now, I'll sign you off."

"My name's Deaver Teague."

"Tell the foreman, he'll write it up." The mechanic lifted the hood to begin the routine checks while the dockboys loaded off the old washing machines and refrigerators and other stuff Deaver had picked up on this trip. Deaver took his mileage reading to the window and the foreman paid him off.

Seven dollars for five days of driving and loading, sleeping in the cab and eating whatever the farmers could spare. It was better than a lot of people lived on, but there wasn't any future in it. Salvage wouldn't go on forever. Someday he'd pick up the last broken-down dishwasher left from the old days, and then he'd be out of a job.

Well, Deaver Teague wasn't going to wait around for that. He knew where the gold was, he'd been planning how to get it for weeks, and if Lehi had got the diving equipment like he promised then tomorrow morning they'd do a little freelance salvage work. If they were lucky they'd come home rich.

Deaver's legs were stiff but he loosened them up pretty quick and broke into an easy, loping run down the corridors of the Salvage Center. He took a flight of stairs two or three steps at a time, bounded down a hall, and when he reached a sign that said SMALL COMPUTER SALVAGE, he pushed off the doorframe and rebounded into the room. "Hey Lehi!" he said. "Hey it's quittin time!"

Lehi McKay paid no attention. He was sitting in front of a TV screen, jerking at a black box he held on his lap.

"You do that and you'll go blind," said Deaver.

"Shut up, carpface." Lehi never took his eyes off the screen. He jabbed at a button on the black box and twisted on the stick that jutted up from it. A colored blob on the screen blew up and split into four smaller blobs.

"I got three days off while they do the transmission on the truck," said Deaver. "So tomorrow's the temple expedition."

Lehi got the last blob off the screen. More blobs appeared.

"That's real fun," said Deaver, "like sweepin the street and then they bring along another troop of horses."

"It's an Atari. From the sixties or seventies or something. Eighties. Old. Can't do much with the pieces, it's only eight-bit stuff. All these years in somebody's attic in Logan, and the sucker still runs."

"Old guys probably didn't even know they had it."

"Probably."

Deaver watched the game. Same thing over and over again. "How much a thing like this use to cost?"

"A lot. Maybe fifteen, twenty bucks."

"Makes you want to barf. And here sits Lehi McKay, toodling his noodle like the old guys use to. All it ever got *them* was a sore noodle, Lehi. And slag for brains."

"Drown it. I'm trying to concentrate."

The game finally ended. Lehi set the black box up on the workbench, turned off the machine, and stood up.

"You got everything ready to go underwater tomorrow?" asked Deaver.

"That was a good game. Having fun must've took up a lot of their time in the old days. Mom says the kids used to not even be able to get jobs till they was sixteen. It was the law."

"Don't you wish," said Deaver.

"It's true."

"You don't know your tongue from dung, Lehi. You don't know your heart from a fart."

"You want to get us both kicked out of here, talkin like that?"

"I don't have to follow school rules now, I graduated sixth grade, I'm nineteen years old, I been on my own for five years." He pulled his seven dollars out of his pocket, waved them once, stuffed them back in carelessly. "I do OK, and I talk like I want to talk. Think I'm afraid of the Bishop?"

"Bishop don't scare me. I don't even go to church except to make Mom happy. It's a bunch of bunny turds."

Lehi laughed, but Deaver could see that he was a little scared to talk like that. Sixteen years old, thought Deaver, he's big and he's smart but he's such a little kid. He don't understand how it's like to be a man. "Rain's comin."

"Rain's always comin. What the hell do you think filled up the lake?" Lehi smirked as he unplugged everything on the workbench.

"I meant *Lor*raine Wilson."

"I know what you meant. She's got her boat?"

"And she's got a mean set of fenders." Deaver cupped his hands. "Just need a little polishing."

"Why do you always talk dirty? Ever since you started driving salvage, Deaver, you got a gutter mouth. Besides, she's built like a sack."

"She's near fifty, what do you expect?" It occurred to Deaver that Lehi seemed to be stalling. Which probably meant he botched up again as usual. "Can you get the diving stuff?"

"I already got it. You thought I'd screw up." Lehi smirked again.

"You? Screw up? You can be trusted with *anything*." Deaver started for the door. He could hear Lehi behind him, still shutting a few things off. They got to use a lot of electricity in here. Of course they had to, because they needed computers all the time, and salvage was the only way to get them. But when Deaver saw all that electricity getting used up at once, to him it looked like his own future. All the machines he could ever want, new ones, and all the power they needed. Clothes that nobody else ever wore, his own horse and wagon or even a car. Maybe he'd be the guy who started *making* cars again. He didn't need stupid blob-smashing games from the past. "That stuff's dead and gone, duck lips, dead and gone."

"What're you talking about?" asked Lehi.

"Dead and gone. All your computer things."

It was enough to set Lehi off, as it always did. Deaver grinned and felt wicked and strong as Lehi babbled along behind him. About how we use the computers more than they ever did in the old days, the computers kept everything going, on and on and on, it was cute, Deaver liked him, the boy was so *intense*. Like everything was the end of the world. Deaver knew better. The world was dead, it had already ended, so none of it mattered, you could sink all this stuff in the lake.

They came out of the Center and walked along the retaining wall. Far below them was the harbor, a little circle of water in the bottom of a bowl, with Bingham City perched on the lip. They used to have an open-pit copper mine here, but when the water rose they cut a channel to it and now they had a nice harbor on Oquirrh Island in the middle of the Mormon Sea, where the factories could stink up the whole sky and no neighbors ever complained about it.

A lot of other people joined them on the steep dirt road that led down to the harbor. Nobody lived right in Bingham City itself, because it was just a working place, day and night. Shifts in, shifts out. Lehi was a shift boy, lived with his family across the Jordan Strait on Point-of-the-Mountain, which was as rotten a place to live as anybody ever devised, rode the ferry in every day at five in the morning and rode it back every afternoon at four. He was supposed to go to school after that for a couple of hours but Deaver thought that was stupid, he told Lehi that all the time, told him again now. School is too much time and too little of everything, a waste of time.

"I gotta go to school," said Lehi.

"Tell me two plus two, you haven't got two plus two yet?"

"*You* finished, didn't you?"

"Nobody needs anything after fourth grade." He shoved Lehi a little. Usually Lehi shoved back, but this time no.

"Just try getting a real job without a sixth-grade diploma, OK? And I'm pretty close now." They were at the ferry ship. Lehi got out his pass.

"You with me tomorrow or not?"

Lehi made a face. "I don't know, Deaver. You can get arrested for going around there. It's a dumb thing to do. They say there's real weird things in the old skyscrapers."

"We aren't going *in* the skyscrapers."

"Even worse in *there*, Deaver. I don't want to go there."

"Yeah, the Angel Moroni's probably waiting to jump out and say booga-booga-booga."

"Don't talk about it, Deaver." Deaver was tickling him; Lehi laughed and tried to shy away. "Cut it out, chigger-head. Come on. Besides, the Moroni statue was moved to the Salt Lake Monument up on the mountain. And that has a guard all the time."

"The statue's just gold plate anyway. I'm tellin you those old Mormons hid tons of stuff down in the Temple, just waitin for somebody who isn't scared of the ghost of Bigamy Young to—"

"Shut *up*, snotsucker, OK? People can hear! Look around, we're not alone!"

It was true, of course. Some of the other people were glaring at them. But then, Deaver noticed that older people liked to glare at younger ones. It made the old farts feel better about kicking off. It was like they were saying, OK, I'm dying, but at least you're stupid. So Deaver looked right at a woman who was staring at him and murmured, "OK, I'm stupid, but at least I won't die."

"Deaver, do you always have to say that where they can hear you?"

"It's true."

"In the first place, Deaver, they aren't dying. And in the second place, you're definitely stupid. And in the third place, the ferry's here." Lehi punched Deaver lightly in the stomach.

Deaver bent over in mock agony. "Ay, the laddie's ungrateful, he is, I give him me last croost of bread and this be the thanks I gets."

"*Nobody* has an accent like that, Deaver!" shouted Lehi. The boat began to pull away.

"Tomorrow at five-thirty!" shouted Deaver.

"You'll never get up at four-thirty, don't give me that, you never get up . . ." But the ferry and the noise of the factories and machine and trucks swallowed up the rest of his insults. Deaver knew them all, anyway. Lehi might be only sixteen, but he was OK. Someday Deaver'd get married but his wife would like Lehi, too. And Lehi'd even get married, and his wife would like Deaver. She'd better, or she'd have to swim home.

He took the trolley home to Fort Douglas and walked to the ancient barracks building where Rain let him stay. It was supposed to be a storage room, but she kept the mops and soap stuff in her place so that there'd be room for a cot. Not much else, but it was on Oquirrh Island without being right there in the stink and the smoke and the noise. He could sleep and that was enough, since most of the time he was out on the truck.

Truth was, his room wasn't home anyway. Home was pretty much Rain's place, a drafty room at the end of the barracks with a dumpy frowzy lady who served him good food and plenty of it. That's where he went now, walked right in and surprised her in the kitchen. She yelled at him for surprising her, yelled at him for being filthy and tracking all over her floor, and let him get a slice of apple before she yelled at him for snitching before supper.

He went around and changed light bulbs in five rooms before supper. The families there were all crammed into two rooms each at the most, and most of them had to share kitchens and eat in shifts. Some of the rooms were nasty places, family warfare held off only as long as it took him to change the light, and sometimes even that truce wasn't observed. Others were doing fine, the place was small but they liked each other. Deaver was pretty sure his family must have been one of the nice ones, because if there'd been any yelling he would have remembered.

Rain and Deaver ate and then turned off all the lights while she played the old record player Deaver had wangled away from Lehi. They really weren't supposed to have it, but they figured as long as they didn't burn any lights it wasn't wasting electricity, and they'd turn it in as soon as anybody asked for it.

In the meantime, Rain had some of the old records from when she was a girl. The songs had strong rhythms, and tonight, like she sometimes did, Rain got up and moved to the music, strange little dances that Deaver didn't understand unless he imagined her as a lithe young girl, pictured her body as it must have been then. It wasn't hard to imagine, it was there in her eyes and her smile all the time, and her movements gave away secrets that years of starchy eating and lack of exercise had disguised.

Then, as always, his thoughts went off to some of the girls he saw from his truck window, driving by the fields where they bent over, hard at work, until they heard the truck and then they stood and waved. Everybody waved at the salvage truck, sometimes it was the only thing with a motor that ever came by, their only contact with the old machines. All the tractors, all the electricity were reserved for the New Soil Lands; the old places were dying. And they turned and waved at the last memories. It made Deaver sad and he hated to be sad, all these people clinging to a past that never existed.

"It never existed," he said aloud.

"Yes it did," Rain whispered. "Girls just wanna have fu-un," she murmured along with the record. "I hated this song when I was a girl. Or maybe it was my mama who hated it."

"You live here then?"

"Indiana," she said. "One of the states, way east."

"Were you a refugee, too?"

"No. We moved here when I was sixteen, seventeen, can't remember. Whenever things got scary in the world, a lot of Mormons moved home. This was always home, no matter what."

The record ended. She turned it off, turned on the lights.

"Got the boat all gassed up?" asked Deaver.

"You don't want to go there," she said.

"If there's gold down there, I want it."

"If there was gold there, Deaver, they would've taken it out before the water covered it. It's not as if nobody got a warning, you know. The Mormon Sea wasn't a flash flood."

"If it isn't down there, what's all the hush-hush about? How come the Lake Patrol keeps people from going there?"

"I don't know, Deaver. Maybe because a lot of people feel like it's a holy place."

Deaver was used to this. Rain never went to church, but she still talked like a Mormon. Most people did, though, when you scratched them the wrong place. Deaver didn't like it when they got religious. "Angels need police protection, is that it?"

"It used to be real important to the Mormons in the old days, Deaver." She sat down on the floor, leaning against the wall under the window.

"Well it's nothin now. They got their other temples, don't they? And they're building the new one in Zarahemla, right?"

"I don't know, Deaver. The one here, it was always the real one. The center." She bent sideways, leaned on her hand, looked down at the floor. "It still is."

Deaver saw she was getting really somber now, really sad. It happened to a lot of people who remembered the old days. Like a disease that never got cured. But Deaver knew the cure. For Rain, anyway. "Is it true they used to kill people in there?"

It worked. She glared at him and the languor left her body. "Is that what you truckers talk about all day?"

Deaver grinned. "There's stories. Cuttin people up if they told where the gold was hid."

"You know Mormons all over the place, now, Deaver, do you really think we'd go cuttin people up for tellin secrets?"

"I don't know. Depends on the secrets, don't it?" He was sitting on his hands, kind of bouncing a little on the couch.

He could see that she was a little mad for real, but didn't want to be. So she'd pretend to be mad for play. She sat up, reached for a pillow to throw at him.

"No! No!" he cried. "Don't cut me up! Don't feed me to the carp!"

The pillow hit him and he pretended elaborately to die.

"Just don't joke about things like that," she said.

"Things like what? You don't believe in the old stuff anymore. Nobody does."

"Maybe not."

"Jesus was supposed to come again, right? There was atom bombs dropped here and there, and he was supposed to come."

"Prophet said we was too wicked. He wouldn't come cause we loved the things of the world too much."

"Come on, if he was comin he would've come, right?"

"Might still," she said.

"Nobody believes that," said Deaver. "Mormons are just the government, that's all. The Bishop gets elected judge in every town, right? The president of the elders is always mayor, it's just the government, just politics, nobody believes it now. Zarahemla's the capital, not the holy city."

He couldn't see her because he was lying flat on his back on the couch. When she didn't answer, he got up and looked for her. She was over by the sink, leaning on the counter. He snuck up behind her to tickle her, but something in her posture changed his mind. When he got close, he saw tears down her cheeks. It was crazy. All these people from the old days got crazy a lot.

"I was just teasin," he said.

She nodded.

"It's just part of the old days. You know how I am about that. Maybe if I remembered, it'd be different. Sometimes I wish I remembered." But it was a lie. He never wished he remembered. He didn't like remembering. Most stuff he couldn't remember even if he wanted to. The earliest thing he could bring to mind was riding on the back of a horse, behind some man who sweated a lot, just riding and riding and riding. And then it was all recent stuff, going to school, getting passed around in people's homes, finally getting busy one year and finishing school and getting a job. He didn't get misty-eyed thinking about any of it, any of those places. Just passing through, that's all he was ever doing, never belonged anywhere until maybe now. He belonged here. "I'm sorry," he said.

"It's fine," she said.

"You still gonna take me there?"

"I said I would, didn't I?"

She sounded just annoyed enough that he knew it was OK to tease her again. "You don't think they'll have the Second Coming while we're there, do you? If you think so, I'll wear my tie."

She smiled, then turned to face him and pushed him away. "Deaver, go to bed."

"I'm gettin up at four-thirty, Rain, and then you're one girl who's gonna have fun."

"I don't think the song was about early morning boat trips."

She was doing the dishes when he left for his little room.

Lehi was waiting at five-thirty, right on schedule. "I can't believe it," he said. "I thought you'd be late."

"Good thing you were ready on time," said Deaver, "cause if you didn't come with us you wouldn't get a cut."

"We aren't going to find any gold, Deaver Teague."

"Then why're you comin with me? Don't give me that stuff, Lehi, you know the future's with Deaver Teague, and you don't want to be left behind. Where's the diving stuff?"

"I didn't bring it *home*, Deaver. You don't think my mom'd ask questions then?"

"She's always askin questions," said Deaver.

"It's her job," said Rain.

"I don't want anybody askin about everything I do," said Deaver.

"Nobody has to ask," said Rain. "You always tell us whether we want to hear or not."

"If you don't want to hear, you don't have to," said Deaver.

"Don't get touchy," said Rain.

"You guys are both gettin wet-headed on me, all of a sudden. Does the temple make you crazy, is that how it works?"

"I don't mind my mom askin me stuff. It's OK."

The ferries ran from Point to Bingham day and night, so they had to go north a ways before cutting west to Oquirrh Island.

The smelter and the foundries put orange-bellied smoke clouds into the night sky, and the coal barges were getting offloaded just like in daytime. The coal-dust cloud that was so grimy and black in the day looked like white fog under the floodlights.

"My dad died right there, about this time of day," said Lehi.

"He loaded coal?"

"Yeah. He used to be a car salesmen. His job kind of disappeared on him."

"You weren't there, were you?"

"I heard the crash. I was asleep, but it woke me up. And then a lot of shouting and running. We lived on the island back then, always heard stuff from the harbor. He got buried under a ton of coal that fell from fifty feet up."

Deaver didn't know what to say about that.

"You never talk about your folks," said Lehi. "I always remember my dad, but you never talk about your folks."

Deaver shrugged.

"He doesn't remember em," Rain said quietly. "They found him out on the plains somewhere. The mobbers got his family, however many there was, he must've hid or something, that's all they can figure."

"Well what was it?" asked Lehi. "Did you hide?"

Deaver didn't feel comfortable talking about it, since he didn't remember anything except what people told him. He knew that other people remembered their childhood, and he didn't like how they always acted so surprised that he didn't. But Lehi was asking, and Deaver knew that you don't keep stuff back from friends. "I guess I did. Or maybe I looked too dumb to kill or somthin." He laughed. "I must've been a real dumb little kid, I didn't even remember my own name. They figure I was five or six years old, most kids know their names, but not me. So the two guys that found me, their names were Teague and Deaver."

"You gotta remember somethin."

"Lehi, I didn't even know how to talk. They tell me I didn't even say a word till I was nine years old. We're talkin about a slow learner here."

"Wow." Lehi was silent for a while. "How come you didn't say anything?"

"Doesn't matter," said Rain. "He makes up for it now, Deaver the talker. Champion talker."

They coasted the island till they got past Magna. Lehi led them to a storage shed that Underwater Salvage had put up at the north end of Oquirrh Island. It was unlocked and full of diving equipment. Lehi's friends had filled some tanks with air. They got two diving outfits and underwater flashlights. Rain wasn't going underwater, so she didn't need anything.

They pulled away from the island, out into the regular shipping lane from Wendover. In that direction, at least, people had sense enough not to travel at night, so there wasn't much traffic. After a little while they were out into open water. That was when Rain stopped the little outboard motor Deaver had scrounged for her and Lehi had fixed. "Time to sweat and slave," said Rain.

Deaver sat on the middle bench, settled the oars into the locks, and began to row.

"Not too fast," Rain said. "You'll give yourself blisters."

A boat that might have been Lake Patrol went by once, but

otherwise nobody came near them as they crossed the open stretch. Then the skyscrapers rose up and blocked off large sections of the starry night.

"They say there's people who was never rescued still livin in there," Lehi whispered.

Rain was disdainful. "You think there's anything left in there to keep anybody alive? And the water's still too salty to drink for long."

"Who says they're alive?" whispered Deaver in his most mysterious voice. A couple of years ago, he could have spooked Lehi and made his eyes go wide. Now Lehi just looked disgusted.

"Come on, Deaver, I'm not a kid."

It was Deaver who got spooked a little. The big holes where pieces of glass and plastic had fallen off looked like mouths, waiting to suck him in and carry him down under the water, into the city of the drowned. He sometimes dreamed about thousands and thousands of people living under water. Still driving their cars around, going about their business, shopping in stores, going to movies. In his dreams they never did anything bad, just went about their business. But he always woke up sweating and frightened. No reason. Just spooked him. "I think they should blow up these things before they fall down and hurt somebody," said Deaver.

"Maybe it's better to leave em standing," said Rain. "Maybe there's a lot of folks like to remember how tall we once stood."

"What's to remember? They built tall buildings and then they let em take a bath, what's to brag for?"

Deaver was trying to get her not talk about the old days, but Lehi seemed to like wallowing in it. "You ever here before the water came?"

Rain nodded. "Saw a parade go right down this street. I can't remember if it was Third South or Fourth South. Third I guess. I saw twenty-five horses all riding together. I remember that I thought that was really something. You didn't see many horses in those days."

"I seen too many myself," said Lehi.

"It's the ones I don't see that I hate," said Deaver. "They ought to make em wear diapers."

They rounded a building and looked up a north-south passage between towers. Rain was sitting in the stern and saw it first. "There it is. You can see it. Just the tall spires now."

Deaver rowed them up the passage. There were six spires sticking up out of the water, but the four short ones were under so far that only the pointed roofs were dry. The two tall ones had windows in them, not covered at all. Deaver was disappointed. Wide open like that meant that anybody might have come here. It was all so much less dangerous than he had expected. Maybe Rain was right, and there was nothing there.

They tied the boat to the north side and waited for daylight. "If I knew it'd be so easy," said Deaver, "I could've slept another hour."

"Sleep now," said Rain.

"Maybe I will," said Deaver.

He slid off his bench and sprawled in the bottom of the boat. He didn't sleep, though. The open window of the steeple was only a few yards away, a deep black surrounded by the starlit grey of the temple granite. It was down there, waiting for him; the future, a chance to get something better for himself and his two friends. Maybe a plot of ground in the south where it was warmer and the snow didn't pile up five feet deep every winter, where it wasn't rain in the sky and lake everywhere else you looked. A place where he could live for a very long time and look back and remember good times with his friends, that was all waiting down under the water.

Of course they hadn't *told* him about the gold. It was on the road, a little place in Parowan where truckers knew they could stop in because the iron mine kept such crazy shifts that the diners never closed. They even had some coffee there, hot and bitter, because there weren't so many Mormons there and the miners didn't let the Bishop push them around. In fact they even called him Judge there instead of Bishop. The other drivers didn't talk to Deaver, of course, they were talking to each other when the one fellow told the story about how the Mormons back in the gold rush days hoarded up all the gold they could get and hid it in the upper rooms of the temple where nobody but the prophet and the twelve apostles could ever go. At first Deaver didn't believe him, except that Bill Horne nodded like he knew it was true, and Cal Silber said you'd never catch him messin with the Mormon temple, that's a good way to get yourself dead. The way they were talking, scared and quiet, told Deaver that they believed it, that it was true, and he knew something else, too: if anyone was going to get that gold, it was him.

Even if it *was* easy to get here, that didn't mean anything. He knew how Mormons were about the temple. He'd asked around a little, but nobody'd talk about it. And nobody ever went there, either, he asked a lot of people if they ever sailed on out and looked at it, and they all got quiet and shook their heads no or changed the subject. Why should the Lake Patrol guard it, then, if everybody was too scared to go? Everybody but Deaver Teague and his two friends.

"Real pretty," said Rain.

Deaver woke up. The sun was just topping the mountains; it must've been light for some time. He looked where Rain was looking. It was the Moroni tower on top of the mountain above the old capitol, where they'd put the temple statue a few years back. It was bright and shiny, the old guy and his trumpet. But when the Mormons wanted that trumpet to blow, it had just stayed silent and their faith got drowned. Now Deaver knew they only hung on to it for old times' sake. Well, Deaver lived for new times.

Lehi showed him how to use the underwater gear, and they practiced going over the side into the water a couple of times, once without the weight belts and once with. Deaver and Lehi swam like fish, of course—swimming was the main recreation that everybody could do for free. It was different with the mask and the air hose, though.

"Hose tastes like a horse's hoof," Deaver said between dives.

Lehi made sure Deaver's weight belt was on tight. "You're the only guy on Oquirrh Island who knows." Then he tumbled forward off the boat. Deaver went down too straight and the air tank bumped the back of his head a little, but it didn't hurt too much and he didn't drop his light, either.

He swam along the outside of the temple, shining his light on the stones. Lots of underwater plants were rising up the sides of the temple, but it wasn't covered much yet. There was a big metal plaque right in the front of the building, about a third of the way down. THE HOUSE OF THE LORD it said. Deaver pointed it out to Lehi.

When they got up to the boat again, Deaver asked about it. "It looked kind of goldish," he said.

"Used to be another sign there," said Rain. "It was a little different. That one might have been gold. This one's plastic. They made it so the temple would still have a sign, I guess."

"You sure about that?"

"I remember when they did it."

Finally Deaver felt confident enough to go down into the temple. They had to take off their flippers to climb into the steeple window; Rain tossed them up after. In the sunlight there was nothing spooking about the window. They sat there on the sill, water lapping at their feet, and put their fins and tanks on.

Halfway through getting dressed, Lehi stopped. Just sat there. "I can't do it," he said.

"Nothin to be scared of," said Deaver. "Come on, there's no ghosts or nothin down there."

"I can't," said Lehi.

"Good for you," called Rain from the boat.

Deaver turned to look at her. "What're you talkin about!"

"I don't think you should."

"Then why'd you bring me here?"

"Because you wanted to."

Made no sense.

"It's holy ground, Deaver," said Rain. "Lehi feels it, too. That's why he isn't going down."

Deaver looked at Lehi.

"It just don't feel right," said Lehi.

"It's just stones," said Deaver.

Lehi said nothing. Deaver put on his goggles, took a light, put the breather in his mouth, and jumped.

Turned out the floor was only a foot and a half down. It took him completely by surprise, so he fell over and sat on his butt in eighteen inches of water. Lehi was just as surprised as he was, but then he started laughing, and Deaver laughed, too. Deaver got to his feet and started flapping around, looking for the stairway. He could hardly take a step, his flippers slowed him down so much.

"Walk backward," said Lehi.

"Then how am I supposed to see where I'm going?"

"Stick your face under the water and look, chiggerhead."

Deaver stuck his face in the water. Without the reflection of daylight on the surface, he could see fine. There was the stairway.

He got up, looked toward Lehi. Lehi shook his head. He still wasn't going.

"Suit yourself," said Deaver. He backed through the water to the top step. Then he put in his breathing tube and went down.

It wasn't easy to get down the stairs. They're fine when you aren't floating, thought Deaver, but they're a pain when you keep scraping your tanks on the ceiling. Finally he figured out he could grab the railing and pull himself down. The stairs wound around and around. When they ended, a whole bunch of garbage had filled up the bottom of the stairwell, partly blocking the doorway. He swam above the garbage, which looked like scrap metal and chips of wood, and came out into a large room.

His light didn't shine very far through the murky water, so he swam the walls, around and around, high and low. Down here the water was cold, and he swam faster to keep warm. There were rows of arched windows on both sides, with rows of circular windows above them, but they had been covered over with wood on the outside; the only light was from Deaver's flashlight. Finally, though, after a couple of times around the room and across the ceiling, he figured it was just one big room. And except for the garbage all over the floor, it was empty.

Already he felt the deep pain of disappointment. He forced himself to ignore it. After all, it wouldn't be right out here in a big room like this, would it? There had to be a secret treasury.

There were a couple of doors. The small one in the middle of the wall at one end was wide open. Once there must have been stairs leading up to it. Deaver swam over there and shone his light in. Just another room, smaller this time. He found a couple more rooms, but they had all been stripped, right down to the stone. Nothing at all.

He tried examining some of the stones to look for secret doors, but he gave up pretty soon—he couldn't see well enough from the flashlight to find a thin crack even if it was there. Now the disappointment was real. As he swam along, he began to wonder if maybe the truckers hadn't known he was listening. Maybe they made it all up just so someday he'd do this. Some joke, where they wouldn't even see him make a fool of himself.

But no, no, that couldn't be it. They believed it, all right. But he knew now what they didn't know. Whatever the Mormons did here in the old days, there wasn't any gold in the upper rooms now. So much for the future. But what the hell, he told himself, I got here, I saw it, and I'll find something else. No reason not to be cheerful about it.

He didn't fool himself, and there was nobody else down here to fool. It was bitter. He'd spent a lot of years thinking about bars of gold or bags of it. He'd always pictured it hidden behind a curtain. He'd pull on the curtain and it would billow out in the water, and here would be the bags of gold, and he'd just take them out and that would be it. But there weren't any curtains, weren't any hideyholes, there was nothing at all, and if he had a future, he'd have to find it somewhere else.

He swam back to the door leading to the stairway. Now he could see the pile of garbage better, and it occurred to him to wonder how it got there. Every other room was completely empty. The garbage couldn't have been carried in by the water, because the only windows that were open were in the steeple, and they were above the water line. He swam close and picked up a piece. It was metal. They were all metal, except a few stones, and it occurred to him that this might be it after all. If you're hiding a treasure, you don't put it in bags or ingots, you leave it around looking like garbage and people leave it alone.

He gathered up as many of the thin metal pieces as he could carry in one hand and swam carefully up the stairwell. Lehi would have to come down now and help him carry it up; they could make bags out of their shirts to carry lots of it at a time.

He splashed out into the air and then walked backward up the last few steps and across the submerged floor. Lehi was still sitting on the sill, and now Rain was there beside him, her bare feet dangling in the water. When he got there he turned around and held out the metal in his hands. He couldn't see their faces well, because the outside of the facemask was blurry with water and kept catching sunlight.

"You scraped your knee," said Rain.

Deaver handed her his flashlight and now that his hand was free, he could pull his mask off and look at them. They were very serious. He held out the metal pieces toward them. "Look what I found down there."

Lehi took a couple of metal pieces from him. Rain never took her eyes from Deaver's face.

"It's old cans, Deaver," Lehi said quietly.

"No it isn't," said Deaver. But he looked at his fistful of metal sheets and realized it was true. They had been cut down the side and pressed flat, but they were sure enough cans.

"There's writing on it," said Lehi. "It says, Dear Lord heal my girl Jenny please I pray."

Deaver set down his handful on the sill. Then he took one, turned it over, found the writing. "Forgive my adultery I will sin no more."

Lehi read another. "Bring my boy safe from the plains O Lord God."

Each message was scratched with a nail or a piece of glass, the letters crudely formed.

"They used to say prayers all day in the temple, and people would bring in names and they'd say the temple prayers for them," said Rain. "Nobody prays here now, but they still bring the names. On metal so they'll last."

"We shouldn't read these," said Lehi. "We should put them back."

There were hundreds, maybe thousand of those metal prayers down there. People must come here all the time, Deaver realized. The Mormons must have a regular traffic coming here and leaving these things behind. But nobody told me.

"Did you know about this?"

Rain nodded.

"You brought them here, didn't you."

"Some of them. Over the years."

"You knew what was down there."

She didn't answer.

"She told you not to come," said Lehi.

"You knew about this too?"

"I knew people came, I didn't know what they did."

And suddenly the magnitude of it struck him. Lehi and Rain had both known. All the Mormons knew, then. They all knew, and he had asked again and again, and no one had told him. Not even his friends.

"Why'd you let me come out here?"

"Tried to stop you," said Rain.

"Why didn't you tell me this?"

She looked him in the eye. "Deaver, you would've thought I was givin you the runaround. And you would have laughed at this, if I told you. I thought it was better if you saw it. Then maybe you wouldn't go tellin people how dumb the Mormons are."

"You think I would?" He held up another metal prayer and read it aloud. "Come quickly, Lord Jesus, before I die." He shook it at her. "You think I'd laugh at these people?"

"You laugh at everything, Deaver."

Deaver looked at Lehi. This was something Lehi had never said before. Deaver would never laugh at something that was really important. And this was really important to them, to them both.

"This is yours," Deaver said. "All this stuff is yours."

"I never left a prayer here," said Lehi.

But when he said *yours* he didn't mean just them, just Lehi and Rain. He meant all of them, all the people of the Mormon Sea, all the ones who had known about it but never told him even though he asked again and again. All the people who belonged here. "I came to find something here for *me*, and you knew all the time it was only *your* stuff down there."

Lehi and Rain looked at each other, then back at Deaver.

"It isn't ours," said Rain.

"I never been here before," said Lehi.

"It's your stuff." He sat down in the water and began taking off the underwater gear.

"Don't be mad," said Lehi. "I didn't know."

You knew more than you told me. All the time I thought we were friends, but it wasn't true. You two had this place in common with all the other people, but not with me. Everybody but me.

Lehi carefully took the metal sheets to the stairway and dropped them. They sank once, to drift down and take their place on the pile of supplications.

Lehi rowed them through the skyscrapers to the east of the old city, and then Rain started the motor and they skimmed along the surface of the lake. The Lake Patrol didn't see them, but Deaver knew now that it didn't matter much if they did. The Lake Patrol was mostly Mormons. They undoubtedly knew about the traffic here, and let it happen as long as it was discreet. Probably the only people they stopped were the people who weren't in on it.

All the way back to Magna to return the underwater gear, Deaver sat in the front of the boat, not talking to the others. Where Deaver sat, the bow of the boat seemed to curve under him. The faster they went, the less the boat seemed to touch the water. Just skimming over the surface, never really touching deep; making a few waves, but the water always smoothed out again.

Those two people in the back of the boat, he felt kind of sorry for them. They still lived in the drowned city, they belonged down there, and the fact they couldn't go there broke their hearts. But not Deaver. His city wasn't even built yet. His city was tomorrow.

He'd driven a salvage truck and lived in a closet long enough. Maybe he'd go south into the New Soil Lands. Maybe qualify on a piece of land. Own something, plant in the soil, maybe he'd come to belong there. As for this place, well, he never had belonged here, just like all the foster homes and schools along the way, just one more stop for a year or two or three, he knew that all along. Never did make any friends here, but that's how he wanted it. Wouldn't be right to make friends, cause he'd just move on and disappoint them. Didn't see no good in doing that to people.

Every great change is taken up by some—and turned down by others.

Robert Charles Wilson is the author of many award-winning SF novels and stories, including Darwinia *and* The Chronoliths. *"The Great Goodbye" was originally written for the science magazine* Nature.

The Great Goodbye

· ·

ROBERT CHARLES WILSON

The hardest part of the Great Goodbye, for me, was knowing I wouldn't see my grandfather again. We had developed that rare thing, a friendship that crossed the line of the post-evolutionary divide, and I loved him very much.

Humanity had become, by that autumn of 2350, two very distinct human species—if I can use that antiquated term. Oh, the Stock Humans remain a 'species' in the classical evolutionary sense: New People, of course, have forgone all that. Post-evolutionary, post-biological, budded or engineered, New People are gloriously free from all the old human restraints. What unites us all is our common source, the Divine Complexity that shaped primordial quark plasma into stars, planets, planaria, people. Grandfather taught me that.

I had always known that we would, one day, be separated.

But we first spoke of it, tentatively and reluctantly, when Grandfather went with me to the Museum of Devices in Brussels, a day trip. I was young and easily impressed by the full-scale working model of a 'steam train' in the Machine Gallery—an amazingly baroque contrivance of ancient metalwork and gas-pressure technology. Staring at it, I thought (because Grandfather had taught me some of his 'religion'): Complexity made this. This is made of stardust, by stardust.

We walked from the Machine Gallery to the Gallery of the Planets, drawing more than a few stares from the Stock People (children, especially) around us. It was uncommon to see a New Person fully embodied and in public. The Great Goodbye had been going on for more than a century; New People were already scarce on Earth, and a New Person walking with a Stock Person was an even more unusual sight—risqué, even shocking. We bore the attention gamely. Grandfather held his head high and ignored the muttered insults.

The Gallery of the Planets recorded humanity's expansion into the Solar System, and I hope the irony was obvious to everyone who sniffed at our presence there: Stock People could not have colonized any of these forbidding places (consider Ganymede in its primeval state!) without the partnership of the New. In a way, Grandfather said, this was the most appropriate place we could have come. It was a monument to the long collaboration that was rapidly reaching its end.

The stars, at last, are within our grasp. The grasp, anyhow, of the New People. Was this, I asked Grandfather, why he and I had to be so different from one another?

"Some people," he said, "some families, just happen to prefer the old ways. Soon enough Earth will belong to the Stocks once again, though I'm not sure this is entirely a good thing." And he looked at me sadly. "We've learned a lot from each other. We could have learned more."

"I wish we could be together for centuries and centuries," I said.

I saw him for the last time (some years ago now) at the Shipworks, where the picturesque ruins of Detroit rise from the Michigan Waters, and the star-traveling Polises are assembled and wait like bright green baubles to lift, at last and forever, into the sky. Grandfather had arranged this final meeting—in the flesh, so to speak.

We had delayed it as long as possible. New People are patient in a way, that's the point. Stock Humans have always dreamed of the stars, but the stars remain beyond their reach. A Stock Human lifetime is simply too short; one or two hundred years won't take you far enough. Relativistic constraints demand that travelers between the stars must be at home between the stars. Only New People have the continuity, the patience, the flexibility to endure and prosper in the Galaxy's immense voids.

I greeted Grandfather on the high embarkation platform where the wind was brisk and cool. He lifted me up in his arms and admired me with his bright blue eyes. We talked about trivial things, for the simple pleasure of talking. Then he said, "This isn't easy, this saying goodbye. It makes me think of mortality—that old enemy."

"It's all right," I said.

"Perhaps you could still change your mind?"

I shook my head, no. A New Person can transform himself into a Stock Person and vice versa, but the social taboos are strong, the obstacles (family dissension, legal entanglements) almost insurmountable, as Grandfather knew too well. And in any case that wasn't my choice. I was content as I was. Or so I chose to believe.

"Well, then," he said, empty, for once, of words. He looked away. The Polis would be rising soon, beginning its eons-long navigation of our near stellar neighbors. Discovering, no doubt, great wonders.

"Goodbye, boy," he said.

I said, "Goodbye, Grandfather."

Then he rose to his full height on his many translucent legs, winked one dish-sized glacial blue eye, and walked with a slow machinely dignity to the vessel that would carry him away. And I watched, desolate, alone on the platform with the wind in my hair, as his ship rose into the arc of the high clean noonday sky.